The Kindred Letters

By

A.L. Crouch

Acknowledgements

I have so many people to thank for making this novel possible. Most of whom, I could not have written it without. First and foremost, I thank God for blessing me with this incredible journey. This was never my story to tell, it was always Yours. I hope I did You proud. What an adventure these three years have been. You always knew it would end up this way. Lead on. I will follow.

Tina Rizzo, you are an inspiration. Your strength is unfathomable. I cannot thank you, Krista and Jeremy enough for inviting me into your family, and for sharing Josh with the world. Thank you for being my kindred spirits. We finally did it, you guys. Now, let's see how far this can fly!

I need to say an incredibly special thank you to Carole Griffin. You are my mentor, my sister, and the best editor money couldn't buy. Thank you for believing in me enough to devote time I know you never had. You are a true friend and I love you.

Thank you, Amanda Joy Rutter, for coming along on this adventure when God called us to move right into it. Your support gave me the confidence to keep going and to dig deeper when I was only skimming the surface. You knew I had more to give. Thank you for reading every word, and for crying with me. Thank you for being my lifeline out of the black.

To all my beta readers, thank you for your invaluable feedback. Your suggestions helped make this story what it is. I offer a special shout out to my girls in the Hope Chapel book club. Thank you for being a part of this adventure. Literally.

Thank you, Skyler Trantham and Ilknur Marlowe, for sharing your culture with me and for making sure I got it right. If the Salids portray only half of your incredible kindness and support, I will have gotten it right. Skyler, I miss you dearly. Keep writing, keep striving, and never stop learning. You are capable of anything.

Last but never least, thank you to my husband, Matt Crouch, and our incredibly silly, loving boys for letting me take so much time away from you to do what I do. Thank you for giving me my year. Matt, you never hesitate to jump into my adventures, and you never cease to hold me up when I think I'm drowning. With you by my side, it's never over. I love you more than you will ever know.

Author's Note:

The True Story Behind the Story

It was February of 2016 when I first traveled down the shore of Sunset Beach to find my story in the mailbox. I didn't know what I was looking for. I just knew that I was meant to make that pilgrimage to the Kindred Spirit in the dead of winter. Little did I know, that one journey would change the entire course of my entire life.

You see, before it all happened, I was an English teacher and writer living in Cary, North Carolina. I'd spent the entire school year preparing to write the 4th book of my *Guardian Series* novels. I was set to spend my summer writing it, just as I had for the last three summers. I know now that God had an entirely different plan.

It feels like only yesterday that I sat at my desk with a note pad ready to outline Book 4 while my students slaved over their first-semester final exams. Though I knew all the characters, the setting, and the general plot, nothing came to me. I just couldn't flesh any of it out. It had always been so easy for me to form my stories during those boring exams, but I found myself completely and utterly blank. So, I got up and circled the room, took a mental break, and sat back down to it. Book 4 never came to me, but an entirely different story did. It's the story you are about to read.

The outline for *The Kindred Letters* took shape in my mind faster than I could write it down. I knew right away that this would be a novel involving young adults, and I knew that it would deal with opiate addiction and depression. I knew that my main character would move to Sunset Beach, NC, after losing his father. I knew he would wander the lonely shore of Bird Island until he discovered the Kindred Spirit. I saw him writing that first tear-filled letter to his dead dad. I knew something magical would happen to him there.

The only thing I didn't get was a sense of who this boy was, which was strange for me. Usually, I know my main characters thoroughly. I let the story revolve around them. That wasn't happening this time. The only detail I was certain of was that this character's name was Josh. I wrote it down in my notebook. I thought that Hurley was a good last name. I wrote that down too.

About a week went by, the new semester started, and I still didn't know anything about my Josh. Nothing was coming to me. So I did what I always do when I need guidance: I prayed about it. A lot. Until one quiet morning, I heard my answer loud and clear. I felt God telling me that my story, my main character, was in the Kindred Spirit.

God bless my husband for driving me all the way back to his mother's house in Sunset Beach on a whim. Our family had just visited a few weeks before. This time I dragged my kids with me down the freezing, windy beach to the mailbox. We were frozen by the time we got there, but I couldn't wait to see what we would find. I took the stack of notebooks out of the Kindred Spirit and divided them among the three of us. We each searched our stack, not knowing exactly what we were looking for.

At first, nothing stood out. I began to think myself crazy. Then a pattern emerged from the notebooks in my pile. I noticed that the same person had written a letter on every other page. She wrote to someone whom she had recently lost. It wasn't until the 5th or 6th letter that she addressed him by name. His name was Josh.

I can't explain to you the feeling of awe that I felt in that moment. I knew I had my main character somehow, but I didn't know what I was supposed to do with this information. The author had signed all of her letters with the nickname, *Masha*. So, I took a few pictures of the letters, we put the notebooks away, and we walked back to the car. The entire ride back to Cary, I Googled, Facebooked, and Twitter searched the name *Masha*. I found nothing. Then I searched the obituaries in Sunset Beach over the past year. Joshua Rizzo's photo came right up. When I typed that name into Facebook, the post of a poem came up. It was signed only, *Masha*. The post was made by Tina Rizzo. I had found my grieving mother. I later found out that Masha was Josh's pet name for her. The reason why is in the book.

I let two weeks go by after that. I just didn't know what to do with all of it. I knew that I needed to contact Tina, but I didn't know where to begin to tell her that I felt led to use her son as the main character for this new book. I was terrified, but also knew that I was now part of something incredible. I woke up at 3 a.m. one morning and knew it was time.

I wrote Tina a Facebook message and tried to explain myself the best I could. I tried to convince her that I wasn't crazy and that God wanted her to have this opportunity for her son to breathe again through fiction. I didn't want to write a story about her son. This story isn't about Josh Rizzo. I could never do that story justice. I was just meant to borrow pieces of who he was to bring my character, and parts of the real Josh, to life.

I figured I would never hear back. I mean, who wouldn't think I was crazy? But within a few hours, Tina wrote me back. She was graciously open to all of it. She was excited even. And she just so happened to be visiting her daughter less than an hour away. We planned to meet the following week.

Tina and her daughter, Krista, met me in a coffee shop in Sanford. They brought pictures, cards, and memories. I brought my notebook. Tina explained that her Josh - the incredible, creative, witty, real Josh - had taken his own life after a long bout with depression and anxiety. He was only 23 years old. When I heard that, everything came together for me. I knew what God wanted me to do. All the blanks filled in.

I explained to them everything that had happened and why I made that journey to the Kindred Spirit. We all agreed that this story was bigger than the three of us, that this story was going to change lives.

When I showed them the place in my notebook where I'd written the name, Josh Hurley, there was no hiding the shock on their faces. Not only was Josh significant to them, but so was the name, *Hurley*. They told me that one of Josh's favorite things in the world had been his Hurley T-shirt. We all cried. There was no denying this book was meant to be. There was no denying that we were kindred spirits, brought together for a huge purpose.

Joshua Rizzo did not have an opioid problem. I need that to be very clear. This story is not his story. But the real Josh did love gaming with his friends. He had a passion for creating songs and uploading them to his YouTube channel, The Cosmic Coud. He loved his family more than anything, and now that I have had the privilege of getting to know them, there is no doubt as to why. Josh never knew an enemy or a stranger. He was a light in a dark world, and though I never had the chance to meet him in person, I thank him with all of my soul for letting me borrow just a piece of who he was to make this story possible. Josh, may be gone, but now I know you will never be forgotten.

Now, dear reader, as you engage with this story, you too will become a part of it. Pass it along to someone. Reach out to someone you know whom might be trapped in the shadows. Talk about your darkness. Depression is real. It is valid, and no one has to go through it alone. Keep up the fight, and keep the faith. Life is full of hope, and it's filled with awe-inspiring coincidences. Let this story be a testament to that. Thank you for being a kindred spirit.

For more information on the story behind the story visit:

https://youtu.be/WLQhL2xaMhg

https://www.youtube.com/user/Grymm

Kindred spirits are not so scarce as I used to think. It's splendid to find out there are so many of them in the world.

– Lucy Maud Montgomery

One

The mailbox wasn't always black. After the storm tore through our small beach town and it was discovered that the old, weathered box had been destroyed, the powers-that-be replaced it with a gleaming white one. To the three of us, the change made perfect sense. The white was a symbol of our rebirth. It represented everything that we'd overcome that summer. It was a testament to our struggles, and a tribute to our pain.

The new mailbox was not as well received by the people of Sunset Beach. After more than thirty years perched in the dunes of Bird Island, the locals insisted that the Kindred Spirit had only ever been, and should only ever be, a plain black mailbox. The white box was replaced with a standard black one within a few months. What the people failed to realize though, is that the color, shape or size of the box was never the key to the Kindred Spirit's magic. We are. It was always us. The only way to explain it, the only way you'll ever truly understand the power of the mailbox, is to tell you my story. It all started the summer we moved to Sunset Beach, and the day I first found the mailbox. Or rather, it found me.

I walked with the world on my shoulders back then. So, I barely noticed that the beach was littered with striped umbrellas that puffed with each gust of afternoon wind. Despite the crowd, it was easy enough to jog down to where the water could cool my feet. The tepid sand made my daily walks more tolerable than the smoldering streets of my new neighborhood. I was able to slosh my way past blankets anchored by discarded sandals and sand-filled buckets. Sunbathers paid me no attention as they lay sprawled on beach chairs beside the water, their hides glistening with coconut-scented lotions.

The farther down the shore I walked though, the fewer kids whipped by on foam boards or inflatable tubes. I no longer had to maneuver around sunken castles or rowdy Frisbee games. Before long, small patches of unoccupied shoreline turned to lengths of barren sand. Soon the chatter and blaring country music was drowned out by the crashing of the waves and the call of seagulls overhead. Though the sun bore down on the back of my neck, I focused on the feel of the water splashing against my ankles and tried to go completely numb.

Low tide spread the firm, grey sand wide from the water's edge to the grass-covered dunes. Ahead, the beach stretched on for another mile. There wasn't a building in sight. It's what I liked best about walking the beach. Once I cleared the crowd, it was easy to pretend I was alone in the world. For a little while at least, there was no one to worry about me, no one to watch for how I was coping.

When I saw the familiar gap between the dunes, I stopped to check the pedometer on my smartwatch. Sure enough, I had walked five thousand steps. Scooping seawater into my hands, I splashed my hot neck. The sunbathers and sandcastle builders I'd passed half an hour ago now looked like a hoard of gnats. They buzzed beside the pier. I noted that the fuzziness in my head was starting to fade, which meant it was time to get back to the solitude of my air-conditioned room. I kicked the wet sand from my heels and started back the way I came. That's when I first heard the call.

Josh . . . Josh.

The whisper was almost inaudible, like a familiar voice traveling to me on the humid Carolina breeze. I almost dismissed it as my imagination. The drug in my system combined with the summer heat was messing with me. There was something about the call, though, that made me pause. The darkest parts inside of me seemed to cry back, *where?*

Behind me, the shore was speckled with fishermen and a couple of excited dogs on strained leashes. Hundreds of seagoing birds flapped the water from their wings and pecked between the rocks of the stone jetty that extended into the ocean farther out. Otherwise, the beach was empty.

With a shrug, I started to turn back. Then something caught my eye. An American flag waved from where it peaked just above the dunes in the distance. It rippled in the wind beside the swaying beach grass in the middle of nowhere. I'd never noticed it before. Curious, I made my way toward it, leaving the cool surf to jog the sweltering sand. I thought that maybe the flag marked some historic site or another public beach access, but the farther down the beach I got, the less likely that seemed. There was nothing around.

As I drew nearer, I saw that it billowed beside two wooden benches planted in the sand. Something odd poked out from the dunes between them. At first, I wasn't sure I was seeing things clearly. When I got closer, I stopped in my tracks. Perched atop a driftwood pole between the benches sat a lonely mailbox. Its black, metal surface reflected the movement of the sea.

I scanned the dunes for some indication that I'd overstepped public bounds or wandered onto someone's private property, but there was nothing but empty beach around me. My legs were tired, and the sand scorched the bottoms of my feet. I thought of turning back. My mom would be home any minute. Before I could though, the call came again.

Josh . . . Come, Josh.

When I could resist no longer, I jogged up to where the mailbox sat in strange seclusion. There were no houses past the dunes, no residence or business for the box to belong to. Instead it sat out of place miles from the pier. Its red flag was raised, suggesting there was mail inside. Beside it, bold white letters labeled the mailbox as the *Kindred Spirit*.

When my curiosity got the better of me, I looked around to make sure no one was coming up the shore. Then I pulled on the lid handle. It opened with a metallic creak. I was expecting to see mail inside. Instead, a half dozen notebooks of all different sizes filled the dark space.

Hesitating only a second, I withdrew a notebook from the rusting metal. The black cover was faded and worn; its pages weathered. I let the notebook fall open to the middle where someone had written a heartfelt letter about a brother who had long ago passed away. The letter was addressed only: *Dear Kindred Spirit.* As I flipped the wrinkled pages, I saw that most of the entries were addressed this way. Replacing that notebook, I drew out another and took it to the bench to give my feet relief from the hot sand. The spiral was warped at its binding, but this notebook looked newer than the last. This time I started at the beginning and skimmed every page.

Most of the authors wrote the date at the top of their letters. The newest entry in this notebook was from a week ago, the letter filled with gratitude for having found such a scenic refuge. A majority of the pages were filled with random thoughts or poems left by tourists and people who frequented the area. Some of the letters, though, were written by people who had lost someone they loved. Those were the ones in which I read every line.

As I took in the words of heartbreak and grief, I felt strangely connected to the people who'd penned them. I'd experienced every span of emotion that I found on those pages. In that way we were alike, like an exclusive club of death-torn strangers. The more I flipped from one to another, though, something started to tug at the flimsy scab on my heart. The letters were all so golden. There was not one harsh word among them, and that angered me. I'd learned that death was far from beautiful. It didn't inspire lovely words and fuzzy memories alone. Loss like I felt wasn't summed up in a single page of a spiral notebook.

Where was the fury? Where was the outrage? Did these people not feel it burning in their veins? Even through the haze of my dying Vicodin buzz, I could feel it. It was always there, diminished only by the drug in my blood but never gone. Did these people just choose to leave all that out? The anger at having been robbed of someone they loved? At being left behind? Did they somehow find their way past it? That couldn't be possible.

Slamming the notebook shut, I withdrew the Altoid tin from my pocket and flicked the lid open with my thumb. The tin no longer contained mints, but the Vicodin I concealed inside was just as curiously strong. I stared down at the chalky tablets and warred with myself. If I took another one, I'd have only six left, and it could be days before my next shipment made it to the new place. But the darkness was creeping back in as I sat there in the company of strangers' grief that fanned the flames of my own. I squeezed my eyes shut as I struggled with the resolve to preserve my stash.

My thoughts were interrupted by the sounds of splashing and laughter just offshore. Startled, I shoved the tin back into my pocket. Then I straightened the notebooks inside the mailbox and shut the lid in case someone was coming. I still wasn't sure I was supposed to be there.

When I heard the commotion again, I walked to the edge of the dunes and peeked out. It was only then that I noticed two bikes discarded beside the beach grass. My eyes followed a pair of mushy footprints out to sea where I spotted a young girl, and an even younger boy, straddling surfboards that bobbed just above the shallows. Though we'd never actually met yet, I recognized them as my across-the-street neighbors.

I couldn't help but to stare at the girl, who despite being in the water, was draped in gauzy fabric. Her white head covering was soaked. It dripped crystalline drops onto her thin turtleneck. Her eyes, black as midnight, commanded my attention. Mesmerized, I watched her delicate face illuminate as she smiled at her brother. Her unrestrained joy pulled me closer to them.

As the ocean swelled, she and the boy paddled out and turned to meet the rise of the tide. To my amazement, the wave lifted their boards into the air. Side by side, they stood atop them and glided across the surf. They looked like they were flying. The boy was the first to bail out, jumping into the frothy water as he laughed. The girl continued to coast across the white-capped surface. On her face was a look of mingled bliss and determination. She was fascinating. When she saw the end of the ride coming, she outstretched her arms and let the wind flow through the layers of fabric that covered her. In the seconds before she finally bailed, she looked like a sea-soaked angel floating just above the ocean spray.

I watched her for so long that I didn't notice the boy staring back at me from where he straddled his board just offshore. The way he sat there with his lip curled and his wet shirt clinging to his bony arms, reminded me of a Chihuahua in a bathtub.

"What are you staring at, Solo?" he shouted to me.

I froze, embarrassed but also confused by the reference. Running a hand through my close-cropped hair, I turned to see if he was talking to someone else. The beach was empty behind me.

"I'm talking to you." He nodded to me. "Did a Rancor catch your tongue?"

"What? No. I . . . I've just never seen anyone surf before," I stammered. "Like, in real life."

Without a word, the girl paddled over to her brother. She looked up at me with her ebony eyes and seemed to study my face. I felt it flush red hot.

"You're the new kid that moved in across the street, right?" the boy asked. He shot a knowing look to his sister before he turned back at me.

"Yeah." I shifted my feet in the sand. "We moved in last week."

"Well, then you were never here. You understand?" he commanded. "You saw nothing."

"I'm pretty sure this beach allows surfing," I tried to counter. "You don't have to worry about . . ."

"You saw nothing," he repeated before I could finish. "You were never here."

The girl laid a gentle hand on her brother's shoulder, but he continued to glare at me, waiting for me to move.

"Right. Whatever," I said, taking the hint and turning to leave. "Carry on. I was never here."

I could feel their stares as I walked away confused. Risking a glimpse back, I took one final look at the mailbox before retreating down the beach the way I came. The whole way back I replayed the encounter and tried to figure out what just happened.

The boy made it seem like I had intruded on what they were doing way out there. He acted like it was some kind of secret, but what was the big deal? They were only surfing. Maybe they didn't like strangers invading their quiet spot. If the dates in the mailbox were any indication, I was the first one in a week to wander that far down.

The crowd had more than doubled by the time I staggered back to the pier. Laughter, music and the sounds of kids at play now drowned out the crashing of the waves. I weaved my way through the masses to reach my shoes. The line for the outdoor showers was too long, so I did my best to wipe the sand from my feet before jamming them into my sneakers. I had to disengage my bike from a tangle of others.

I was panting, and my shirt was drenched with sweat by the time I barged into the back door of our trailer. Thrusting my head under the faucet, I filled my mouth with cold water and swallowed until my parched throat was soothed.

"You know, I unpacked the cups three days ago," my mom said, her slender frame appearing in the doorway. She raised an eyebrow at me.

I took one more gulp and dislodged my head from the sink. "I'm just saving you dishes."

"Nice try." She smirked and held out her hand. "So, let's see it."

I extended my arm so she could read my watch. She looked impressed.

"No wonder I beat you home," she said, crossing her arms. "You don't get to add extra steps to tomorrow."

"What, no rollover plan?"

She poked a playful finger into my chest. "It's ten thousand steps per day. That was the deal. You come up short tomorrow and no gaming tomorrow night."

"I know, I know." I rolled my eyes at her. "I just lost track of steps today. Can I go log in? The gang will all be online by now."

"Help me put away these groceries first." She motioned to the paper bags on the counter. I positioned myself at the fridge, ready to receive inventory.

"Now, I don't want you to panic." My mom tossed me a bottle of ketchup. I put it inside the door with the other condiments. "But you should know it's happening already."

"What is?" I asked, helping myself to a cold can of Mountain Dew.

"One week in this trailer and you've developed a red neck." She giggled.

"Funny." I pressed the cool can against the sunburn below my hairline and winced. "I guess this should be a can of Budweiser then."

"Nope, that's not until phase two. There's still hope for you." She reached back into the bag. "So how was the beach today?"

"Hot," I said, swigging the last of my soda. "And crowded."

"It's summer." She flung a bag of shredded cheese at me. "It will die down when school starts."

"I guess," I said, tossing it into the drawer. Next came a carton of milk. I used both arms to catch it.

"See anything cool?" she asked.

When I remembered the mailbox and the way the letters inside had made me feel, I contemplated not telling her about it. I didn't want it to lead to a discussion about how I was doing or what I really thought about having to move away from my friends and family before my junior year. I couldn't talk about any of that. Not without taking more pills first. However, my mom had spent her summers with my grandparents here as a child. I wondered if she knew anything about it.

"Actually, I found a mailbox out in the middle of nowhere," I said, shelving the milk. "It was really weird."

My mom turned to me, a far-away look on her face. "You met the Kindred Spirit? It's still out there?"

"Met?" I said with a laugh, though my pulse quickened with the intensity of her glare. "It's a mailbox."

"Oh, it's more than a mailbox," she said, coming over. "I can't believe you wandered all the way over to Bird Island. I need to make my way down there. It's been so long . . ."

"Island? I didn't swim anywhere," I said, confused. "I just turned right at the pier and walked to the end of the beach."

"That's Bird Island. Well, it used to be an island anyway," she said, excited. "You used to have to swim to the Kindred Spirit, or wait for low tide to wade across. It's a very special place."

"So, it was here back when you used to visit?" I crossed my arms. "How old is this mailbox?"

"It's got to be over forty years old by now." She leaned against the counter and stared off into the past as if she were remembering a long-lost love. "I'm sure they switch out boxes from time to time, but one way or another the Kindred Spirit has been around forever. I used to beg your grandmother to take me out there."

"But why a mailbox in the middle of nothing?" I shrugged. "There are all these notebooks inside. People actually write personal stuff in there."

"Why not?" she asked, her smile growing. "Whoever put the mailbox there all those years ago brought people together from all over. I can't even imagine how many folks have found her over the years."

I raised my eyebrow. "Her?"

"I always thought of the Kindred Spirit as a 'her.'" She shrugged. "She's got a kind soul."

"You keep talking about a mailbox like it's alive or something."

She patted me on the head on her way back to the bag where she tossed me a sack of mandarin oranges. "Maybe it is."

"Whatever," I said, stealing one before I put them away. "I'm beginning to think that people around here get too much sun. Makes them loopy. I don't know what your excuse is."

My mom only laughed, then emptied the canned goods onto the counter.

"You know," she said, slyly changing the subject. "I saw a flyer for some internships they're offering over at Ocean Isle Beach. You'd get a college credit rescuing sea turtles. It's for high-school kids, so you might get to know some of the people you'll go to school with."

I snorted. "I'll pass on the sea turtles."

"Aww, I think it's a great opportunity." She paused to look at me. "Don't you want to meet people your age?"

I glared at her. "You know I don't."

She crossed her arms at her chest, and I braced myself for a lecture. "This is why we made you a step goal, remember? You can't spend the whole summer in your room in front of your Xbox. You're supposed to be getting out there and talking to people. That's the only way this will ever start to feel like home."

"This isn't home," I said before I could stop myself.

Her face fell, and I knew I needed to change the direction of this conversation or escape to my room immediately. I hated the way her jaw tightened as she fought to hide her discouragement.

"I know it doesn't feel that way now," she conceded. "That's why I want you to meet people. Once you get some new friends, you'll feel a lot better."

"I have friends," I mumbled.

"I'm talking about people you can physically see and talk to, not just your gaming friends," she qualified. "And what about your music? You used to love mixing songs. That's why we bought you all that equipment. You haven't even touched it since . . ."

"I haven't felt inspired," I interrupted.

My mom shook her head and took a loud breath before she continued. "You're just so talented. I'm worried that you're going to throw that away. You have to start living your life again, Josh."

And just like that we were back to our old argument. The one that would keep me trapped in the shadows for days, and my mom crying into her pillow at night when she thought I couldn't hear her.

"I am living, Mom," I said, defeated. "You don't have to worry about me. I'm fine. I promise."

I longed to duck into my room and take another pill. It was the only way to keep the darkness from ruining everything. It was the only way to pretend I was still myself. I'd know the things to say to make her stop worrying. I could pretend that I wasn't exhausted, that my body didn't constantly ache to stay in bed. I could appear as happy as I used to be. Without them my head was a tangle of memories and sorrow, but there was no time to sneak a pill. I had to say something now, or things would only be worse later. If I left it like this, my mom would worry even more that I wasn't moving on with my life or that she'd made the wrong decision to start over in a new town. I had to stop doing this to her. She'd been through too much for me to keep ruining her attempt to find happiness in our new beginning. I struggled to come up with something to say that would help.

Then I remembered the strange encounter out past the mailbox. I recalled the way our neighbors had looked at me when I tried to speak to them, but I had tried to talk to someone my age. That should count for something, right?

"Actually," I turned back. "I did see our neighbors from across the street today. The two teenagers were way down the beach by the mailbox."

"Oh, yeah?" She brightened.

I leaned against the counter and started to peel my mandarin, relieved that her disappointment had turned to curiosity.

"Yeah. I mean, they didn't say much." I didn't want to tell her how annoyed the boy had been by my watching them. "They were . . . busy."

Her brows furrowed. "What were they doing?

"They were surfing."

"Surfing?" My mom seemed impressed. "Out by the Kindred Spirit? That's a pretty cool spot."

"You should have seen the girl, Mom. She's really good. She was out there fully clothed, head covering and all."

"It's called a hijab."

"What?"

"The head-covering. It's called a hijab. One of my best friends in high school wore one," she said. "Did you introduce yourself? What are their names? Tell me everything."

"There's not much else to tell. I didn't ask their names," I admitted. "but I did try to talk to them. They just seemed . . . busy."

"You know what?" My mom said, going back to the grocery bags. "I know what you should do."

When she turned to face me again, she had a log of cookie dough in her hand.

"You're rewarding me with cookies?"

"You're not going to eat it," she said, thrusting the dough at me until I took it from her. She pressed a few buttons on the oven and then turned back to me. "You're going to make these cookies and take some over to them."

"Oh, no, no, no . . ." I set the dough on the counter and backed away. "No way."

"It's what new neighbors do." She reached into a cabinet and produced a cookie sheet.

"But we're the new neighbors," I qualified. "Aren't they supposed to bring us stuff?"

"Semantics . . ." My mom picked the log of dough up and thrust it at me again. "It's time to clutch it. Isn't that what you always say?"

"Don't use my words against me. You're not even saying it right." My heart pounded in my chest at the thought of walking up to the rusted trailer across the street. "This is a horrible idea. I forgot to mention that I'm pretty sure the younger one hates me."

"Well, then, they can be a peace offering," she said, rubbing my shoulder. "You'll thank me later."

"But, Mom . . ."

"If you don't go, I'll just have to go over there myself. Do you really want that?" My mom squared her shoulders and waited for me to weigh my options.

I imagined the best and worst-case scenario of each. If I went over there, I could hand them the cookies, say a quick word and be gone. Most likely they would stare at me like I was growing a second head. At worst, the boy would hurl more bizarre insults at me until I left.

If my mom went over there, though, she would rattle on and force a chat out of them. She could elicit conversation from a mute. More likely than not, she would just call me over there anyway to formally introduce me. I'd stand there all awkward while my mom rattled off my favorable attributes. Worst case? She would inform them of just how much I needed new friends to change my anti-social ways.

No, it was better to just go over there myself. It was the path of least humiliation. I remembered the mint tin in my pocket and felt marginally reassured.

"Fine," I said, snatching the dough from her. "What do I do?"

Fifteen minutes later the smell of burning sugar wafted into my room. My heart sank as I jumped up from my chair and dropped my headset.

"JOSH!" my mom yelled from her room. She smelled it too.

Running down the hall, I grabbed a dish towel from the counter. I threw open the oven, snatched the tray out and set it on the stove. The cookies were dark brown, their edges singed.

My mom followed me into the kitchen. "You did that on purpose."

"I did not," I protested. "I just got caught up in the game."

She investigated the damage. "They're not that bad."

"Mom, they're burnt."

She poked at the tray. "Only the ones on the edges. The rest are a little overdone, but fine. I'll bag them up for you once they cool."

"You're going to make me take burnt cookies over to the neighbors?"

"They're not burnt." She broke off a piece of one and popped it into her mouth. "See? All good."

Defeated, I grabbed a new can of Mt. Dew from the fridge and skulked back to my room. Making sure my bedroom door was shut tight behind me, I took the tin from my pocket and plucked out two Vicodin. I threw them into my mouth and chased them down with my soda. This was an emergency. Now I had only four left.

I grabbed my headset and controller and tried not to look at my neglected music equipment. My mom was right. I knew she was. Mixing music and uploading my songs to my YouTube channel had been my greatest passion. Now my sequencer and interface sat like paperweights, collecting dust on my desk. Ignoring them, I tried to concentrate on the game until the numbness carried away the anxiety. My crew was still at it when I rejoined the mission though the screen showed that my avatar had been hit and was respawning.

"Great," I said into the mic.

"Where'd you go?" rED asked. "You just took a critical hit to the face."

I considered rED the best friend I had in the whole world, not just in our online gaming crew, The Stranded. Of course, he had a real name, but we had been gaming brothers for so long his gamertag held more significance. We all had them. I was known as Grymm to the group. I felt cooler as Grymm. He could save worlds and destroy whatever stood against him. I was literally in control of life when I was him. On days when I felt like things outside of the game were swallowing me whole, my avatar smiled for me. In the game I was indestructible, and if I did screw up one of my lives, I always got another. The Stranded understood that. That's why we'd all grown so close. We'd been playing together since I got my first console for Christmas almost a decade ago.

"My mom was just freaking out on me as usual," I complained. "She wants me to take cookies over to the neighbors."

"But aren't YOU the new neighbors?" Stephy asked.

"That was my argument!"

"What kind of cookies?" Zoso asked. Stephy and Zoso were married with a kid and everything. I looked up to them. They seemed to have life figured out in a way I doubted I ever would. "Cuz if you bring over oatmeal raisin and they get all excited thinking you brought them chocolate chip, you could have a turf war on your hands."

I sighed into the mic. "Try burnt peanut butter."

"You burned them?" Blank laughed. "Oh, man. That's classic."

Blank was older than the rest of us, but that only made him cooler in our eyes. He was a schoolteacher, so we figured that was how he stayed in touch with what it was like to be a kid. Perhaps he'd just never really grown up himself.

"I can't wait to hear how this goes," Stephy laughed.

Ignoring them, I looked to see if our sixth member had logged in yet. "Anyone talk to Biggles? He hasn't shown all afternoon."

"He said he'd be on later tonight," Zoso said, leading the clan into heavy fire. "Just in time to hear all about your cookie catastrophe."

Before I could think of a retort, the sound of raised voices and clicking bike spokes drew me to the window. The sunlight was fading, but I could see the girl from across the street pedaling ferociously toward her trailer. The damp material around her shoulders flowed behind her like vapor as she raced around the corner. She paused to look back; her dark eyes were wide.

"Ani!" Her frustrated shout penetrated the thin walls of my room. "Hurry up!"

I looked down the street in time to see the scrawny, dark-skinned boy round the corner so fast that he almost skidded into the neighbor's bushes. He corrected, his twiggy legs breaking his fall, then mounted the pedals again as if his very life depended on it.

"Save yourself!" he yelled back.

When the girl reached the rusted trailer across the street, she hopped off her bike and yanked it into the yard behind the home. As she came back to the front, the boy jumped the curb, lost his balance, and skidded to a sideways stop beside her. The girl grabbed his arm and pulled him firmly to his feet. He too dumped his bike in the back, and together they sprinted into the house and shut the door.

Bewildered, I stared after them for a minute before turning back to the game. The flicker of sunlight off a car easing down the street drew my attention back to the window. The old Chrysler squeaked as it maneuvered the gravel drive of the rusted trailer. It came to a stop beside the discolored front porch. When the door opened, a short, solid man got out. His skin was as dark as tanned leather, and his forehead was beaded with sweat. He looked tired.

As the man plodded toward the trailer door, he turned and caught me staring at him through my opened window. I stiffened. My first instinct was to dive to the floor, but it was too late for that. It was dark enough outside by now that the light from my room shone on me like a spotlight. Instead, I raised my hand in an awkward wave and held my breath. The man stared at me a moment, then simply nodded and went inside.

I sunk into my chair. Now I was even more anxious about bringing the cookies over. They were going to think I was crazy. Clinging to the emptiness that was creeping into my consciousness, I continued the game. Slowly, my muscles began to ease, and my mind melted into blissful numbness.

When my mom called me for dinner, I told The Stranded I would be back and ignored their cookie-themed jokes. My mom and I sat across from one another at the wicker table and said nothing. I felt her look up at me between bites of taco. She knew I was contemplating what was to come. What she didn't know was that thanks to the Vicodin, I felt dull and outside of myself. Only part of me was even present.

That part was still anxious about meeting the neighbors, but nothing felt real now. It was the sensation of having a nightmare but knowing you're dreaming. Life was happening around me, but thanks to the pills, I was on the outside looking in. Even through the Vicodin fog, though, my mind continued to play out possible scenarios. Best case? No one would answer the door. Worst case? They'd slam it in my face.

Shaking the thought from my mind, I stood from the table and grabbed my plate.

"I'm ready," I announced, dumping my half-eaten meal into the trash bin. "Where are the cookies so I can get this over with?"

My mom studied me a moment. Then she pointed to a small paper sack on the counter.

"Make sure you introduce yourself first this time," she said.

"I know, I know." I took a deep breath and stormed out of the house.

Fireflies danced in the breeze beneath the fading summer sun, and crickets chirped their evening songs as I crossed the gritty yard. Across the street, light glowed from behind the crooked blinds of the rusted trailer. When I saw movement inside, I froze. For a second, I just stood there, wrapped in the thick humidity that threatened to strangle me. I suddenly wasn't sure if I could go through with this.

Behind me, a tapping sound broke my trance. I turned to see my mom at the living room window. She shooed me forward with her hand and then gave me a thumbs-up. I considered returning a hand gesture of my own but turned instead and crossed the street.

When I knocked on the front door of the trailer, I was startled by the hollow, metallic thud that rang into the quiet night. I held my breath as I listened to shuffling from within. Someone yelled in a language I didn't recognize. Then footsteps hastily made their way toward me. The door opened, and the young boy peeked his head out, holding the door close to his side. He was shorter and even scrawnier up close.

He blinked in surprise. "Solo?"

"WHY do you keep calling me that?" I asked but was cut off by a deep voice from within.

"Anas," it commanded. "Who is there?"

Before the boy could answer, the stocky man came forward. He opened the door wide.

"Can I help you?" he asked.

"Hi. My . . . my name is Josh Hurley. My mom and I just moved in across the street." I tried to keep my voice calm, but I sounded like an idiot to my own ears. The man waited for me to continue, but the aura of authority that emanated from him left me speechless.

"It is pleasant to meet you, Josh," he finally said. I'd never heard his accent before. "Won't you come in?"

I scrambled to think of an excuse to not go inside, but nothing came to me in the awkward seconds after he asked. So, I forced a smile and stepped in. "Thank you."

Though the interior was well kept despite its faded wallpaper and dated furniture, I was suddenly grateful that our home was a double-wide. I couldn't imagine living in such a confined space. Family photos lined the low walls adjacent to a small corner kitchen. The smell of exotic spices from a recently cooked meal lingered in the air. I scanned the tiny living room, but there was no sign of the girl.

When the man cleared his throat, I spun to face him and the boy.

"I am Youssef Salid," he said, and then motioned to the boy. "This is my son, Anas."

"It's nice to meet you both," I said. "Is it just the two of you then? I thought . . ."

"It's the three of us. My sister isn't decent for company just now." Anas glanced nervously from me to his father.

"Oh," I said, squeezing the paper sack in my hands.

"Yes, my daughter Irsa lives here as well." Mr. Salid raised an eyebrow at me. "Have you met her already?"

"No, not exactly. I saw her earlier . . ." I said, stopping short when I saw Anas's eyes grow wide. He shook his head at me behind his father's back, pleading. I remembered how adamant he'd been that I hadn't seen them surfing today, and how frantic they'd been to get home. It was all starting to come together. He didn't want his father to know they were out there. I cleared my throat and backpedaled.

"I mean, I thought I saw a girl," I explained. "My bedroom window faces your house."

Mr. Salid nodded. "I see."

Did I seriously just tell this man I was peeping his daughter through my window? I didn't know what to say to make it better, so I said nothing. My palms were sweating in the awkward silence. I shifted the bag of cookies to the other hand.

"What's that?" Anas asked, pointing to the bag. He was in just as much of a hurry to change the subject as I was.

"Oh, yeah." I handed the bag to Mr. Salid. "I made you guys some cookies."

"How gracious of you," he said. "Thank you."

To my dismay, he opened the bag and lifted out a charred, peanut butter disc. He inspected it like an exterminator would a musty basement.

"They're a bit overdone." He chuckled and dropped the cookie back into the bag.

I let out a nervous laugh. "Yeah, it was my first attempt at baking. Usually meeting new people makes me want to toss my cookies. I thought I'd try baking them instead."

Neither Anas nor Mr. Salid laughed at my terrible joke, but a soft chuckle sounded from behind a door in the hallway. The girl was listening.

Mr. Salid patted my shoulder. "Well, thank you so much for the gesture."

"Sure." This was my chance to excuse myself. I made a move for the entryway. "Well, I should get going. It was nice to meet you both."

Anas was quick to hold the door open for me.

"Likewise," Mr. Salid said. "Do come again."

My butt was barely past the threshold when Anas shut the door and locked it. I stood there numb, taking in the last few minutes. Movement from across the street caught my eye, jarring me from my stupor. The blinds from my dining room shook and then fell back into place. My mom had been watching. Of course she had.

I trudged back home feeling as though my head had deflated. When I walked into the house, my mom was still sitting at the table, casually sipping her evening decaf.

"How did it go?" she asked.

"Mom, I know you were at the window the whole time."

"They invited you in. That's great!" She didn't bother to deny it. "What happened inside?"

"Well, I met Mr. Salid and his son, Anas."

"And the girl you saw?"

"She was there, but I didn't see her because . . . and I quote: 'she was not decent for company.' Whatever that means," I said with a shrug.

"Oh." My mom contemplated. "Well, besides that how was it?"

I walked past her to grab another soda from the fridge.

"It was weird. All of it," I said. "but I did what you wanted. I'm going to my room now."

"Okay," she agreed. I got half-way down the hall when she called me back. "Hey, Josh?"

I turned reluctantly. "Yeah?"

"I'm proud of you," she said with a smile.

"Whatever," I said, continuing to my room. "You owe me some unburnt cookies."

Her laugh traveled down the hall. "It was worth it."

The Stranded were all too eager to hear about my cookie encounter. I relayed every detail as we cleared a field of an enemy horde.

"Man, I still can't believe she made you go over there with burnt cookies," rED sympathized.

Blank snorted in the mic. "I thought your mom wanted you to make friends."

"Can we change the subject now?" I asked.

My head wasn't in the game. So much was swirling around inside my mind, making my aim as off as my thoughts. Images of burnt cookies, Anas's pleading face, and a mysterious mailbox could not be erased by the digital world on my screen.

"Where's Biggles?" I asked, anxious.

"Why, you going to offer him some cookies?" Zoso laughed so loud that I had to turn the volume down on my headset.

"You know Biggs," Stephy said. "He'll be on eventually."

"He should have been online by now." I sighed.

A year ago, Biggles got into a car accident coming home from school. He injured his back badly enough to have to finish his senior year from where he was laid up on the couch. That's when he first got a prescription for Vicodin. Though his back recovered by the end of summer, he'd come to enjoy the numbness as much as I did. He faked the pain for as long as he could until his doctor refused to prescribe them anymore. That's when he took to the Internet and found a cache of online pharmacies. Armed with a copy of his medical records, Biggles was able to hop from one pharmacy to another and score enough pills to sedate a rhino.

It was different for Biggles, though. He enjoyed the high, but he didn't need it like I did, or else he would have never considered sharing. When he first offered to sell me a portion of his stash, I was hesitant, but only for a minute. My original bottle had long ago run out, and I was drowning in the darkness. Without the drug, my thoughts were free-falling farther and farther into the shadows. It was the first time I'd thought about ending my life and hadn't immediately dismissed the idea.

I thought about my dad a lot back then. At that point, he'd only been dead a few weeks. I didn't know how to deal with life without him. If it weren't for Biggles and the pills, I might have joined him in the peaceful oblivion, or the great beyond, or wherever he is now. Biggles was saving my life by handing me a parachute. He was the only one who understood what I needed.

It was nearing midnight before he logged in at last. I sent him a direct message as soon as his avatar appeared on screen.

"Where've you been?" I typed. *"I need a hookup."*

It took a lifetime for him to message me back.

"I have good news and bad," it read when he finally did. *"Which do you want first?"*

I sucked in a breath and then typed, *"Hit me with the bad news."*

An interminable minute passed while he typed. I still held my breath.

"The party is over, Grymm. I can't say much, but I'm taking a lot of heat over some certain online purchases I've made. There are eyes on me, man. I'm tapping out."

The room began to close in on me. It was hard to take a breath. The panic vibrated from my shoulders down my back. I tried to remain calm.

"What's the good news?"

This couldn't be happening. Biggles was my only hope. I'd plummeted, head first, into this new life—a life in which I was the sketchy new neighbor, the grief-ridden anti-social, the teenage boy without a father. If I didn't have my parachute, I was as good as dead.

"I sent you everything I had left. I have to get it out of here. Don't worry about paying me anything. This last one's a gift, man."

"How many did you send?"

"A few dozen."

"That's as much as a normal tin!" I could barely type. My hands were shaking. *"That's everything you had?"*

"I'm sorry, brother. We knew this day would come eventually."

"Isn't there something you can do? Can't you say your back is giving you hell? Something? You can't just leave me hanging."

Only once had I felt this kind of desperation. When I walked into my father's room six months ago and found him on the floor, the same panic had raced through my body. I thought of ways that I could get a prescription for my own Vicodin, Percocet, anything. There had to be a way to get my hands on more.

"I'm out of excuses and out of luck," Biggles wrote. *"Use this last shipment to wean yourself off, man. It's time. I overnighted it, so it should be there tomorrow. I have to warn you; I was out of Altoid tins. I had to improvise."*

There was nothing I could say, nothing I could do. I could barely breathe. Staring at the screen, my mind was a useless slush pile. If it weren't for my heart galloping in my chest, I would have thought I'd died. I wished it were that easy to.

Biggles signed out of the chat. Somewhere in the churning seas of my mind someone called to me.

"Grymm!" rED hollered in my headset. "You in this game, or what?"

I watched as the avatars on the screen dodged enemy fire across rooftops. Mine did not move. It was frozen, just as I was, trapped in a terrifying new reality.

"Grymm!" rED yelled again. "Josh!"

Blinking to life I grabbed up the controls, but it was too late. My character took a shot to the back of the head and went down.

"What are you doing, man?" Blank asked. "You flaking out on us?"

"I . . . I've got to go," I stammered. "Sorry, guys. Go on without me."

"What?" Zoso huffed. "This party just got started."

"I'm . . . not feeling well," I said, preparing to log off.

"It was the cookies." Stephy laughed.

rED sounded concerned. "You okay, man?"

There were so many things I wanted to say to him. *No, I'm not okay. I'm drowning. It feels like I'm being burned alive from the inside, like every breath I take only fans the flames. I feel worthless, and small and massive at the same time . . . completely out of control.*

Instead I said, "I'm fine. I just got too much sun today or something."

"You've got to be careful in the South," Blank said. "That humidity is nothing like Pittsburgh. You'll get used to it."

"I'll catch you guys tomorrow." I was about to switch off my headset when rED cleared his throat, making me pause.

"Hey, Grymm?"

"Yeah?"

"You'd tell me if you weren't okay, right?" he asked.

My heart plunged to the pit of my stomach as I answered and then quickly signed off.

"Of course I would," I lied. "I'm fine . . . promise."

Two

I woke up face-down on my desk. This wasn't the first time I'd spent the night fully clothed and hunched over in my chair, but it was the first time since the move. Confusion flooded my senses when I opened my eyes. It took me a minute to recognize the grey-washed walls of my room in the bright morning light. At least, I hoped it was still morning. I'd spent the entire night researching online pharmacies and reading stale discussion boards until my body had completely given out. I was too exhausted to even crawl into my bed.

As I detached my face from my desk, flapping yellow caught my eye. I reached up and plucked a sticky-note from my forehead.

Maybe make an effort to talk to the Salids today? And get your steps in. Also, try the bed next time. – Mom

Crumpling the note, I checked my watch. It was only a quarter past nine. I hadn't slept the morning away for once, which was a perk of sleeping face-to-desk. Life looked marginally better in the light of a new day, but the panic from the night before lingered like a bad hangover. I was grateful that more pills were on the way, even if it was my last shipment. In order to ease the anxiety, I'd taken another dose last night. Though it warded off the darkness for a while, I was now down to my last two pills.

Stumbling down the hall for a bowl of cereal, I contemplated what to do with my day. I needed to get back to my Internet search. That much I knew. There had to be a way to purchase more pills. I just needed to keep looking. I also needed to get my steps in, or else I wouldn't be allowed online at all tonight.

I looked out the dining room window between bites of Frosted Flakes. The cloudy morning sky presented an easier walk than if I waited for the sun to emerge and attack my already peeling neck. So, I rinsed my bowl and changed into a fresh shirt.

A mild breeze drifted ashore from the ocean as I grabbed my bike from under the porch, but I was still taken aback by the humidity. The air felt thick in my lungs, like I was breathing in briny chowder. I wondered if I'd ever get used to it. Thankfully, Mr. Salid's car was still in the drive, and Anas and Irsa's discarded bikes were still behind the trailer. There would be no more awkward encounters with the Salids, at least not this morning. I wasn't in a rush to speak to them again for a while, despite what my mom wanted.

Making sure my tin was secure in my pocket, I mounted my bike and took off down the street. The ride to the Sunset Beach Bridge was a short and easy one. Getting over the bridge was a different story. As I walked my bike up the steep curve, I looked out at the waters of the Intracoastal Waterway. The tide was low. Plush green marsh grass poked up between rivers of shallow saltwater. Men in waist-high waders whipped fishing poles into the deeper recess and waved at me as I walked by above.

Hopping back onto my bike at the crest of the bridge, I coasted toward the beach entrance beside the pier. The parking lot was already full. Cars traversed the main road, pulling in and out of their rented beach homes. Kids laughed and tugged their parents toward the Italian Ice shop on the corner while others browsed the small beach stores for souvenirs, or waited for the bike rental to open.

I secured my bike among the others beside the pier and ditched my shoes as seagulls cackled overhead. My clothes clung to my body and whipped behind me as I walked against the wind down the shore. The sand was cool beneath my feet, the sun unable to reach the grains from where it hid behind the clouds. I struggled past the growing crowd and kept walking. With so much on my mind, my pace was faster than the day before. I thought about taking my last two pills to keep the panic at bay, but I wasn't sure when the new tin would arrive. I might need a dose if things got tense with my mom when she got home from work, or worse . . . if she sent me back across the street. So, I kept the tin in my pocket and tried not to think about what would happen if I couldn't score more pills.

My mind was uninhibited, so my thoughts wandered to my dad. Without the pills, they always did. I noted that it was getting harder to remember the exact shade of brown of his eyes, or the precise pitch of his voice. I did remember clearly the way the corners of his mouth would curl upward when he made one of his jokes. I remembered the feel of his hand against my head as he tussled my hair. What I missed the most, though, was the way he always seemed to know what I needed to hear. I could tell him anything. He always understood. He always had the answers, mostly because he'd made enough mistakes in his own life to know what not to do. He was imperfect, but loved me perfectly.

I was so deep in thought that I lost track of how far I'd walked. The crowd behind me was barely distinguishable now, and nothing but the rocky jetty lay ahead. Looking down at my watch, I saw that I'd surpassed my step count. So, brushing the sand from my legs, I started back.

Then I heard the voice call to me again. *Josh . . . Come, Josh.*

Whipping around, I searched the dunes. The American flag waved to me in the near distance, beckoning me over. I tried to dismiss the voice as the whipping of the wind, but it couldn't be a coincidence that I'd heard this strange call two days in a row, could it? Someone or something was out there, and it was waiting for me.

Cautiously, I made my way toward the flag until the mailbox came into view. It sat like a sentinel, guarding the barren dunes surrounding it. For a minute, I just stared at it. I wondered what it was about this mailbox that was so obviously special. How could it reach out to me like that from down the shore? I shook my head with a sigh. This wasn't possible. I was imagining things. The stress I was under was making me paranoid.

I was about to turn back when I noticed a lone spiral notebook sitting open on the bench beside the mailbox. Its pages flailed in the wind. I looked around at the barren sands and the rising tide. Whoever left it was long gone. The soft-packed sand of the dunes swallowed my feet as I jogged over to pick it up. The notebook had a simple, green cover. I flipped through its crisp, new pages. All of them were blank except for the first page. Someone had written the date at the top. It was today's date.

The best I could guess was that someone started to write something and had changed their minds. I was about to put the notebook back, but the blank page compelled me. Not knowing how or why, I suddenly felt as though that page had been prepared just for me. I knew whom I wanted to write to. He was the only one who could understand all that I'd become.

It was my dad who taught me that how someone reacts in a crisis reveals who they truly are. He was right. My crisis happened almost six months ago, and what it revealed about me is that I am just like my father. In most ways that wasn't exactly a shock. I'd been told my whole life that I had Hurley genetics to thank for my wiry frame, nearsighted vision, and aversion to social situations. My father's love for greasy food, hockey, and solitude was passed down to me like a treasured family heirloom. He taught me to put family first always, and to stay strong for them no matter what. He taught me that on days where you had nothing left to give, to always give a smile. In those ways I was proud to be like him.

But when I walked into my father's bedroom that morning and found him lifeless on the floor beside his bed, I discovered something else about myself.

For a minute, I had just stared into his glassy, vacant eyes and yelled his name. I knew he was too far gone, but I'd screamed for him anyway. Then I saw the prescription bottle laying open on the beige carpet beside his pale, open hand. Before I even thought to perform CPR, before I called for help, or even shed a single tear, I grabbed the near-full bottle. For reasons I can't explain, I replaced the cap and shoved the bottle into the pocket of my jeans.

I tell myself it was a compulsion, that I had grabbed the pills in order to protect my father's not-so-secret addiction, but even as I dialed the police with the trembling fingers of one hand,

I clasped the cool plastic container in my pocket with the other. I knew there were other bottles scattered throughout the house. I knew that the one in my pocket would never be missed.

It didn't matter to me that the pills had killed him. The overdose had wrecked his heart like they'd wrecked his marriage, his job, and his resolve. They'd torn his life apart, those chalky branded assassins, deployed by the touch of a pen to a prescription pad. Yet in that moment before the sirens screamed in the distance, I understood what my father had always known.

Within each 300-milligram dose was the potential for escape; escape from pain, from feeling. From life. The pills wielded the power to feel something apart from the shadows that seemed to cling to some people and spare others. When I saw that my best friend in the world was gone, I knew that the darkness in my heart would swallow me whole. I did what I had to do to survive. My dad would have understood that. There was so much I wish I could tell him. He would know what to say.

Having a seat on the bench, I opened the notebook back up to the first page. Then plucking a pen from the mailbox, I closed my eyes and pictured my dad. I imagined his scruffy brown hair lifting in the wind as he smiled his sideways smile at me. I thought of all the things I would say to him if he were here beside me. In this remote and mysterious place, it almost seemed possible.

When I opened my eyes, I had to blink back the tears in order to see the lines on the page. I decided to address the letter like so many had before me.

Dear Kindred Spirit,

I don't even know where to begin. There is so much I wish I could say to my dad. I wish I could tell him that I turned out more like him than he ever thought I would and that I need him now more than I ever thought I could. Funny how things work out that way. Maybe that's why I'm holding onto him, to who he used to be anyway. when he left me, he took away all the good. All that's left of me are all the worst parts of him.

Sometimes I get so angry at him for leaving me, for letting go so easily. It feels like I'm burning alive inside. Was I not worth staying here for? Fighting for? We could have figured things out together. We could have found a way, but now it's too late.

Most of the time, I just miss him. I miss our talks, our games. I miss the way things used to be when our family was still together. He was always the one person who really understood me, and when I felt like I was all wrong on the inside, I could look at him and know that I'd turn out all right. That seems so funny now because he was never all right. And now, neither am I.

Just look at us. My dad's gone forever, and now I'm writing to some weird mailbox in the middle of nowhere. He's never even going to read this.

I swear, though, it's almost like I can feel him in this place.

I can hear his voice calling to me . . .

A tear hit the page, jarring me from my thoughts. I slammed the pen down beside me and wiped at my eyes, suddenly feeling stupid. All at once I felt out of place, like a foreigner in some distant country.

"What am I even doing here?" I asked myself out loud. "This is crazy."

With an angry huff, I shut the notebook and jammed the pen back into the binding. I was mad that some imagined voice had brought me here, mad that I actually came, and mad at the sharp turn my life had taken. Kicking the sand, I took the notebook to the mailbox and opened the lid. I thought about tearing my letter out. I wanted to crumple it up and throw it into the sea, but a thought stopped me.

As I stared at the small pile of notebooks inside, I remembered all of those other letters, the ones void of pain and burning. I decided to let my letter be the one truth in a pile of poetic words and memories. Maybe someday someone like me would come along and see that death is not all sentiment and nostalgia.

Lifting the pile of weathered notebooks inside the box, I slid the green one underneath and then shut the lid with a sigh. A part of me felt better, like my soul was lighter after letting go of some of the words I'd longed to say. All the other parts of me ached. Though the sun was peeking out overhead and soaking the landscape in brilliant light, I felt drenched in shadow. The pain of my father's death, all of the anger and grief, was now at the surface. I needed to stuff it back down so I could breathe and make it back home. There was only one way that I knew how.

Grabbing the tin from my pocket, I opened it and stared at the last two ivory pills inside. If I took them now, I was risking another encounter with my mom without any backup. Last night had been a close one. I might not be as lucky tonight if my new tin didn't arrive.

None of that seemed to matter as much as it should. The pain was too much. The shadows were too strong. I was about to throw them into my mouth when I saw sunlight glint off of something in the dunes. When it happened again, I shoved the tin back into my pocket. Then I walked past the mailbox to the deep ridge behind it. Something was sticking out among the beach grass and layers of sand. I bent down to inspect it. Its smooth, waxy white sheen caught just enough sunlight to glint from where it lay, buried.

Brushing the sand away, I found that the object was even larger than I anticipated. Much larger. I wiped and blew away the sand until I found an outer pointed edge. Then I heaved it free from the sand. The surfboard was worn and scarred, and almost a foot taller than me when I stood it on its end. When the dust settled, I saw another pointed edge sticking out of the displaced sand. Another board . . .

I was about to pull it free when an angry voice stopped me cold.

"What the hell do you think you're doing?" It yelled.

Dropping the board, I spun on my heels and came face to face with an irate Anas.

"Why are you suddenly always around?" He asked, irritated. "You're like an ass rash, Solo. I feel like I need to apply ointment to get rid of you."

"Ass rash?" I stammered.

He bumped my shoulder as he passed me to pick his board up from the ground. That's when I saw that his sister, Irsa, was behind him. She stared at me with those ebony eyes as the gauzy fabric that covered her head flowed in the wind behind her.

"Cool it, Anas," she said, keeping her eyes on mine. I felt my face flush again as Anas brought the other board over to her. "It's fine."

"It's fine? Really, Irsa?" Anas said, throwing up his hands. "Solo here could ruin everything for us. One word to Father, and it's all over."

"WHY do you keep calling me Solo? We're not on the Millennium Falcon!" I yelled.

Anas cocked an eyebrow at me, obviously pleased that I knew my movie references.

"Look," I said, "my name is Josh, okay? And I'm not going to ruin anything for you."

"You'll have to excuse my brother." Irsa smirked. Her voice was soft. "He's been obsessed with Star Wars since he could barely walk. He thinks he's some kind of Jedi."

"Excuse me," Anas huffed, holding his pointer finger in the air for emphasis. "Not just a Jedi, but a Jedi master. Thank you very much."

Irsa rolled her eyes. "You're a thirteen-year-old who barely passed the eighth grade."

I turned to him, waiting for his response. He seemed unfazed, holding his head high as he walked past us both.

"I find your lack of faith disturbing," he said.

"Just explain to me why you keep calling me Solo," I called after him.

Anas let out an impatient sigh. He turned and placed a hand on his scrawny hip.

"One look at you and I knew you were a rebel," he said. "The haircut, the gauges in your ears . . . your clothes? Rebel all the way. However, you lack the discipline to be a Jedi."

"Wow. I don't know if I'm insulted or impressed." I shrugged.

"I have that effect on people," Anas said, and then turned to his sister. "If he tells, it's on you."

With that he picked up his board and ran into the choppy water with a wild cry. Irsa stood beside me, holding her board under her right arm.

"Sorry about that," she said. "He takes a bit to get used to, I know."

"No, I'm the one who is sorry," I waved him off. "You have to live with him."

Irsa giggled. I recognized it as the laugh I'd heard in her house the night before. I remembered that she'd heard me stumble through that awkward introduction to her family. Before I could feel too humiliated, Irsa smiled at me and put me at ease. Now that she was standing beside me, I could see that she was almost as short in stature as her little brother. The way she carried herself, though, and the way her chocolate eyes looked right into me made her presence just as commanding as her father's.

"He's not so bad once you get to know him. My name is Irsa Salid, by the way," she said extending her hand. "We haven't formally met yet."

I hesitated, not wanting her to notice my clammy hands or that my pulse was racing beneath my skin.

"Josh Hurley." I wiped my hand on my shorts before taking hers. "It's nice to meet you."

"Walk with me?" she asked, picking up her board.

I followed her to the water where Anas was paddling out. Inside, I told myself over and over not to make an idiot of myself again.

"You should know that as irritating as my brother can be, he's really just worried about me," she said as we walked. "You see, my father can't know I'm out here. He wouldn't approve."

"Wouldn't approve?" I asked. "Of you surfing, you mean? Is that why you hide the boards?"

"That's exactly why we hide the boards," she confirmed.

"I don't understand," I shrugged. "From what I saw, you're really good. Why hide that?"

"Thank you." Irsa giggled again. "But my father is a very religious man. He's strict in that he believes it is indecent for a woman to do what I do. My place is supposed to be in my home. So, when I am not focusing on my studies, I'm supposed be attending to things there."

"Oh, I see," I contemplated. "It's kind of like when my Uncle Frank freaked out on me when I got the gauges put in my ears. He said I was desecrating my temple or whatever."

"And you did it anyway." Irsa's brows raised. "I guess we have a lot in common."

"I guess so."

When we reached the water, Irsa bent over to secure her board to her ankle.

"So, it's just the three of you?" I asked. "Where's your mom?"

"My mother died when I was very young, and we've lost . . . a lot since then."

"I'm sorry," I looked down to where the tide embraced my feet. "My dad died last year, so I know what that's like."

"Then we do have a lot in common," Irsa said. "I'm so sorry. Were you close with him?"

"Extremely. I miss him a lot." It was easy to talk to Irsa for some reason. She made me feel comfortable, like she wasn't judging me or sizing me up like other people so often did.

"My mother loved the sea. I always feel connected to her out there." Irsa turned toward the ocean and extended her arms, her smile barely contained in her delicate face.

"Did she surf too?"

"No way." Irsa chuckled. "There aren't many women surfers in Iran where we're from. I think she would have loved to watch me though. She was much more open-minded than my father is, but I understand why he is the way he is. He's lost so much, so he's protective of me. Just sometimes a little too protective."

I tried to wrap my mind around it. "So, you two have to pretend that you've been at home all day?"

Irsa dropped her arms and turned back to me.

"I don't want to hurt my father, so I let him believe what he wants to believe about me. He'd never understand that this is a part of who I am. It's everything," she said. "Have you never kept a secret from someone because you knew the truth would only hurt them?"

I thought about the mint tin in my pocket, and imagined the look on my mom's face, the pain in her eyes, if she were ever to find out about it. "Actually, I know exactly what that's like."

"Then see?" she said jumping into the water as it rushed to meet her heels. "You get it. You won't tell."

"I won't say a word," I promised.

I watched Irsa slide onto her board and start to paddle away. Then with a sigh, I turned to leave.

"Hey!" She called after me. "You want to try?"

When I looked back, Irsa was already gliding across a small crest, her knees slightly bent beneath her. She waved me over with a laugh. When she jumped into the water, I saw Anas straddling his board behind her. He watched me with clinical interest, as if at any moment I would turn to the Dark Side.

I waited until Irsa surfaced to answer. "I don't think your brother would like that very much."

"Sure he would." She wrung out her hijab. "He likes you."

"Yeah, right," I said with a nervous grin. "That's funny."

"No, really," she insisted, waving me over again. "You know how I know?"

"By the way he's glaring at me as if I chopped off his hand?"

Irsa laughed and walked her board over to where Anas sat on the water.

"Because other than Luke Skywalker, Han Solo is his favorite character," she called. "Join us. Please."

Looking at Anas, I waited for another barrage of insult or objection. I actually hoped he would give me an excuse to not make a fool of myself. There was no way I could do what they did.

Instead, though, Anas just looked at his sister and sighed. His shoulders dropped with a shrug. "You a snitch, Solo?"

I looked from him to Irsa. Then I raised my right hand. "I pledge my allegiance to the Rebel Alliance."

"Yeah, okay," Anas nodded. "Let's see what you've got."

My heart raced as fast as my thoughts. As happy as I was that Anas had finally let down his guard, as happy as I was that my mom would be proud of me for interacting with our neighbors, I still needed to get out of this. I imagined myself wiping out in grand fashion over and over again in front of them.

"I don't know how to surf," I argued. "I never even saw anyone surf for real until you guys yesterday."

"No one knows how to surf until they try," Anas huffed. "Come on, man."

"I'll probably break your board or something," I stammered.

Irsa smirked at me and put her hand on her hips. "Do you always make this many excuses to not try something? Tell me what scares you more: trying and failing or failing to even try?"

She had me pegged. There was nothing I could say. I knew she was right. If I didn't try, I would feel pathetic, like I always did when I ran away from people and situations because I was afraid of what they'd think of me. I imagined how I'd feel later when my mom asked what I had done today and I'd have to tell her I had walked away yet again.

More than anything, though, I was scared of being seen. Irsa seemed to be able to look right through me. What would she see if I let my guard down, even if just for a minute, to join them? What did she see in me as I stood there frozen in indecision?

"I don't have on my swim trunks," was all I could think to say.

Irsa laughed and motioned to her own wardrobe, now soaked through. Anas shrugged beside her, his T-shirt and shorts clinging to his bony frame like a second, sagging skin.

"Then you will fit right in." He laughed.

They were watching me, waiting to see what I would do. Again, I weighed my options. If I walked away, they might mock me. They might hate me forever. At the very least, I would let Irsa down, which for some reason scared me more than just joining them. I'd make a fool of myself for sure, but that didn't seem to matter to them. I felt like failing to try would be more embarrassing than the magnificent wipeout they were about to witness.

So, taking a deep breath, I walked back over to them. They raced to meet me at the shore, smiles broadening their faces. I clasped the tin in my pocket and longed to take my last dose. It would make me less of a scared wreck. When I lifted it from my pocket, Anas's eyes widened.

"Oh, I love the wintergreen ones!" he said. "Can I have one?"

"No!" I said more urgently than I should have. "I mean, I only have a couple left, and this kind is hard to find."

"No, they're not," Anas argued. "They sell them at the surf shop next to my dad's bike rental."

"Oh, cool," I said. "Still, I'm sort of . . . Well, I'm addicted to them."

"Whatever," Anas shrugged. "Let's just do this."

Irsa watched, a hint of suspicion in her eyes, as I kicked off my shoes. I dropped the tin into the heel of one of them, not daring to open it.

"What do I do?" I asked to distract her.

"Well, first we have to work on your pop-up," she said, looking away from the tin at last.

"Pop-up?"

"The ride is short at this beach," Anas said. "You've got to get up fast, or you miss it."

Anas tossed his board into the sand to demonstrate. He flopped down on top of it.

"So, you're paddling, right?" He demonstrated. "When you get up enough speed, you put your hands up by your chest like you're about to do a push-up. Then as fast as you can, you bring your legs beneath your body and . . ."

Anas put his hands beneath him and drew his legs up into an instant crouch atop the board.

". . . pop up."

"Right, okay." I lay on the board when he got up.

"You're paddling, you're paddling . . . Now, pop up!" Anas said as I went through the movements. When I snapped up, he and Irsa clapped their hands. "Good!"

"One more time," Irsa said, and I got back down.

When I snapped up a second time, she smiled. "You're ready."

"Already?" I asked, my voice cracking. "I mean, shouldn't I practice some more on the shore first?"

"There's really only one way to learn how to surf." Anas bent down beside me to secure his board to my ankle. "And that's to just do it."

"Let's go." Irsa ran into the water with her board. "The water's perfect."

When Anas stood back up, I looked him in the eye. "I have no idea what I'm doing."

"You say that like it's a bad thing, like it's your first day of kindergarten or something. You gonna cry for your mommy?"

"Maybe . . ."

"Just look at this like an amazing first experience. You know, like when you found your penis for the first time."

"And what a glorious day THAT was," I laughed, despite myself.

"See? Only this is going to be even better. You, my friend, are about to be bitten." Anas slapped me on the back.

"Bitten? By what, like a shark?" My heart beat so fast I thought I might pass out before I made it to the water.

"Dude, that'd be awesome!"

"WHAT?"

"That's not what I meant, though." He ushered me into the water. "I meant by the bug. You'll always remember your first ride."

"Come on!" Irsa called. When I looked up, she was twenty feet from the shore and paddling out farther.

"Carry the board out until you pass the breakers. Then you can hop on like Irsa and paddle out," Anas said. "Just watch her."

With one final look at Anas, I turned and followed Irsa out.

Though the morning hot beneath the summer sun, the water was cool against my bare legs. Irsa turned and waited for me as I lifted the board above the crashing waves. The water was choppy, throwing its weight against me and threatening to knock me down.

"Hold the board up, and jump the waves," Irsa called, and I followed her instructions. "Good, now hop on top, and use your arms to paddle to me."

It took me three tries to get my body on top of the board once I'd passed the breakers, but once I was on, it was easy to paddle out to where she waited for me. Irsa took hold of my board and rotated me until I was next to her facing the shore.

"Now what?" My heart was thundering in my chest.

"Now we wait for the right wave," she said. "When I say go, paddle toward the shore. If the wave picks you up, you'll feel the front of your board rise in the water. Wait for it to take you, and then pop up onto the board."

"You make it sound so easy."

Irsa's smile lit up her face. "Having fun is easy. What you do is much harder."

"What do you mean? What do I do?" I asked.

Irsa looked behind us and readied herself atop her board.

"You worry about what could go wrong instead of taking the bad with the good," she said. "There can't be any good without the bad. If you wipe out ten times before you succeed, it just makes it that much better when you get it."

I stared at her, at the way her eyes twinkled with mischief as she smiled at me. Once again, she had me pegged. I wondered what gave the inner parts of myself away to her. How could she look at me and see so clearly what I didn't even understand?

"Get ready." She tightened her grip on her board. "Here comes a good one."

The ocean billowed behind me, but there was no time to look back. I copied Irsa's grip on the board and watched her for what to do next. Every fiber of my flesh screamed at me to abandon this stupid idea and find an excuse to leave, but Irsa's words kept me glued to the surfboard. *Take the good with the bad.*

With a cry of joy, Irsa turned and paddled toward the shore as the water swelled beneath us.

"Go now!" she yelled, and I paddled beside her as best I could.

Within seconds the front of my board lifted and began to carry me back to shore. I watched Irsa pop up on her board, and I knew it was time. I struggled to get my shaking arms beneath me. Everything was going so fast that there was no time to think, just to react. The water rushed around me in a roar like thundering applause. I found my balance and pulled my feet beneath me.

Then I was flying.

It was only for a second or two, but in those blissful seconds the world melted away, and I soared. Beside me Irsa let out a joyous cry and outstretched her arms. Anas was in the water now, fist pumping in the air as he cheered me on.

Then suddenly my board kept going, and I did not. My legs flailed in the air, and I crashed down on a hard, twiggy surface in the shallow water. It took me a second to find which was way up, but when the twigs beneath me pushed, I shot out of the water.

Anas flailed in the water beside me. I grabbed his T-shirt and yanked him up.

"Sorry, man," I said as he coughed.

"My fault. I hould have told you how to bail," he said once he caught his breath.

"Woooohooo!" Irsa shouted as she ran up to us. "You did it!"

"What'd I tell ya?" Anas slapped me on the back as I pulled the board back to me. "Is that the best feeling or what?"

"Better than discovering my penis," I said, and then immediately regretted it when Irsa frowned at me. She contemplated for a minute and then smirked.

"Actually, I know the feeling," Irsa said with a wink. "It's the same joy I felt when I discovered that I DIDN'T have one."

I turned to Anas, my mouth agape. "She's just as nasty as you are."

"You have no idea," he said, and we all laughed as the waves crashed around us. "You want to go again?"

The excitement in their eyes matched this new feeling that was welling inside of me. The adrenaline still coursed through my veins. It was the opposite of what I felt when I took the pills. Instead of a calming numbness, I felt alive with thrill. It felt good to feel something other than the numbness or the shadows. For the two seconds I was flying on the water, I was free from everything. For those two seconds there was no time to think or doubt, no time to fear. I wanted that feeling to last forever.

"Hell, yeah," I said. "Hell, yeah."

So, we went again, and this time I stayed up for a second longer, maybe two. We took turns on the two boards. When I wasn't surfing, I was watching Irsa and Anas, studying the movement of their bodies atop the boards. Always, though, I was drawn to the smile on Irsa's face as she glided above the waves. I understood her now, I thought. We both had secrets to hide. We both had to be someone we weren't in front of those we loved the most. In the water, though, none of that mattered. You couldn't carry your burdens with you onto the waves.

We surfed until the sun began to dip in the other direction. Then with tired limbs and growling stomachs, we carried the boards back onto the beach. When I reached for my shoes, I discovered that they were soaked through, wetted by the rising of the tide. I picked up my tin and water poured from its cracks.

"Oh, man, your last mints," Anas said.

"It's okay," I said, hiding the panic that pricked my spine. "I'll get more."

I flipped open the lid and let the water and dissolved pills spill onto the sand. Then I put it back into my pocket and helped them carry their boards back to the mailbox. We buried them in the dunes behind it and smoothed out the sand to look undisturbed.

"You want a ride back?" Irsa asked as they mounted their bikes. "You can sit on the handlebars."

I waved them to go ahead. "I should walk."

"Same time tomorrow?" Anas asked.

"Yeah." I shrugged. "Maybe."

Irsa and Anas rushed to get home before their father returned from work. I watched them pedal down the beach as I lingered. Then I turned back to the Kindred Spirit. I thought about the letter I'd written that morning. It seemed like a lifetime ago now. Again, I contemplated tearing my letter out. The anger and bitterness that had consumed me only hours earlier felt detached from me now. I knew this new euphoria wouldn't last. I knew that the shadows would return as they always did, but for now anyway, I felt content.

I opened the box and fished out the green notebook. I flipped it to my page and removed the pen from the binding. Then I added one more line to my letter.

Today I did not fail to try. Maybe we aren't so alike after all.

For privacy, I signed it using only my first initial,

J.

Then I put the notebook back in the bottom of the pile and closed the lid.

Three

My mom beat me home again that afternoon. Her truck was parked in the driveway when I pedaled up to the trailer. I couldn't wait to tell her about my day. Irsa was lowering the blinds of her living room when I glanced across the street to see if she and Anas had made it back in time. She was dressed in dry clothes, her head covered with a fresh hijab. Mr. Salid was not yet home. When Irsa smiled her reassuring smile at me, I waved. Then she disappeared behind the layers of white aluminum.

Setting my bike against the porch railing, I jogged up to the back door. My skin felt tight from hours of baking in the sun, and my limbs were aching. None of that mattered to me though. I was too busy reveling in this newfound excitement. I couldn't wait to see my mom's face when I told her what I had done all day.

"Mom, you're never going to guess what . . ." I said, barging through the door. I stopped dead in my tracks when I saw my mom standing with her arms crossed in the kitchen. An opened FedEx package sat on the counter in front of her.

"Do you want to explain this to me?" she said, shaking a small tin concealed in her palm. The tablets inside tinkered against the metal.

My heart galloped in my chest. My palms began to sweat. She'd opened the package from Biggles. With all that happened today, I'd forgotten it was coming. I meant to intercept it while she was at work. *How could I have been so careless?*

Now she knew about the pills. There was no way out. It was all over. I was as good as dead.

"What are you talking about?" I played dumb. It was all I could think to do. I felt like a kid caught with his hand in the cookie jar—only instead of a jar, I had reached into my mother's chest and yanked out her heart. My red hands had stolen her trust and her peace of mind. The guilt was too much.

My mind raced with possible excuses. I could tell her it was a mistake. I could blame it on Biggles, but I couldn't bring myself to do that to him. He'd already put himself at risk for me. No, this was on me. My mom would send me away to rehab or worse. She would have to quit her new job and move us back home to Pittsburgh. All because of me. It was all my fault. I'd ruined everything, just like I always feared I would.

"Don't act like you don't know what I'm talking about, Joshua Hurley," she said, her lips pursed into thin slats. "Do you have something you need to tell me, young man?"

"Mom, I . . . I can explain."

"This is pretty self-explanatory, I think."

"But you don't understand . . ." Tears burned the brim of my eyes and threatened to fall.

"There's nothing to understand here, Josh! You may be seventeen years old, but you are still living under my roof, and THIS is just inappropriate!"

"Inappropriate?" I repeated, confused. "What . . .?"

She stalked over to me in a huff of impatience and slammed the tin onto the counter in front of me. For a minute it didn't register that this tin was NOT the same Altoid tin that Biggles usually sent. When I blinked back my tears, the hot-pink packaging became clear. I read the label.

"Sex Mints?"

Then I remembered that Biggles had warned me that he ran out of the usual tins. THIS was how he improvised?

"Mmmmhhhhmmm!" My mom crossed her arms. "That's disgusting, Josh."

A rush of breath escaped from my lips, and I doubled over. All of the panic and tension turned to uncontrollable laughter. My mom glared at me. She was not amused, but I didn't care.

She didn't know what was really inside the tin. Biggles had sealed it with shiny tape. It looked brand new. So instead of a pill addict, my mom just thought I was a pervert. I tried to stop laughing, but I couldn't. At least it was better than the truth.

"There must have been a mistake when I ordered my mints," I said once I'd gathered myself with a ready lie. "I didn't order these! I promise you, Mom."

My mom's eyebrow raised, but her arms lowered.

"Mom, seriously. Why would I want these? What are they even for? Wait . . . please don't tell me. I don't want to know."

My mom glared at me. Then her shoulders relaxed. She let out a deep sigh and tossed me the opened Fed-ex packaging.

"You'd better write a complaint and send those back first thing tomorrow. The post office is just up the street," she said. "I don't want those things in my house. And DON'T look up what they're for!"

"I will. I mean, I won't." I laughed again. "They're as good as gone, I promise."

"Disgusting," she mumbled as she walked down the hall to her room.

When she was gone, I clung to the counter and caught my breath. I wiped my eyes with the heels of my hands and collected myself. My heart rate slowed as I picked up the new tin and put it safely into my pocket. Then I cleared my throat and followed my mom down the hall.

"How was work?" I asked. "Still liking it at the bank?"

"It's going so well," she said from inside her room. I heard her kick off her shoes. "The other tellers are super nice. They keep asking if I need anything. I almost want to make something up just so they'll stop asking. Southern hospitality is no joke."

"That's great, Mom."

"Where have you been all day?" She emerged from her room in her lounging clothes. She looked me over as if it were the first time she'd seen me all day. "You're as red as a baboon's ass. I assume you got your steps in?"

"Oh, I did more than that," I said, regaining my excitement. "I went surfing."

She was taken aback for a second as it registered. "Surfing? Really? But you don't know how to surf."

"No one knows how to surf until they learn how." I repeated Anas's words.

"But you don't even have a surfboard."

"Anas let me use his," I said before I could catch myself.

"The kid from across the street?" She couldn't contain her enthusiasm as she shimmied to the kitchen. "I KNEW those cookies would do the trick! Oh! Was the girl there?"

I went to her, pleading. "She was there, but Mom, you can't tell their dad. He doesn't know she surfs, and if you tell him, he'll make her stop. Please, Mom."

"Whoa, whoa, whoa. Hold on a sec. I haven't even met the man yet, and you want me to lie to him?" She passed me to go into the kitchen.

"I'm not asking you to lie. Just don't mention it to him. Like, ever."

"Does he really care that much?" She grabbed a jar of spaghetti sauce and a box of pasta from the pantry.

"Yes," I said. "He's religious or something. He thinks that a woman's place is at home."

"Yeah, well, there are plenty of non-religious men who think that." She waved the box of pasta at me. "Maybe I could go over there and talk to him. You know, single parent to single parent. He might just need a woman's point of view."

"No, Mom," I begged. "You can't do that. You can't. Look, you wanted me to get out there and meet people and do something this summer. Wasn't that the whole point of the step count? Please, please don't ruin it."

"You really got out there and surfed with them?" She handed me a clean pot.

"I did." I beamed.

My mom's smile spread wide. "What was it like?"

"It was incredible," I said, taking the pot to the faucet. "It was . . . freeing."

"Something tells me that grin has more to do with that young lady over there than surfing," she said with a wink. Then her face fell. "Wait. Is that why you need the mints?"

"Ewww! No!" I set the pot on the stove and glared at her. "Gross! We're just friends, Mom. You wanted me to make friends, and I did."

"Yes, you did." She smiled again, and I knew I had her. "I'm really proud of you, Josh."

The look on her face was everything. To be able to make my mom happy, proud even, was all I'd wanted this year. It meant more than the new friends I'd made or the bliss I'd discovered on the waves. For a moment, a second even, I remembered the pills in my pocket and thought that maybe, just maybe, I could wean myself off of them after all.

"Then you won't say anything?"

"Oh, okay. Fine. Her secret is safe with me," she conceded. "But I expect details. Tell me everything about today."

We sat down to dinner, and as I devoured almost the whole pound of pasta, I told my mom everything about surfing with Anas and Irsa. I told her about our conversations and about how much I'd learned. The only thing I didn't share was that I had written to my dad in the Kindred Spirit. That I would keep for myself. Telling her would only give her a reason to ask how I was dealing with his death. I wasn't ready for that conversation. I didn't think I'd ever be ready for it. Instead, I basked in my mom's proud gaze as she relished every detail.

"That Anas sounds like quite the character," she said with a laugh.

"You have no idea."

My mom stood to clear the table. "Okay then. If you're going to be doing this, then you have to promise me something."

"What is that?" Skeptical, I followed her into the kitchen with my dishes. "I promise I'll be careful, and I won't stay out too late, and . . ."

My mom held up her hand and looked me sternly in the eyes. "Please, for the love of God and all things holy, wear sunscreen, will you? You look like you absorbed enough solar power to charge your phone for a week."

"That's it?" I smiled wide. "You're not worried about me drowning or becoming shark food or something?"

"Of course, I worry about you. That's my job." She patted my cheek. "But I haven't seen that smile for a long time, Josh. And if this is what is bringing it back, then it's what you need to do. In fact, if this is what you're going to be up to while I'm at work, I don't think we have to worry about steps anymore."

"REALLY?" I brimmed.

"You were right. The point of the step count was to get you out there and doing something with your summer. Now you are."

"Thanks, Mom."

"I'm really proud that you're turning things around, Josh." My mom's voice broke as she patted my cheek. "I knew that you'd find your way back."

The pill tin burned in my pocket as guilt began to creep into my momentary happiness. I told myself that if I could just hang onto this new feeling forever, I could become the person that she wanted me to be. For the first time since my dad died, it felt possible.

"We have some sunscreen below the sink in the bathroom. Use it tomorrow, will you?" she said with a satisfied smirk. "Now, help me with these dishes."

It was late by the time my mom went to bed. As soon as she did, I dumped the Vicodin from the hot pink tin into my empty one. Then I pitched the disgusting pink one into the trash bin.

I logged onto my Xbox. The whole gang was already online when I joined them—everyone but Biggles, that is. I fell behind Blank, who was point man.

"Hey, Grymm!" Zoso yelled into his mic. "Feeling better?"

"Are you okay?" rED asked. "I messaged you last night, but I never heard anything back. I've been worried all day, man."

"Yeah, I'm better," I said. "Sorry, dude. Last night was a bad night. Everything's good now."

"You sure?" rED asked.

"Absolutely."

"Was it the cookies?" Stephy laughed. "You know, I could send you my grandma's recipe next time. Guaranteed to make you the most popular kid on the block."

"You should listen to her, Grymm. Those are some darned good cookies," Zoso agreed.

"Hey, my cookies weren't THAT bad," I argued. "Besides, they did the trick."

"They liked the burnt cookies?" Blank asked, his avatar clearing a floor of humanoids while the rest of us covered him.

"You'll never guess what I did today," I dodged the question like my character dodged the bullets on screen. "I went surfing."

"Well, holy crap. You ARE becoming a beach bum," rED laughed. "That was fast."

"I'll be damned, Grymm," Zoso said. "Good for you."

"My little brother surfs," Stephy said. "He loves it. Surf is life."

"I've only done it for one day, and I can see that." I laughed.

"I'll need to see some footage of this. Recorded proof or it didn't happen," Blank said.

"No way. I was in the water more than I was on top of it."

"You'll get the hang of it if you stick with it," rED said. "I'm jealous. When can I come visit?"

"Soon, man," It was my usual answer. "Soon."

rED had asked to visit from Chicago ever since my dad died, but I couldn't see him. Though we had never actually met in person, he was my best friend, the one person who could see through all my fronts and masks. One look at me would reveal the brokenness behind my smile. I couldn't fake it in front of him. He would see, and he would want to talk about it. He'd find out about the pills, and I would never hear the end of it. He didn't understand them the way Biggles did.

Soon the conversation turned back to the normal things, like who sucked worse with a longshot rifle in the game or who could discover points on the map first. Before I knew it, it was after eleven. I was starting to doze in my chair when a subtle knocking roused me.

I sat up and muted my headset. A series of knocks reverberated throughout the quiet room. It was coming from my window. A second later there was another series, louder and more frenzied than before.

"Hey, guys, I'm tapping out this round. Might catch the next one." I exited the game before anyone could protest.

Going to the window, I raised the binds. Smooshed, bronze butt cheeks were pressed against the glass, leaving round impressions on its surface.

"What the hell?" I said, raising the window.

The cheeks squeaked against the glass until their owner jumped away with a shout. Anas pulled his pants up and turned to me with a satisfied grin.

"That's what you get for making me wait so long, Solo."

"What are you doing here?" I asked.

He slapped his leg. "Bro, let me in. These bugs are loving my sweet Persian blood."

I stepped back, and he crawled inside. "Seriously, what are you doing here? It's almost midnight."

"I'm sorry, baby. Is it past your bedtime?" He smacked me on the back. "I was bored. Thought we could hang."

"Hang?"

"You know, hang out. Do nothing. Chill?" Anas inspected my room. He took in the hockey posters on my walls before his gaze landed on the picture of my dad I kept on my dresser. He picked it up and studied it. "This your old man?"

"Yeah." I considered snatching it away.

"Irsa told me he died and all." He shrugged and put the picture back. "That sucks, man. What happened to him?"

"He overdosed on pain medication," I said, righting the frame. "They think it was accidental."

"Man, I'm sorry," Anas whispered.

"Thanks." I shrugged. "It's sucks about your mom too. Do you remember her?"

"Never met her." He shrugged. "She died giving birth to me."

"Man, that's rough," was all I could think to say.

"Yeah, but it was rougher on the three of them."

"Three?" I asked, confused.

"We don't really talk about it." He made a beeline for my desk and picked up my sequencer. "Dude! Do you mix music on this thing?"

"Please put that back. If you break it, I am screwed."

"Then you do make music!"

"Yeah. I mean, I used to." Anas put it back down but continued to examine my equipment.

"Used to?" Anas raised a bushy eyebrow at me. "You any good? You got a YouTube channel or anything?"

Walking to my desk, I closed out my gaming screen. Then I clicked a new tab and my YouTube page loaded. "I've got a few thousand followers, which is good, I guess. I haven't uploaded anything for a while, though."

Anas gawked at the screen.

"Wait a minute. You're the Cosmic Cloud? YOU are the Cosmic Cloud. Holy crap!" Anas all but shouted. I slapped my hand over his mouth.

"Ssshhhh. My mom is asleep." I slowly removed my hand. "I would really like to keep it that way."

"Sorry. It's just that your channel is like my favorite dubstep channel." His whisper was almost as loud as his shout, but his excitement made me smile. My shriveled ego puffed a bit in my chest.

"Seriously? Thanks, man."

Anas grabbed my arm and motioned me to the desk. "Show me how you do it!"

"What? No way," I protested. "I told you, it's been a long time."

"You've GOT to show me how you do it." Anas sat on the edge of my bed. "It's not every day that you find out your neighbor is the sickest mixer on the Internet."

"And to think, just yesterday you couldn't stand me," I muttered, sitting at my desk.

"No, yesterday I didn't trust you." He pointed a finger at me. "There's a difference."

"And now?" I asked over my shoulder.

"Now?" he slapped me on the back again. "Now you caught the bug, like I said. You want to keep surfing, so you won't tell. Plus, you're about to show me how you mix those sick beats. That's brownie points, bro."

"I'm a bit rusty," I warned though his excitement was sparking something in me I hadn't felt for a long time.

"I bet you've still got it," he assured. "You just need a kick in the ass, metaphorically or physically. You choose."

We both laughed. I couldn't argue with his blunt logic, and I was getting used to his quirks. After I showed him how I arranged my songs, he talked me into mixing a whole new beat into a classic tune. It was Anas's idea to weave choir vocals in and out of the bass chords. It sounded awesome. We kept at it until almost two in the morning. When we were finally satisfied with how it came together, we sat back exhausted.

"Dude, you have to upload this to the channel." His eyes were weary but beaming.

"You might be right," I agreed. "I need to clean it up a bit, but yeah, it's a good one. You've got a good ear."

Anas slapped me on the back once more before going to the window. He turned with a wink. "I've got more than that."

"You really are gross," I laughed.

"It's one of my many talents." Anas swung one leg over the windowsill, but stopped dead when he saw what was in my trash can.

"And you call ME gross?" He wrinkled his nose. "Sex mints? What the hell, bro? I don't know whether to congratulate you or run home to get my hand sanitizer."

"Those are a mistake." I felt my cheeks flush red. "They sent them to me by mistake when I ordered my wintergreens."

He seemed to accept this, but then a mischievous look spread across his face.

"Can I try one?"

"What? Hell no. Get out of here!"

"Man, you've got a real hard-on for your mints." Anas attempted to swing his other leg out the window with a flourish. Instead, his shoe caught the frame, and he hit the ground outside with a thud.

"I'm good!" he whisper-shouted. I rushed to the window in time to see him stand and brush himself off. "You going to be out there in the morning? It's supposed to be windy tomorrow. Makes for some good breakers."

"It is morning," I said with a yawn.

"Welcome to surf life." He ran off toward his trailer. "See you there."

"Yeah, I'll be there," I said as I shut the window.

Then without even bothering to turn off my computer or change into pajamas, I crashed, exhausted, onto my bed. The Internet search could wait until tomorrow. My hand went to my pocket, ready to pop a couple of pills to help me sleep, but I reconsidered.

For the first time since my father died, I thought I could sleep without them. The song, the surf, and the overwhelming excitement of the day made me more tired than the pills ever could. With a content smile, I set the alarm on my phone, closed my eyes, and let thoughts of crashing waves and new friends lull me to sleep within seconds.

Four

By the time I got to our spot on the beach, Irsa and Anas had already unearthed their boards and were hopping swells beneath the low-hanging clouds. I'd wanted to beat them there. It was my intention to get up early so I'd have a chance to sit at the mailbox alone for a minute. I thought that I might leave another letter in the notebook. The last one weighed heavy on my mind. Yesterday started as such a dark day. I almost regretted my harsh words to my father, knowing that a stranger's eyes would see them. I wanted to write another, to balance the darkness of yesterday morning with the light of the afternoon, but it would have to wait. I was late.

Irsa waved to me as she balanced atop her board on the choppy surf. Today she wore a shade of violet-blue that shamed the sand-churned water around her. The sky loomed grey with an impending storm, but Irsa's smile seemed to light up the world around her. Her joy was palpable, addictive, and entirely contagious. I understood her love of these moments now, and the feeling of being free and unbound on the water. I doubted that anyone could match her passion for gliding across the surf.

"You made it," she called. Then she dove into the dying wave.

Anas turned to me from where he waded beside her. "There he is, Mr. The-Man-Music-Guru."

I hopped off my bike and dropped my backpack in the sand in front of him. "You know, you could just call me Josh."

"What fun would that be?" He shrugged and turned to paddle against the breakers.

Out of nowhere, Irsa grabbed onto his board as he tried to pass. She flipped him into the water before he knew what was happening.

"I know how you can get him to call you by your real name from now on," she said once his head was under water. "Just ask him how his name is spelled in our native language."

"What?" I called.

"Just do it!" she yelled as her brother flailed to the surface.

"What the hell, Irsa?" he spat.

"Whoops." She shrugged, hopping atop her board and paddling away.

"So . . ." I crossed my arms over my chest and smiled. "Just how DO you spell your name in your language?"

Realization flashed into his eyes. He turned to grab Irsa's board but was too late. She'd paddled out of his reach with a teasing laugh.

"You said you would never tell!" he yelled after her.

"A-N-A-S-S," Irsa shouted over him with a giggle.

Anas ditched his board with a frustrated cry and did his best to run toward her against the crashing waves.

"He dropped the last 'S' when we moved here, but it's there," she continued, dodging his grasp. "It's there!"

"You know that back in Iran it's a masculine name!" he huffed, his tan cheeks turning red. "You're a disgrace to our people!"

"Wait, wait, wait . . ." I laughed as I put it together. "Holy crap. You really are an ass!"

With another scream, Anas doubled back and came straight for me. I ditched my shoes in the sand and dove for his board, which floated just in front of me. Grabbing hold of it just in time, I jumped aboard and paddled for my life. Anas's dramatic anger made me hoot and laugh as he clawed through the water to get at both me and Irsa while we caught wave after clumsy wave beside him.

We played this game of keep-away until the humor wore off and Anas's face returned to its normal bronze hue. Exhausted and in need of a break, we dragged the boards ashore and sat in the sand. I dug into my backpack for the bag of pre-made sandwiches I'd found waiting for me on the counter that morning.

"Your secrets are safe with me," I said, handing them both a peanut butter and jelly. "I won't tell your dad that you surf, and I won't tell anyone about your extra *S*."

"Thanks, Solo . . ." Anas began. Then I swiped his sandwich away.

"I mean, Josh," he corrected and snatched it back. "You're lucky I don't chuck your mints into the ocean."

I looked up and met Irsa's eyes, scared that she would look as suspicious as she had the day before. Instead, their rich, brown depths warmed my soul against the cool breeze that whipped around us.

"I left them at home," I shrugged. "I knew I wouldn't need them."

It was the truth. That morning I'd grabbed the tin automatically and was shoving them into the pocket of my shorts when I thought better of it. I hadn't needed them at all yesterday, and I was pretty sure I'd slept better than I had in months.

So, there I was, standing in the doorway of my room, considering leaving the pills behind for the first time since I had picked up that first bottle. I thought of the waves and the liberation I'd found on the water. It was almost too easy to chuck them in the drawer of my desk and walk away.

"Oh, yeah!" Anas's eyes grew wide. "I just thought of something."

"What?" I asked biting into my sandwich.

"You know, I wasn't going to say anything." His bushy eyebrows raised into mischievous arches that reminded me of bowing caterpillars. "But now that I've been savagely humiliated and all, I feel I should redeem myself. I think I'll tell Irsa what kind of mints you really have sent to your house."

I jumped to my feet. "I told you that was a shipping mistake!"

Anas dropped his half-eaten sandwich in the sand with a scream and scrambled away. He ran into the water as I lunged for him, both of us laughing as his scrawny legs narrowly escaped my grasp.

I gave up my pursuit when he grabbed his board and paddled away. Then I sat back down beside Irsa and tried to not make eye-contact. I could feel her staring at me, waiting for an explanation.

"It's nothing." I shrugged, taking another bite of my sandwich. "He's just full of it."

"No need to tell ME that," she said. "Does this have anything to do with him sneaking over to your house last night?"

"You know about that?"

"I watched the whole thing from my window." She giggled. "He's lucky my dad was sound asleep. He's not exactly stealthy, my brother."

"No. He's definitely not." We both stared ahead at the water where Anas was hooting with each wave he conquered. "He told me about how your mother died in childbirth. That has to be hard on the kid."

Irsa nodded, sadness coming to her eyes. "I know he takes it hard. He feels responsible. I think that's why he hides behind *The Force*. He needs the fantasy, you know?"

"Like you need the waves?"

Irsa considered a moment before answering. "I guess everyone learns to cope with grief in different ways."

For a second the guilt, shame, and self-loathing threatened to return, but when I took in a deep breath of the ocean air, it settled me. I focused on the breaking waves that rose to catch the wind.

"Your brother was right about the waves today. They are better with the wind. There are less people around too. It looks like a storm is coming."

"It's my favorite time to be out here." Her voice was barely louder than a sigh. "I love it when the waves are choppy and the sky looks like it's about to unleash. I've always wanted to stay out here when it really gets going. With all that rain, wind, and lightning, I bet the waves are intense."

"Why not stick around to surf a storm then? You make it sound like a rush."

"We can't stay," she continued. "My dad always closes up the shop whenever we get a good storm and heads straight home. He's afraid our trailer will fly away or something whenever we get a good storm."

"So, when it starts storming, you guys have to leave before he gets home? How do you know he won't leave before you do? How do you know he's not home right now?"

"Oh, no," she said. "He'd never shut up the shop unless it actually started storming and he was sure no customers would come in for the rest of the day. This is peak season. It's the time of year where he makes the most money. We don't have to worry until rain falls, but when it does, we're out of here."

Irsa explained this with a smile and another giggle, but the yearning on her face as she looked out to the water tugged at my heart. I could see the conflict raging inside of her. Maybe I recognized it because I felt the same longing for a life I could no longer have.

"One day though," she continued, examining the sky as though her lofty promise was written in the clouds, "I'm going to come out here during a storm and surf the biggest swell this beach has ever seen."

"Of course you are," I agreed.

"And I'm going to compete." She continued the fantasy. "I'm going to show the world what I can do."

"You want to compete?" I imagined Irsa in front of a crowd gathered at the beach. In my mind's eye, I saw her glide across the waves like when I'd first seen her, the crowd as breathless as I had been.

"Someday," she said. "They have surf competitions the next beach over at Ocean Isle. You think I have a shot?"

I considered a moment and then followed her gaze out to sea. "I think you'd blow them away. I say go for what you want in life. Just clutch it!"

"Clutch it?"

"Yeah, you know . . . grab hold of life. Go for what you want. Clutch it."

"Clutch it," Irsa repeated. "I like that. What it is you want out of life, Josh? What do you want to clutch?"

My father's face flashed into my mind, his smile erasing the past year as if it were nothing more than a bad dream. I thought of life before he died. I thought about the things I wanted before all I wanted was to see him again.

"You know," I finally said, "before my dad died all I wanted was to create my music. I thought I might become a DJ someday. I always wanted to see a crowd dancing to my stuff."

"And you don't want that anymore?"

"I don't know," I said. "Now things are so different. Now it all seems . . . unimportant."

Irsa leaned over and patted my hand. "Sounds like when you lost your dad, you lost yourself too. It was the same way for me as well."

My hand heated beneath her touch. I'd said too much, revealed too much, but I'd never met anyone like Irsa before. Wise beyond her years, it was easy to talk to her. When she looked up at me with those brilliant chocolate eyes, I thought she could see straight into my soul. It felt good to talk to her, to let her light penetrate the darkness in my mind.

"How did you find yourself again?" I asked.

"I didn't." She shrugged. "I had to accept that who I was before had died too. That's the hardest part, figuring out where to go from there. I had to let my losses change who I was. I had to try to find a new me."

"And did you?" I watched as a double-crested cormorant dove into the sea from above and emerged with a full beak. "Did you find a new you?"

"I'm still figuring things out," she said with a proud grin, "but I have discovered that I am a determined, surfing, stereotype-breaking woman of Islam. I am a trendsetter, an enigma, and an all-around badass."

I laughed with her as I watched the strengthening wind lift the damp fabric from her shoulders, but my smile fell when I considered her words. *Who was I now that my father was gone?* So far, I'd been nothing but a pathetic pill addict, a liar, and a disappointment. I was a fraud. Familiar guilt clawed its way up my back to cling to my shoulders. The weight of it made it hard to breathe.

"Do you ever feel guilty for pretending to be something that you're not?" I asked, sheepishly.

"What do you mean? You don't think I'm a badass?" She squinted her eyes at me, and I backpedaled.

"No," I said. "You totally are. I just meant that with your dad you have to pretend to be someone that you're not. Does that bother you? Does it bother you that your religion says you can't do what you love?"

Irsa furrowed her brow. "My faith does not hold me back, just my father's outdated vision of it. I believe differently from him. It's that simple."

"Then why do you wear that," I pointed to her head. "The hijab, I mean. You could take it off out here, couldn't you?"

"I could, if it were not my choice to wear it," she explained. I was afraid that I'd offended her with my ignorance, but then she winked at me.

"It's okay. I like when people ask me about it. Most people just judge me based on my hijab alone," she explained. "You see, I choose to wear it because to me it is a way to express myself while still holding onto my beliefs. To me it is a sign of strength. It forces people to see me for what I am rather than judge me by whatever standard of beauty women are forced to conform to at the moment. I've chosen to rise above all of that."

"Because you're a badass," I confirmed.

"Exactly," she agreed with a laugh.

"So, what about you?" Irsa perked up and turned in the sand to face me. "What is it that you believe, Josh?"

I thought through my answer before I spoke. "Well, I believe what you said about your old self dying with your loved one is true. I don't think I'll ever be the same. Unlike you though, I feel like I've changed for the worse."

Irsa patted my knee. "That can only mean one thing," she said, matter-of-factly. "You, my friend, are not done finding yourself."

I let that sink in. The way she explained life made it all sound so simple, and maybe it was. Maybe it was too soon after my father's death to know who I was on the other side of it. There were so many questions I wanted to ask her. She seemed to know so much. Before I could say anything, though, Anas flung water into our laps, drenching the rest of our lunch with warm seawater. Just like that, the reflective spell was broken.

"Why don't you two just make out and get it over with so we can catch some of these killer waves before it rains?" he yelled from where he sat perched on his board in the shallow tide. "You want me to go get your special mints for you, Josh?"

With a sigh, I turned back to Irsa. "If you'll excuse me, I need to go kill your brother now."

"Not if I get to him first," she said, jumping up.

Anas let out another scream as we both charged the water after him.

The clouds darkened and lowered as we took turns riding the turbulent waters. We didn't even notice that, little by little, the tourists and locals alike had left the beach for shelter. It wasn't until the sky turned dark as slate that we finally stopped to examine our surroundings. Fragile raindrops floated from the sky and scattered in the rough wind.

"We stayed too long. It's time to go." There was a hint of fear in Irsa's voice. "Now."

Anas looked to the sky, saw the rain that fell, and his face went rigid. The two of them jumped off their boards and ran as fast as they could against the rough tide. I followed, picking Anas up under his arm when he lost his balance. They dragged their boards ashore, almost frantic.

"We'll never make it home in time!" Anas cried. "We still have to bury the boards."

"I'll do it," I offered. "You guys hurry home."

Irsa looked torn.

"Don't worry about me," I assured her. "I wanted to write something in the mailbox anyway. I don't mind."

"Bro, you're going to write something in that ratty mailbox?" Anas plopped his board beside me in the sand. "Don't you know that thing is cursed?"

"Cursed? Yeah, right."

"No, seriously. Our father is adamant that we never go near that thing. It has some kind of voodoo power or something that makes people crazy enough to share all their thoughts and feelings with strangers. Folks write to dead people in there," Anas said, his eyes wide. "That's just nuts. My father says that it's wrong to write in that thing instead of taking your prayers to god, and for once I agree with him. Why do you think we bury our boards here? This is the last place he'd look for us."

"You don't think people just like having a place to get out their thoughts?" I remembered how much better I'd felt after finally getting to write what I wished I could say to my father.

"We don't have time for this nonsense." Irsa tugged on her brother. "Are you sure you don't mind, Josh?"

"Go," I assured, already picking up the boards. "I've got this. Run, you'll make it."

Irsa and Anas ran for their bikes and hopped on, both looking back at me before they took off.

"Seriously, don't go near that thing, or you'll be cursed!" Anas yelled back at me before they disappeared down the beach.

"I'm already cursed!" I yelled back with a laugh, but I knew my words were lost to the intensifying wind.

It took a little longer to bury the boards in the now dampened sand, but I did my best to make the dune look undisturbed. Then with Anas's warnings in mind, I turned to the

Kindred Spirit. I remembered how it called to me from the deep recesses of my pain. Even though I didn't believe in curses or superstition, as I watched the wind whip bits of seagrass and sand against the black surface of the mailbox, I could see why someone would think it cursed. Just standing on the deserted beach as the early afternoon sky around me turned as dark as dusk was starting to give me the creeps.

A flock of pelicans flew overhead in a V-formation as I shook off the feeling of foreboding. I was just buying into one of Anas's dramatic fancies. When I'd written in that notebook the day before, this place had been so peaceful and inviting. Besides, I saw nothing wrong with writing your thoughts down. In fact, it was kind of cool how people shared their lives with other people in that way.

My only regret was how harsh my letter was. As good as it had felt to let all that anger and hurt out, I didn't want people to think I felt that way about my dad all of the time. Maybe it would be better if I just ripped it out.

"Cursed," I mumbled to myself, going to the mailbox. "Whatever."

The lid opened with a metallic squeak, and I reached inside. To my surprise the green notebook was on the top of the pile inside. Strange, since I was sure I'd buried it at the bottom somewhere.

I grabbed it out and flipped through its pages, determined to rip mine out before they all got soaked in what was becoming a downpour. Lightning flashed above, startling me, and I dropped the notebook in the sand just as I'd finally found my page. I hesitated, motionless, considering what I thought I'd just seen. Though rain was whipping across my face, I thought I saw writing below my letter.

Thunder roared above as I scrambled to pick the notebook back up. Brushing off the wet sand, I shielded it from the wind and rain with my body as I hunched over it. The pages were starting to stick together, and I fumbled with wet hands to turn to my page. When I found it again, my breath caught in my throat. There, written below my letter, was something scribbled in small, neat handwriting. When I read the greeting, I realized with crushing dread that it was not just a random letter, it was a response to mine. It was from my father.

Son, is that you?

You don't know how long I have waited to hear from you. I don't understand how this is possible. I don't care. I am just so grateful to hear from you at last. When I read your letter, I knew it was you reaching out to me somehow. I knew you would come to me here.

My brave boy, you are nothing like me. You never were. You have to know that. The mistakes you made are because of me. I see that now. I should have done so many things differently. I should have stayed with you instead of allowing anything to come between us. Nothing is as important to me as you, my son. You were always a better person than I ever was. I should have told you that every chance I had.

You will never know how sorry I am that I left you. I should have fought harder to stay with you. I should have been the father you needed me to be.

I failed you.

I failed your mother.

Please tell her that I am so, so sorry.

There is not a minute that passes when I don't think about you both.

May God forgive me, and maybe he has. Maybe that is why He has given me this chance to speak to you once more.

I love you, my son

I am with you always.

There was no signature, no name to close the letter, just those last words: *You are with me always*.

Tears fell from my eyes to mingle with the rain that dropped onto the page, smearing the black ink. My dad had said those same words to me after my parents split up. He said them to me every time my weekend visitation with him was over and I had to go back home without him. My dad had written me back.

How was that possible? Again, I remembered how the mailbox had called to me in a familiar voice. My dad's voice.

Then reverie broke and real life took over. There was no way my father had written me back. It couldn't be him. This was crazy. There had to be another explanation.

When I found enough resolve to take a breath, I slammed the notebook shut and threw it back into the mailbox. For a moment I just stood there and let the now heavy rain soak into my flesh. The rapid drops pelted the sand around me, matching the rhythm of my speeding heart. My mind searched every possibility for a reasonable explanation.

My father was dead and gone. He'd been in the ground for months. There was no way he had written that letter, I told myself. Maybe someone had mistaken me for somebody they knew, I rationalized, but in the core of my being that didn't seem likely. Who would make that kind of a mistake? Who would answer someone's letter in a mailbox in the middle of nowhere? Who would do something like that?

As the thunder roared overhead, an answer came to me.

This had to be some kind of a sick prank, and there were only two people who had ever seen me near the mailbox. Besides my mom, there were only two people in all of Sunset Beach who knew about my father's death. I realized with sinking dread that my new friends, my newfound happiness, was all a big joke. There was only one person I knew of who would do something like this and think it was funny. This was low even for him.

"Anas . . ." I hissed, anger heating my chilled skin.

My thoughts turned dark as my emotions spun out of control. *How could he do this? I trusted him. I thought we were friends. Did Irsa know about this? Oh, God, she had to have seen him do it. Why wouldn't she tell me something like that? Did she help him? They never cared about me at all, did they? They've just been laughing at me this whole time. I'm nothing but a joke to them.*

I reached into my pocket for my pills. When I remembered I'd left them at home, I rushed to my bike. I couldn't think. I could barely breathe. There was only one thing I could do, one way to help myself. I had to get home to my pills.

Five

Rain came down in heavy sheets, making it hard to see the road. I didn't care. I just kept pedaling even as the thunder exploded and my bike wheels sprayed sludge across my calves. By the time I turned onto my street, I was soaked, mud splattered, and crushed. I noticed two things right away. As much as I tried not to look over at the Salid trailer, my periphery caught a glimpse of burgundy in their driveway. Mr. Salid was home. Unfortunately, so was my mom.

My heart sank as I rode up the driveway and dumped my bike beside her truck. She wasn't supposed to be home yet. I couldn't talk to her right now. Not yet. I needed to get to my pills. It was the only way to show her a brave face. She couldn't know that my new friends had played me for a fool. She'd been so proud.

Taking a deep breath, I dumped my shoes by the back door and tried to plaster on a smile. A list of excuses rolled through my mind like movie credits as I readied myself to dodge her questions and enthusiasm.

"Wait, don't come in yet," she yelled to me as I started to open the door. "Let me grab you a towel."

Hurried footsteps scrambled to the bathroom and back before the door finally opened to my mom's smiling face. She handed me a towel. I hid my tears in it, posing as though I were drying my head off.

"I thought you might have gotten stuck in this craziness too," she said. "I came home for lunch, and the skies opened. I'm waiting for it to let up a bit before I go back."

"Yeah, it's really bad out there," I mumbled. "I'd better go get changed."

"Good idea," she said.

There was excitement in her tone as she followed me down the hall. Something was up, but all I could think of was getting to my pills. I was so close. When I reached my bedroom door, she hovered behind me, a stupid grin plastered on her face. Excitement radiated from her like radio waves. I prayed she wouldn't follow me inside.

When I opened the door, the source of her excitement took my breath away. She jumped up and down with a squeal as I gawked at the shiny, eight-foot surfboard that leaned against my desk.

"Do you love it?" she asked. "I was talking to Jan, one of my new co-workers, about how you're getting into surfing, and she had this board just sitting in her garage. Her son didn't get much use out of it before he left for college, so she just gave it to me. All I had to do was go by her house and pick it up. What do you think?"

Think? I could barely breathe, let alone think. My head raced. I tried to put myself in the mindset that I had yesterday. I tried to remember the excitement, but the happiness from yesterday withered inside like a blade of grass beneath a blizzard of betrayal. It was hard to even conjure the idea of it. I needed my pills. I needed the false euphoria only they could provide. Without them I couldn't pretend. I couldn't stop the darkness from taking over.

"You're not saying anything." My mom was suddenly concerned. "It's the wrong kind of board, isn't it? I don't know the first thing about surfing. Maybe we can trade it in for another one somewhere?"

"No, Mom," I said at last, trying my best to sound excited. "I'm just so surprised. I don't know what to say. It's perfect. This is great, really. Thank you so much."

"You mean it? You don't sound very excited." She crossed her hands over her chest and looked sideways at me through the doorway. I had to be more convincing.

"No, I . . . I totally am," I stammered. "I'm just bummed that it's supposed to rain the rest of the day. I can't wait to get this baby out there. I can't believe you did this. I'm just in shock."

I ran my hand down the smooth, rounded edge of the board as if admiring it. It was a beautiful board, detailed with blue with white and yellow pinstripes, which made the pain in my chest all the worse. How could I tell her that it was all over? The surfing? The friends? All gone as easily as they had come.

"Well, don't get too down." Her smile returned, and I knew that she'd bought it. "It's supposed to be mostly sunny the rest of the week. You can take it out first thing in the morning."

"That's great."

"I'll let you get cleaned up. You're a mess," she said. "I've got to get back to work. See you in a few."

"Mom," I called her back into the room, but I didn't dare face her. "Thank you for this, really. I love you, Mom."

"Aww, you're going to make me all emotional." I knew she put her hand to her heart when she said it, like she always did when overcome with emotion. "I'm just so glad you found something to be passionate about. I love you too."

With that she left the room. Part of me wanted to call her back, wanted to cry into her arms as she held me against her. I was scared of being alone with my thoughts and of having her come back to see me like this all at the same time. The splintered parts of me cried out for her to see my pain, to come rescue her baby boy from the hurt. Part of me was mad that she didn't see me, really see ME. The one person who should know me better than anyone, was blind to what I'd become.

But it was my fault that she couldn't see. I'd hidden myself from her. I'd concealed what was going on in my mind from the world, from my mom, and from rED and the others. Irsa was the first person I'd really started to talk to about what was going on inside of me, and she and Anas had made a joke of it all. They'd seen Me, the real Me, and just as I feared, I didn't measure up. The real Me, THIS Me, wasn't worth anything at all. I knew that for sure now.

I waited motionless, the darkness and pain consuming me, until I heard my mom's truck pull out of the driveway. Then I threw the surfboard out of the way, tears stinging my eyes, and reached into my desk drawer for my tin. I swallowed two pills at once, but found myself staring at the open tin. Without thinking, I took two more. And still, I couldn't shut the lid.

I looked down at the surfboard lying on the floor. What was I going to do now? My mom was so proud, so excited to see me happy. She was eager for me to be the little kid who used to be so full of joy, the kid who died the day my dad did.

Though she said the surfboard was free, I knew better. I knew she'd pay anything, sacrifice anything, for me to be okay. Instead, I was going to disappoint her like I always did now. How could I stand to see the disappointment in her eyes? How could I stand to let her down again? It wasn't worth it. I wasn't worth it.

The pain in my chest was too much. The gloom was so heavy that I was sure it would never clear again. As I looked down at my trembling hand, I wondered how many pills it would take to stop my miserable existence. How many pills had it taken my dad to die? What was the magic number? I wondered if it would hurt, if I would even know I was dying. Maybe I would just drift off to sleep as he had, and just stop breathing.

I imagined life without me in it. Mostly I thought about my mom. She would finally be free to live her life without having to worry about me. Sure, she'd be sad for a while, maybe even depressed, but she would be free of me, the REAL Me, the Me who was holding her back from the life that she deserved. The son she loved, the one she was holding onto? He was dead and gone already anyway. She didn't even know THIS Me, the unlovable Me, the Me who'd been born from her worst pain.

If I ended it all right now, she would never have to know who I really was. She would never find out, never have to experience the horror of knowing I'd turned out just like the man she couldn't love anymore. Didn't she deserve that? Didn't I owe her that much? If I really loved her, I would put Me out of her misery.

And I'd be free too. Finally, free. No more pretending to be someone that I wasn't anymore. No more trying to be strong and failing over and over again. No more fighting the darkness. I imagined what that would be like. To just not exist anymore. To fade into the shadows, into nothing. No more pain, no more anxiety. No more Me.

I wondered if my dad would be there, on the other side of this hopeless life. The possibility of seeing him again made death less scary. It made it welcoming. Maybe he was waiting for me right now. It could be like we were never apart. *You are always with me.*

Now I could be.

Taking in a shaky breath, I dumped the rest of the tin into my hand. Twenty parachutes rested in my palm, ready to carry me above the storm that was ravaging my resolve. I grabbed the half-empty can of Mountain Dew off my desk with the other hand and told myself to just do it. Do it before I lost the nerve.

My heart pounded even as the Vicodin I'd already taken eased my tense muscles and numbed my thoughts. I took a few purposeful deep breaths and readied myself. In my mind's eye I held onto my dad. He waved to me from the bench perched on the deserted dunes beside the Kindred Spirit. *Come to me, Josh. I'm waiting.*

"I'm coming, Dad," I mumbled. "I am coming."

With one last breath, I tilted my head back and opened my mouth wide.

Just as I raised the pills to my lips, a loud banging reverberated from my window and made me jump. The pills hit the floor and scattered at my feet. For a moment I stood, stuck in a haze, watching them settle into the cracks of the carpet. Another knock sounded at the window as impatient knuckles assaulted the glass. Even in my drug-induced stupor, I knew it was Anas.

"Go away!" I yelled, sluggishly stooping to gather my pills.

"My dad went back to work. It stopped raining," he yelled from the other side of the window. "Let's get back out there. We still have a few hours."

"Not interested!" I yelled back, dropping the pills back into the tin.

"Dude, I will seriously press my butt against this glass in broad daylight!" he yelled. "I have no shame. Think of the neighbors."

With a sigh, I slammed the tin shut and shoved it into my pocket and then went to the window. I raised the blinds to find Anas bent over, lowering his pants. I raised the window, and he pulled them back up, a satisfied smirk on his face.

"I knew the neighbor thing would get you," he said.

"What do you want?" I asked, not looking at him.

"What do you mean, what do I want?" I could feel his eyes on me. "Bro, don't take this the wrong way, but you look like something I flushed down my toilet this morning."

When I didn't answer, he made a move to come through the window. I blocked him with my legs.

"I'm busy right now," I said.

"You working on the song, Solo?" He forced his head between my calves. "Dude! Is that a new board? Holy crap, it looks like a hybrid too!"

The Vicodin made it hard to focus, hard to stay in the moment, but I could feel the anger and hurt bubble up past the numbness in my mind.

"Yeah, it's a new board," I yelled, finally looking at Anas. "But there's no way I'm going back out there with people who think I'm a joke."

"What are you talking about?" He backed out of the window, his face a mask of confusion. "You don't want to surf anymore?"

"No, I don't want to surf with YOU anymore. Not after what you did. Don't think I don't know it was you."

"What did I do?" Anas took a step back. His eyes were wide. "What the hell are you talking about? What's wrong with you, Solo?"

"STOP CALLING ME THAT! And don't play dumb with me!" I screamed, and Anas flinched. "I know it was you! I know you're the one who answered my letter in the Kindred Spirit!"

"What letter? You mean . . . wait, you mean the mailbox?" he stammered. "You wrote a letter in there?"

I heard a door slam across the street. Irsa stood on her front stoop watching the spectacle at my window.

"You're the only one that could have done it," I continued. "Stop acting like you didn't!"

"I told you, I don't go near that thing!" Anas yelled back. "It's cursed, I told you. It's cursed."

"Get out of here!" I shouted at him, lowering the window. Before I shut it all the way, I looked across the street right into Irsa's concerned glare. Our eyes met.

"I want you to leave me alone. Just leave me alone."

I slammed the window the rest of the way shut and closed the blinds on them both. My hands were shaking, so I balled them into fists and waited for Anas to leave. For a minute he just lingered at my window. Then I heard his footsteps trudge back across the street. He mumbled to Irsa, and then the sound of their bike spokes passed my house and continued down the street.

Groggy and numb, I collapsed onto my bed. The pills made my body relax and the tension ease, but the pain in my heart was still there. Curling into a ball above the sheets, I didn't have the strength to hold back the tears. They flowed until the world around me faded away and I was lost to dreamless sleep.

Six

When I opened my eyes again, it was dark. Shadows formed confusing shapes against my bedroom wall, and I stared at them until I realized where I was. I sat up, my head cloudy, and stretched my stiff limbs. Then I walked to my door and peeked out.

The hallway was black. I turned back to look at the clock on my desk. It was after ten o'clock. I'd slept the entire day and evening away.

My stomach growled as I felt my way down the hall in search of food.

"Josh, is that you, sleepy head?" my mom called from her bedroom.

"Yeah, sorry . . . I,"

I tried to think of an excuse for having slept for so long, but nothing came to me. The lights were out in her room when I peeked in. The streetlight shone just outside her window, and I could see her lying in bed. She sat up and smiled at me.

"Man, all that sun and surf finally caught up to you, huh?" she said with a chuckle. "I would have woken you up for dinner, but you looked like you needed your rest. You feeling better?"

"Oh . . . yeah," I stammered. "I guess I was pretty worn out. Late nights and early mornings don't mix. I feel better now though."

None of it was a lie. I had been worn out and exhausted, and I did feel clearer now that the grogginess was fading and the Vicodin was wearing off. Things felt tolerable now that the anxiety had passed. The sting of betrayal remained, but I tried not to think about it. I was free of the shadows for now at least, and I wanted to keep it that way.

"Is there any dinner left?" I asked.

"I left a plate for you in the microwave," she said. "Don't stay up too late tonight. You've got a new board to try out in the morning. I wish I could be there to see it."

My heart sank. I still couldn't bring myself to tell her that I had no intention of going back out there. I'd have to lie about that now too.

"Thanks, Mom. I can't wait to get out there," I mumbled. "Good night."

"Good night," she said as I made my way down the hall. "Oh, and Josh?"

"Yeah?" I turned back.

"Take a shower, will you?" she asked. "You're still a mess."

I looked down at the mud still caked on my legs and at my wrinkled shorts and T-shirt, sullied with sand and dirt.

"Good idea," I agreed, closing the door to her room behind me.

As hungry as I was, I left my food to wait for me in the microwave as I opted for a shower. The hot water washed the remainder of fog from my mind down the drain along with the sand and mud. I couldn't help but think of the mailbox and the response to my letter. The shock of seeing what looked like my father's writing below my own was still with me.

Then I thought of Anas. The shock on his face when I yelled at him didn't add up. He'd looked so hurt and confused. Would he have looked that way if he had written the letter? What if he didn't do it after all? What if this whole thing was a mistake somehow? What would that mean?

I shook the thought from my mind. It had to be Anas and Irsa. They were the only ones that knew enough of my story to have done it. They were the only ones that had ever seen me near the mailbox. Wasn't it just like Anas to pull this kind of prank? It just had to be them.

Somehow, I didn't feel as anxious or upset about it as I had this afternoon. As much as the whole thing still sucked, it didn't feel as helpless as it had only hours ago. I felt calmer now. *What was that about?* This afternoon I was ready to end everything over it. That thought sent a wave of fear, like an electric shock, through me. *What the hell was I thinking? Would I really have done it?*

Once I dried off and dressed in clean clothes, I grabbed my tin from my dirty shorts. I thought about taking another, just to make sure the shadows stayed away. There were thirty-two left. It couldn't hurt to take another one.

Then a thought struck me.

What if the pills were causing me to go crazy? That could explain why the darkness had been so overpowering earlier. I'd taken more than I usually did. Maybe it wasn't just me overreacting. Maybe it was the pills making me irrational. If that was the case, I'd have even more reason to quit. I could do it.

Then I remembered that I hadn't taken any pills for almost twenty-four hours before I'd returned to the mailbox. In fact, the four I'd taken hadn't kicked in until after I'd almost swallowed the rest. If anything, it was the LACK of Vicodin in my system that had sent me off the rails. What I'd always feared was true. Without the pills, the darkness was too much to bear. It would overtake me again. It was just a matter of time. I only had one tin left.

Not bothering to re-heat my dinner, I snatched it out of the microwave. The smell of the tater-tot casserole made my stomach rumble despite the tempest in my mind. Plopping down in front of my computer, I took a tepid bite and waited for the system to come to life. When the screen came up, I saw that there were numerous messages from rED. He was asking where I was, asking if I was all right. I knew I should respond, but I had something more important to do. I needed answers to questions that he would never understand. Someone out there had to know how to score more Vicodin. There had to be a way.

I started again with stale forums, where people had asked the same questions I had. It was both a comfort and startling that there were so many people like me out there. I felt like I didn't belong to this alliance of prescription drug abusers. I felt better than them somehow, like I had a valid reason. I needed the pills for survival, not just for recreational fun. The more I read from these people though, people my age, the more I realized that they were just as desperate as I was. I wasn't any better than them. I was one of them. *Kindred Spirits*, I thought disgusted.

My empty plate sat next to me as I chased lead after lead about online pharmacies, prescription forging, and doctor shopping. I was deep into a thread about the art of faking injuries when I heard a knock on my window.

Anas, I sighed.

I had to give it to him. He was a tenacious one for sure. I ignored his knock, hoping he would just give up and go away. I wasn't ready to talk to him yet, but when I didn't answer the knocks grew louder and louder until I was forced to answer before they woke my mom.

I stomped to the window and threw up the blinds, ready for the site of butt cheeks on glass. Instead, deep chocolate eyes stared up at me from beneath a row of thick lashes. My breath caught in my throat.

"Irsa?" I opened the window. "What are you doing here?"

"We need to talk." Her voice was a tight whisper.

I looked across the street. Her father's car was in the drive. "What about your dad? If he finds out you're here . . ."

"Then you'd better let me in quickly."

She didn't wait for an invitation or permission before she started to climb in. There was no time to tidy up or to even think before she was standing in my room looking around. When her gaze fell on my computer screen, I scrambled to turn it off. I hoped she hadn't seen what was on it. She glared at me, suspect, until she saw the new surfboard that was now leaning against the wall.

"So, I wonder why someone with a brand-new board decides to no longer surf," she said, going to admire it. "Seems like a waste to me."

I didn't know what to say. Guilt, anger, betrayal and embarrassment went to war where coherent thoughts should have been at the ready. So, I said nothing, only watched her study me with those warm eyes. With a sigh, she sat at the edge of my bed and seemed to consider her words carefully.

"Anas didn't do whatever you think he did."

My heart sped. I didn't want to fight with her, but I could tell by Irsa's demeanor that she wasn't going to let this go.

"Irsa, he's the only one that saw me at the mailbox. He's the only one that could have done it besides . . ." I sounded pathetic even to myself, the doubt making my voice waver.

"Besides me?" she asked, lowering her head.

"Yes," I whispered. "But . . ."

"Why don't you explain to me exactly what you think we did?" Irsa interrupted.

I expected her to yell at me, but she didn't. She just crossed her hands in her lap and waited for me to explain. So, I told her everything about the mailbox, starting with how I thought it had called to me. I told her about my letter and about how I'd buried the notebook at the bottom of the pile inside. Her eyes widened when I told her that my letter had been answered, that the notebook was on top. I told her what it said and how detailed it had been. When I was done explaining myself, she took a minute to process. Then she cleared her throat and looked up at me, sympathy in her eyes.

"I can see now why you are so upset."

I rushed to her side, relieved that she understood. "That's why the only thing that makes sense is Anas."

Irsa sighed. "Do you know what my brother spent the entire afternoon doing at the beach today?"

"Surfing?"

"How I wish," Irsa huffed. "He spent it trying to sum up enough courage to tear that mailbox apart."

"What?" I sat down next to her. "Why?"

"He said that if he broke the curse, you'd want to surf with us again," she explained. "But he's too afraid of the thing to touch it. Do you understand what I am saying to you?"

"He didn't do it." I bowed my head.

"My brother is a lot of things," she said, rising, "but he's not someone to make a joke about such a loss. Neither am I."

"Then who? Who would do this?" I asked. "Who even could?"

"I don't know." She patted my hand.

Guilt won the war in my mind as I recalled the hurt in Anas's eyes when I'd screamed at him. I thought about how I'd overreacted. More than anything I wanted to explain to her that I wasn't myself earlier, that I wasn't thinking clearly. There was no way I could tell her any of that without giving away my secret. She must have thought I was insane, that I was a pathetic, horrible person. To my surprise, though, she stood and slugged me playfully in the shoulder.

"We'll meet you out there tomorrow," she said as if nothing had ever happened. "We have a mystery to solve."

"A mystery?" I tried to grasp how she didn't hate me.

"We've got to figure out who wrote that letter," she declared.

"Wait . . . you're going to help me?" I asked. "After I accused you guys?"

"That's what friends do. They help each other investigate creepy, cursed mailboxes," she said, going to the window. "They also let each other try out their new surfboards."

Her patience was unfathomable. It scattered the darkness like clouds after a storm. I smiled back. "Of course, they do."

"Good." Irsa's smile lit up my room. "Meet us out there at noon."

"Wait, why so late? What if we miss our letter writer?" I asked, confused.

"We go into Wilmington on Fridays," she said. "They have the closest mosque for us to attend Jumu'ah. It's the only day my father opens the shop late. Don't worry. We'll think of something."

Irsa peeked through the blinds. When she was satisfied that she wasn't being watched, she opened the window.

"Jumu . . . what?"

Irsa laughed. "Jumu'ah. It's our prayer service, kind of like Sunday church."

"Oh," I said. "I don't really go to church unless my mom drags me."

"Do you not believe like she does?"

"I used to, I guess," I struggled to explain. "I'm not sure what I believe anymore."

"Maybe you should go with her then." She hopped to the ground outside. When I went to the window, she turned back to me with a smile.

"Why?" I asked.

"Because a man without faith is a man without hope," she whispered.

I thought about her words for a minute. "Is that a famous quote in your religion or something?"

"Actually, I just made that up." She shrugged. Then she ran off before I could say anything else, before I could even thank her for not being mad at me.

I stared after her as she disappeared into the shadows beside her trailer. Then I shut the window and returned to my computer to resume my research with renewed vigor. I couldn't run out of pills and end up back at the edge of destruction again. There had to be a way to get more pills and stay ahead of the darkness. I wouldn't let it threaten everything again.

Seven

Cradling my new board under my left arm, I pedaled as fast as I could over the bridge. The tide was high. I looked down at the crystal waters that filled in the green space of the Intracoastal Waterway below. The sun punished my cheeks from where it glared high in the sky. I was late again.

Hours of Internet searching had finally yielded contact info for someone who had Vicodin to sell. I left him an email at four o'clock in the morning, just before taking another two pills and falling asleep at my desk until well past noon. I prayed this new source would come through.

By the time I got to our spot by the mailbox, Irsa and Anas were already taking a break from the waves. They sat dripping in the sand staring out at the ocean, deep in conversation. I wondered if it was about me.

"Slackers," I teased as I rode up and dumped my bike.

Irsa's face lit up when she turned to watch me lay my new board next to theirs. "It's about time you showed up."

Her smile reassured me. Anas, however, didn't look at me at all, only continued to stare out to sea. Guilt slammed my chest as I plopped next to him in the sand.

"Anas, I'm sorry," was all I could think to say. He remained stoic, staring straight ahead.

"Jedi Master," he finally said.

"What?"

"You will address me as Jedi Master from now on," he clarified. I waited for him to laugh or even crack a smile, but he just stared ahead and awaited my response.

I leaned over to Irsa. "Is he for real?"

"Oh, yes. He is very serious," she said. "Be grateful. At first, he was going for Grand Master of the Jedi Order. I convinced him it was too long."

"Jedi Master," I repeated.

"AND I get to call you Solo," Anas added.

"What?" I laughed. "I thought we were over that."

"These are my terms for reconciliation," he said, still not looking at me. "Do you accept?"

"So, if I call you Jedi Master from now on and let you keep calling me Solo, then you'll forgive me for yelling at you yesterday?"

"That's the idea," Irsa said, restraining a giggle.

"Do you accept these terms?" Anas asked again. I wondered how long he could keep up the serious pretense, but knowing him, it could be forever. With a laugh, I fell back into the sand.

"Fine," I said. "Oh, mighty Master of the Jedi, I accept your conditions. Please restore order to the Force and elevate it to its previous greatness."

Anas stood up; his demeanor completely reversed. It was as if nothing bad had ever happened. He smiled down at me and offered his hand. "Now you're just taking it too far."

I grabbed his hand and let him heave me out of the sand. "Can we just surf already?"

"Finally!" Irsa jumped up. "You couple of drama kings."

Grabbing her surfboard, she bounded into the water. Anas and I followed suit, grabbing our boards and racing each other to the surf.

The new board soared atop the waves like a jet hovering above the clouds. Irsa was the first to get a turn after she showed me the proper way to apply wax to keep my feet from slipping. She took command of the board within seconds, a true pro.

Anas had a harder time handling the sleeker board, but once he heaved his skinny legs aboard, he got a few good rides. Ultimately though, they left me to learn my new board. Irsa said getting to know your board was like breaking in a wild stallion. She said you have to lose your fear of it in order to gain control of it.

She was totally right, of course. At first it felt like the board was controlling me, tossing me about or making me bail whenever I was afraid that the ride was going wrong. Once I mastered my fear of a rough fall, though, I was able to keep the board beneath me. Soon I was riding the waves as long as Anas and even Irsa.

We took a break after an hour and plopped down in the sand beside the receding tide. As content as I was that my new friends weren't mad at me, I couldn't stop looking up the beach at the Kindred Spirit. The mystery of who had answered my letter still hung in the air like a foul odor. If it wasn't Anas, then who had done it? Could it really be my father writing me from beyond the grave? *You are with me always.*

"Are we ever going to address the elephant in the room?" Irsa broke the silence once she caught me gazing toward the Kindred Spirit for the thousandth time. "Or, more accurately, the mailbox on the beach?"

"Irsa, you don't have to . . ." I started.

"No," Irsa interrupted, "we're going to get to the bottom of this."

"She's right." Anas pounded his fist into the sand beside him. "We have to break the curse, Solo."

"You and your curses."

"Okay, let's figure this out." Irsa wrung the water from the front of her shirt before she turned to me. "How was the letter signed? Did you recognize the handwriting? How do you know some stranger didn't just write their letter randomly on the same page?"

"No, it was a direct response to my letter," I explained. "Whoever wrote it didn't sign it. They just said stuff that my dad used to say. He always just texted me or called me up, so I don't really know his handwriting that well. I mean, it looked like his. Here, why don't I just go get the letter so you can see for yourselves?"

I started to get up, but Anas grabbed my arm and yanked me back down.

"Do you want to curse us too?" he shrieked. "Keep all that stuff over there, or else we'll all start getting letters."

"You don't actually believe that there's a curse, do you?" I sighed. "Your dad was probably just trying to scare you."

"My dad believes a lot of things." Anas stared me in the eyes. "But when it comes to that mailbox, I'm with him. There's something about that thing. Don't tell me you don't feel it."

"Feel what?" I asked.

"Like it's watching you or something." He took a chill despite the blanket of summer heat upon our shoulders.

I wanted to tell him that he was crazy, that his superstitions were getting the best of him, but I couldn't. The mailbox had called to me that day. Of that I was certain. It had drawn me to it from the depths of my soul.

"So, what if you're right? What if the mailbox really is cursed?" I asked. "What does that mean?"

"It means that you have to see this thing through," Anas said. "To break the curse."

"What do you mean, see this thing through?" My pulse quickened. "Do you think that letter really is from my dad? That's not possible."

We all watched the wind blow wisps of sand past the mailbox as the seagrass beside it swayed in the breeze.

"There's only one way to find out if it was your dad or someone messing with you," Irsa said.

"How?" I asked.

"You have to write back."

"You want me to write another letter?" I shrieked. "After what happened the first time?"

Anas nodded in agreement. "We can stay here as late as possible to see if anyone goes to the mailbox and be here first thing in the morning. Anytime we see anyone write in one of the notebooks, we'll check to see if it's them. It's the only way to know for sure if someone's messing with you, or . . ."

"If it really is my dad," I finished.

The idea of writing in the mailbox again made my palms sweat. I wasn't sure I could do it. What if some stranger really was messing with me? How could I respond to someone who had taken my deepest wound and made a sport out of my pain?

More so, what if it wasn't someone messing with me? What if it really was my father writing to me from beyond the grave? What was I supposed to do with that? What would I even say?

"What if no one responds?" I asked.

Irsa shrugged. "Then we know it was probably just some jerk who's long gone by now."

"You have to do it," Anas insisted. "I'm telling you. It's the only way you're going to break the curse. You have to face your fear of it because fear leads to anger and anger leads to hate. Fear is the path to the dark side."

"Okay, Yoda." I snickered. "I'm not the one who's afraid of the mailbox. You are."

"Maybe he's right though," Irsa said. "Maybe this is your chance to face your fears."

"Like I said, I'm not afraid of the mailbox," I repeated.

Irsa raised her eyebrow. "Maybe it's not the fear of the mailbox you need to face. Maybe it's what you put into it."

"Dude, that's deep," Anas whispered. "I have no idea what you mean, but it sounds deep."

"I don't get it either," I said, confused. "What did I put into it? I just wrote a letter."

"You put into it what everyone else who discovers the Kindred Spirit does," Irsa explained as if it were obvious. "It's the same reason my father tells us to stay away from it. People come, and they pour their hearts out onto those pages for the world to see. They leave a piece of themselves in that mailbox. You left a part of you on that page when you wrote that letter. Maybe that's what you're afraid to face."

There was silence for a minute as Irsa's words washed over us like the ocean spray. I didn't know how she did it. We hadn't known each other a week, and Irsa seemed to understand me better than I understood myself. She was right again. I'd left all of my anger and brokenness in that mailbox. It was the pain that scared me the most, and what it had done to me. I was afraid of myself and of what I was becoming.

Anas laughed and slapped his sister on the shoulder. "Holy crap. That really is deep. The Force is strong with this one."

"So, are you going to write a response?" Irsa asked. "If you do, we've got your back."

I considered it for a second as they both stared at me, awaiting an answer. Again, I considered my choices. If I wrote another letter, we might find out that some stranger was messing with me, but at least I'd have an answer. Or maybe, just maybe, we'd discover that the mailbox really was cursed. We'd discover that my father was somehow contacting me from the great beyond. I didn't know if I could handle that.

If I didn't write the letter, though, Irsa and Anas would be disappointed. They would bug me about it until I gave in. Irsa would think I was too much of a coward to face my fears, and I would never know who wrote the letter.

"Okay," I decided, with a sigh. "I'll write another letter."

"Yes!" Anas jumped to his feet.

"But you guys can't watch me," I added. "I have to do this alone."

"That won't be a problem," Anas said. "Just scream at us if zombie hands come out of the mailbox to choke you, or if you hear evil chanting or something."

I stood up and brushed the sand from my legs. Then I extended a hand to Irsa. She took it, and I pulled her to her feet. "What help are you going to be if I start screaming, Anas? I mean, Jedi Master? You won't go near the thing, remember?"

"Oh, no, I just want you to scream so I know when to run for it." He smiled at me, his white teeth glinting against his tan cheeks.

"My hero." I rolled my eyes. "You can ride my board while I'm over there."

Anas squealed for joy and bounded over to the boards. He picked mine up, the size of it making him stumble all the way to the water.

"Good luck." Irsa saluted me before turning to grab her board.

Taking a deep breath, I turned to the Kindred Spirit. It didn't look very ominous from where it sat beneath the afternoon sun. I jogged to it, the sand scorching the bottoms of my feet until I threw myself onto the bench. For a second, I just stared at the mailbox, trying to imagine it as some kind of mystical portal to the afterlife. *Did Heaven get mail?*

The Kindred Spirit looked like a plain old metal mailbox. It was hard to believe that the box was anything other than an innocent heap of aluminum, but it was easier to think I was writing to my father rather than some weirdo stranger. So, I conjured his image into my mind's eye as I had done a thousand times since he died. What would I write if I knew he would actually read it?

I had to dig through the pile inside the mailbox to find the green notebook. The pages were crinkly from getting damp the day before, but I was able to flip to my page right away.

There it was, the response to my letter.

I examined it again. The ink had run some from the rain, but it was still legible. I tried to compare the writing to what I remembered of my dad's. It could be his. The edges of the letters had the same sharp angles my father used to sign his name, but a lot of people had jagged handwriting. It didn't mean anything. It was that last line, that familiar phrase that got to me. *You are with me always.* No one could have known that was something he used to say to me.

Grabbing a pen out of the mailbox, I checked to make sure Anas and Irsa weren't watching. They were belly down on their boards, racing each other against the tide. Once I knew I wasn't being watched, I closed my eyes and tried to imagine my father was in front of me. Then I put the pen to the stiff paper.

Dad?

Is it really you? How is this possible? When I wrote that letter, I never thought you would see it.

All of those things I said . . . I'm sorry. It's just that sometimes I get so mad I don't know what to do. You say that I am a bigger person than you are, but the hole you left in my heart is bigger than the ocean that rages beside me now. I am just like you, Dad. Mostly, that makes me proud, but it also scares me. I don't want to end up like you did. I'm afraid that there's no way to stop that from happening.

Mostly, though, I just miss you. I miss you all the time. I miss watching hockey games together and eating your homemade sauce. I miss Sunday morning coffee runs and our talks. You always used to know how to make me feel accepted. I needed that in my life.

I know Mom tries, but I always let her down. I try to stay strong for her, but I know that I remind her of you. I know she misses you too.

It's funny, I've wished so many times that I could just talk to you one more time. Now that I might be getting that chance, I don't know what else to say.

I'm sorry for whatever I did that made you leave me.
I love you.

I hope this is really you, Dad.

I made sure to sign it with my first initial, just as I had the first time. Then I nestled the notebook into the bottom of the pile and shut the mailbox. For a minute I sat there alone to gather my thoughts. Drying my eyes, I told myself that there was a logical explanation for the response to my letter.

A big part of me wanted it to be my dad, though. As freaky as it was, it would be like I hadn't lost him after all. He wasn't gone forever because he could meet with me in this place at the edge of the shore. Would that really be a curse?

"Did you do it?" Anas yelled, snapping me out of my thoughts.

I gave him a thumbs-up, and he waved me over, offering me back my board. We waded in the water, looking back at the Kindred Spirit.

"Now what?" I asked.

"Now we wait," Irsa said.

So, we waited as the tide clawed its way up the beach, drawing us closer to the Kindred Spirit. It was the end of the week, so the crowd was growing. People mostly congregated by the pier miles down the beach. Only a handful of joggers, dog walkers, and curious explorers made their way down to us. They all passed by, watching as we caught shallow waves off shore.

A few stopped at the mailbox and had a seat on the bench. We went on high alert whenever they took the time to leave their thoughts. None of them looked suspect, but Irsa sent me racing to check for a response to my letter each time they left. Every time, I found the green notebook still at the bottom of the pile. The space below my letter remained blank.

It wasn't until late in the afternoon when much of the crowd had packed it up for the day that a man wandered down the beach. His grey hair fluttered above his weathered forehead as he walked against the wind toward the Kindred Spirit. A solemn look creased his rugged face. Just behind him, a wooly dog sniffed at shells and ran to dip its legs in the surf before returning to his side. When the man sat on the bench beside the mailbox, the dog found a spot of shade beside the dunes to rest his paws.

"Are you guys seeing this?" Anas paddled up to where Irsa and I waded.

"Oh, I'm seeing it," I said.

The man looked out to sea from where he rested on the bench and spotted us staring at him.

"Quick," Anas whispered. "Look natural."

He attempted to paddle away but got swept up by a strong wave that knocked him off his board. His twiggy legs kicked the humid air as he sank, bottom end first, into the water.

I paddled past him. "Oh, yeah, very natural."

"Actually, that was about right." Irsa shrugged as she caught a shallow wave and stood up.

"Shut up," Anas spat when he surfaced. "Is he still looking?"

I chanced a look back at the beach as I struggled to pop-up onto my board. The man had turned his attention to the mailbox where he removed the small stack of notebooks and placed them on the bench beside him. Then he picked one from the top and began to read through its pages.

"He's reading the letters," I reported, paddling back to where Irsa and Anas waded. "I think he's looking for something."

"Your letter?" Anas asked.

"I don't know."

The wind picked up, causing the waves to push us farther and farther down shore from the mailbox and the man. We watched him from a distance as the sun dipped farther in the sky. He flipped through each and every page, reading with solemn interest.

"We have to go," Irsa said to Anas. "It's late. We'll be cutting it close as it is."

"How are we supposed to hide the boards with that guy sitting there?" Anas asked. "He's been there for over an hour."

"I'll take care of the boards," I offered, not taking my eyes off the man on the bench.

"Thank you, again." Irsa's voice was tense as she made for the shore. "Anas, move it."

Anas let out a huff and started for the beach.

"Wait," I said, and they both froze. "He just picked up my notebook. The green one, that's the one."

We all sat down in the shallow water, watching the man but pretending not to. When he finished reading the letters, he reached into the mailbox for a pen. We held our breaths as he touched the pen to the paper in my notebook.

"He's going to write something," Anas whispered. "This is definitely our guy."

"It has to be," Irsa agreed. "Do you recognize him at all?"

"I've never seen him before in my life," I said, studying the man's furrowed brow.

Then as if he sensed us watching him, the man glanced up. He looked straight at us, and his eyes narrowed. He shut the notebook and replaced the pile in the mailbox. Then he closed the lid and walked off, calling for his dog to follow.

"Damn it," I whispered.

When he passed us, the man kept his eyes forward, ignoring us altogether. The dog bounded up to us and greeted us with a soggy tail-wag before falling in at the man's heels. Soon they were nothing but specks moving down the beach.

"We have to go," Irsa urged, running ashore.

"Wait," Anas pleaded. "Let's see if he left a message."

Not waiting to hear her answer, I plopped my board down and ran across the hot sand to the mailbox. Dripping and out of breath, I yanked the mailbox door open and found the green notebook on the top of the pile. I flipped to the page where I'd left my last letter. There was no response.

"Did he write back?" Anas kept a few feet's distance between himself and the mailbox. "Was it him?"

"No, there's nothing here," I said.

"Man, I was so sure we had him," Anas cried.

"Ani!" Irsa yelled for him down the beach.

"Wait," I said as he turned to leave. "There's a pen mark right below my letter. That wasn't there before. Maybe he was about to write something, and we scared him off."

"Anas, we have to GO!" Irsa yelled again.

"I'm telling you, that was our guy." Anas backed away toward his sister's urgent calls. "We're going to catch him. To be continued, Solo."

"Yeah, maybe. You guys get out of here," I said, still contemplating. "I'm right behind you."

I made quick work of burying Anas's and Irsa's boards. The wind blew in just the right direction to help cover them with a thick layer of sand. Hopping on my bike, I raced toward the pier. I thought I might be able to catch up to the man with the dog. It had been hours since I'd taken any pills, and their effects had long worn off. I needed to get home, but if I could just get a better look at the man, it might help me figure out who he was. That thought was enough to keep me pedaling as fast as my tired legs would go.

By the time I got to the pier though, neither the man nor the dog was anywhere to be found. Disappointed, I jogged my bike up the embankment and onto the wooden planks of the beach access. I looked across the street at the bike rental parking lot as soon as it became visible. Mr. Salid's car was no longer there. I wondered if Irsa and Anas had made it home in time.

When I turned onto my street, I had my answer. Irsa and Anas were parked behind a row of high shrubs on the corner looking out at their father's car parked in the driveway of their trailer. For the first time, I saw fear on Irsa's face as she and Anas argued in excited whispers.

"Oh, no. You didn't make it." I pulled up beside them. "What can I do? This is my fault."

"No, we knew this would happen eventually," Irsa said.

Anas turned to me, his eyes pleading. "We're trying to come up with a plan."

"What do you have so far?" I set my bike down to hide with them behind the brush.

"I could distract my dad while she sneaks back in her window. She could change and sneak back out . . ."

"It will never work," Irsa interrupted.

"She could say she went to the store, or for a walk or . . ." Anas tried to continue before Irsa spoke up again.

"The walls in there are as thin as cellophane," she argued. "Even if you could distract him for long enough, he's going to hear me. If he sees me soaked like this, he is going to figure it all out. My father is trusting, but he is not stupid."

I considered the plan. Irsa was right, if the walls of their trailer were anything like mine, then their dad would hear her. Unless . . .

"I have an idea." I looked over at my trailer. My mother was home, which would make things more difficult, but not impossible. "You need a loud distraction so you can make it into your room unheard. I'm going to open my window and blare my music as loud as I can. The bass from my subwoofer could register on the Richter Scale."

"That could work." Anas jumped up. "He might even go across the street to ask you to turn it down. Then Irsa might have enough time to change and make it down the street before he comes back. I can say she told me she was running to the store. This could work, Irsa."

Irsa looked hopeful for a second and then lowered her eyes and nodded toward my trailer.

"Your mom is home," she said. "I can't ask you to get in trouble for me."

Thrilled by the thought of being able to help Irsa for once, I was ready to do whatever it took. It was finally my turn to be the one taking the risks.

"Let me worry about my mom." I hopped back onto my bike. "Just be ready to run for it as soon as you hear the beat drop."

Putting my feet to the pedals, I started to take off when Irsa yanked me back. Before I knew what was happening, she kissed me on the cheek.

"Thank you, Josh," she whispered as my face flushed.

"You'd do it for me," I said before pulling back onto the street toward my trailer.

The blinds were open in the Salid trailer as I passed by, but I couldn't see if Mr. Salid was freaking out inside. I assumed he was as I parked my bike beside the banister of my back porch. For a minute I just stood there, trying to figure out a way to convince my mom to let me do this. I knew she wouldn't like my plan. In fact, she would hate it because it involved not only being sneaky, but also pissing off our neighbors. All of them.

I took a deep breath, deciding that if worse came to worse, I would just have to lock my bedroom door and let my music blare against her wishes for as long as I could. Better for me to be grounded than for Irsa to be found out and no longer able to surf. I couldn't let that happen.

Looking back, I saw Irsa and Anas peek their heads above the bushes. Anas gave me a thumbs-up while Irsa looked on, concerned. I wished that I had my pills. I needed their chemical courage. They were in my room, I reminded myself, their proximity spurring my confidence. I could do this. Not hesitating another minute, I threw open the back door ready for battle.

"Mom, I need to do some . . ."

When my eyes adjusted to the shade of the indoors, I froze. My mom sat at the dining table, a plate of fresh cookies in front of her. She stared at me, eyes wide, as I took in her guest. Mr. Salid sat beside her, sipping coffee from my favorite Pittsburgh Penguins mug. He raised his eyebrows at me as I burst in, obviously interrupting their conversation.

I stood staring, not knowing what to do, until my mom cleared her throat and looked me in the eyes.

"Oh, good, you're home. Josh, you've met Mr. Salid," she said, tense. "I caught him coming home from work and just *had* to have him in for coffee."

The inflection in my mom's voice told me what she'd done. She'd stopped Mr. Salid from going into his house on purpose. She saved us.

When I still didn't move, she cleared her throat again.

"Yeah . . . I mean, yes," I stammered. "It's nice to see you again, Mr. Salid."

"Likewise," he nodded. "Your mother has been telling me a lot about you."

"I promise you," I said with a shy smile, "only half of it is actually true."

Mr. Salid laughed, which softened his stern demeanor. He wasn't nearly as intimidating when he smiled.

"She tells me you like hockey too," he said, holding up my mug with a nod. "Was that part true?"

"You like hockey?" I asked, surprised. "I love hockey."

"I enjoy a Carolina Hurricanes' game every now and again," he said. "Does that make us rivals?"

"Yes, I mean, well . . . sort of, but only if we're playing each other." I had to think of a way to escape to my room long enough to flag down Anas and Irsa. "I would love to talk to you more about that. Would you excuse me a minute while I clean up? I'm a mess."

"Of course." I thought I saw a hint of suspicion in his eyes. My mom must have sensed it too.

"Yes, go change for Heaven's sake. You're getting sand all over my clean floor." My mom laughed nervously, giving me a *hurry up* look behind Mr. Salid's back.

"My son does the same thing . . ." I heard Mr. Salid say as I rushed to my room and shut the door.

Before I could think of doing anything else, I threw open my desk drawer. My heart pounded as I popped two pills into my mouth and swallowed. Twenty-six left. Then I opened my bedroom window as quietly as I could and slipped out. Irsa and Anas looked confused as I ran up to them, my words coming out fast and breathy.

"Your dad is at my house," I panted. "My mom stopped him before he went home. You have to hurry and get inside. He doesn't know you're not home yet."

"He's at your house? He hasn't gone inside ours yet?" Anas asked, shocked. "Holy crap!"

"Oh, praise Allah." Relief washed over Irsa as she grabbed her bike. "Your mom is the best."

"Quietly," I warned as they passed me running back to my room. I watched them dump their bikes behind their trailer as I climbed back into my window. They made it in the front door before I turned to change into dry clothes. Relief and a pill-induced euphoria flooded my senses and washed away the sting of nerves. By the time I walked out of my room, my mom and Mr. Salid were engaged in conversation about single parenthood.

"Irsa does an amazing job keeping up the house," Mr. Salid was saying. "She's had to learn her household duties without a mother to teach her. My wife died many years ago, you see."

"I'm so sorry to hear that. Josh's father died recently, so I can definitely relate." From the hall I watched my mom pause, think, and then lean in closer to Mr. Salid. "I hope you don't mind my asking, but what does Irsa do for fun? That's one thing I worry about the most with Josh. I don't want him to lose the rest of his childhood because of what happened to his father. What does your daughter do that, you know, is just for her? Does she ever get out of the house?"

Typical. My mom was pushing it. I glared at her as I entered the room, but her eyes were fixed on Mr. Salid who smiled politely and took a sip of coffee before answering. I knew that I needed to interrupt, to stop this line of questioning from my mom. She could give us away, but I was too curious about Mr. Salid's answer to say anything.

"Irsa has a lot of girlfriends at school that she sees frequently during the school year," he explained. "Unfortunately, they all live in Shallotte, a few towns over. You'll see when school starts, most of the children live closer to the school. One of the prices you pay, unfortunately, for living this close to the beach. It's hard for Irsa to see them during the summer with me working seven days a week."

"Seven days a week?" My mom laid a hand on her chest. "That has to be hard."

"It is, but this is the shop's busiest season, you see," he said with a smile. "I look forward to next summer when my son will be old enough to join me at the bike rental."

"But shouldn't Irsa . . ." my mom started.

"In my culture," Mr. Salid interrupted, "a young lady's place is in the home. She must learn how to care for a family if she is to have her own one day. You understand?"

"I . . ." my mom started again. Only this time I cut her off before she could argue Mr. Salid's views on a woman's place in society. This was not an area they were ever going to see eye to eye. I knew she would only pry and that could lead to the truth coming out.

"Sorry," I said, entering the room. "You were saying you watch hockey, Mr. Salid?"

Mr. Salid seemed to welcome the change of subject, turning his full attention to me as my mom scowled beside him.

Spurred on by the pills, I engaged Mr. Salid in conversation about my favorite sport and about why he should consider pulling for the Penguins instead of the Hurricanes as the Penguins were the best team of all time. His face lit up when he talked about the game, and I found him surprisingly easy to talk to.

"I don't know," he chuckled. "Now that you live in North Carolina, you might have to start pulling for the Hurricanes. They're a decent team if you give them a chance."

"I'll think about it," I said.

My mom sighed happily from where she sat, resigned, in the corner. "I'm just glad Josh is talking hockey again. He's been more interested in his video games than real life up until recently."

"Sounds like my son as well," Mr. Salid agreed. "Always on the game system. Anas is a bit younger, but perhaps you two would get along."

I smiled. "Maybe we would."

"Speaking of my children, I have to be getting home. They are probably wondering where I am." Mr. Salid stood, took his mug to the sink and then turned back to us. "Thank you very much for the visit, Tina."

"It was a pleasure to meet you, Mr. Salid," my mom said standing with him.

"Please," he said, "call me Youssef."

"Youssef," my mom repeated, walking him to the door. "How would you and your kids like to join us for dinner this weekend? Sunday night maybe? We would love to have you all."

I glared at my mom, eyes wide, as Mr. Salid thought it over. His sable brown eyes met mine, and I gave him what I thought was a neutral smile. Then he turned back to my mom.

"That would be very nice, thank you," he said with a smile. "Perhaps I can bring my specialty recipe. I don't cook much, but you might enjoy it."

"That would be lovely." My mom clapped. "We'll have a potluck of sorts. Say, seven o'clock?"

"I look forward to it," he said, and then he left the house with a nod goodbye.

From the window I watched him cross the street before I let out a long, relieved sigh.

"Mom! I can't believe you did that," I said. "You know you saved our lives, right? Irsa didn't make it back on time. It was almost all over."

"That's what I figured when I pulled up and noticed that none of your bikes were here." She put her own mug in the sink. "Then I saw him pull up and panicked. I ran over to him as he was checking his mail."

"Mom, you're our hero." I went to her with arms as wide as my smile, ready to embrace her in a grateful hug. She held her hand up and stepped back.

"Not so fast." She stuck her pointer finger into my chest. "That's the last time I cover for you. Do you understand me? You know how much I hate dishonesty. Youssef is a perfectly nice man. I won't lie to him again."

"You didn't lie," I assured her. "You did the right thing. You heard how he talked about Irsa. He expects her to live out her days trapped in that trailer."

"That's a little dramatic, don't you think?" she argued. "There's a cultural difference here that I don't want to disrespect."

"Disrespect?" I cried. "What about what he's doing to Irsa? Isn't that disrespect?"

"I don't have the answers here, Josh. My heart goes out to Irsa, it really does," she said. "I just know that if you were struggling with something major like that, I would want to know about it. I think that if you really want to help Irsa, you should encourage her to talk to her father. Keeping things from him isn't fair to either of them."

Guilt dug its sharp talons into my chest as I thought about the struggles I was keeping from her, and from everyone.

"If she tells him, he'll never understand," I said, knowing it would be the same if I told her about the pills. "He'll only be disappointed in her. He'll make her stop surfing."

My mom sighed and leaned back on the kitchen counter. She looked at me with sadness in her bright eyes.

"That's one thing you just won't understand until you have kids of your own," she said. "There is nothing a child could ever do that could make a parent feel any differently about them. Disappointment comes with the package. It's our job to pick you up, brush you off and get you back onto your feet. I'm sure that man over there feels the same way about his children."

I tried to stay focused on Irsa and her dad, but I couldn't help but think about how much I wanted my mom to be able to brush me off and make everything all right again. The hard fact was, there was no way she could put the broken pieces of me back together again. I knew that she would try, but how could I let her? Knowing that she would only fail? It would break her heart, just like it would break Mr. Salid to know that Irsa snuck out every day. If I told my mom about the pills, she would take them from me and force me to live without them. She wouldn't know that she was killing me. I knew that Mr. Salid would do the same to Irsa. He would keep her from the waves. Only he'd be robbing her of her passion. The pills kept me living, but the waves made Irsa come alive.

"He'll make her stop," I said again.

"Maybe." My mom hugged me to her. "But he may just surprise you."

With that she tapped my nose with her finger before disappearing into her room to change. I stood there in my pill-induced numbness and took in her words. Then I made my way into my room and shut the door.

The sun was setting on another summer day, showering my room with an array of oranges and pinks. Going to the window, I looked out across the street. Through the blinds, I could see my new friends and their father gathered for their evening prayers. As if she sensed me watching, Irsa looked up at me and grinned. I smiled back and lowered the blinds.

Eight

"Do you really think it was your dad?" rED asked as my avatar followed him through a scorched landscape.

"The whole thing is super creepy, if you ask me," Stephy said. "You don't really think the mailbox is cursed, do you?"

I sat back in my desk chair and tried to focus on the game, but my mind was in a million places. Luckily, my mom didn't bring up Irsa or Mr. Salid again that evening. She left me alone with my thoughts for the most part. The biggest weight on my mind was the fact that my new Vicodin source still hadn't emailed me back. There was no way I could deal with all the other things in my life without first figuring out how to get more pills.

"I don't know what I think right now," I said into my headset. "It's all so weird."

"My money is on the shady guy with the dog." Blank's avatar raced to join mine at the front of the clan. "I mean, who sits there for hours reading other people's personal thoughts like that if they aren't looking for something. Maybe the guy is lonely and looking to be part of someone else's story. You said he picked up the pen like he was going to write something, right?"

"Yeah, until we spooked him," I said. "There was a pen mark right under my letter like he was going to reply before he saw us watching him."

"Creepy," Stephy repeated.

"What if it wasn't him, though?" Zoso asked. "I totally believe in curses. Besides, how would this guy know what to say like that? As crazy as it sounds, I think it could your dad writing you from beyond."

"What?" rED snorted.

"Think about what you're saying," Blank interjected. "Think about what that would mean."

"Haunted mailbox," Stephy whispered.

"I'm saying that things happen that we can't always explain, is all," Zoso said. "Like the Bermuda Triangle, the pyramids, Roswell, and yes, ghosts. Maybe this mailbox is something like that. What if it is some kind of portal to the afterlife?"

"You've been playing too many horror RPG's," rED mocked.

"Zoso, all of those things you just mentioned have scientific explanations," Blank argued. "Just because we haven't figured out what they are yet, doesn't mean they're supernatural. Same goes for this mailbox."

"The teacher would say that." Zoso chuckled. "What is it you teach again, Blank?"

Blank paused before answering. His avatar charged past me, its gun raised.

"Philosophy and Earth Science," he said with a cough. We all laughed, scurrying to catch up.

"My point exactly," Zoso said.

"Look alive, boys," Stephy warned. "There's a horde ahead."

Teasing turned to battle cry as we charged at the enemy. Just as we neared the front lines, a small text box popped open at the bottom of my screen announcing that a new player had entered the game. I ignored it, assuming Biggles had finally arrived to round out the group. I made a mental note to make sure to touch base with him. Maybe he would have a lead on more pills. It wasn't until Stephy started laughing that I realized it wasn't Biggles.

"What the . . ." she said, her avatar wavering. "Who the hell is R2Deez2Nutz?"

"What?" I asked, unable to contain a chuckle as I looked down at the new player's gamertag. "I thought that was Biggles."

"Biggles hasn't logged on in days," rED said. "His spot's been open to just anyone. We got stuck playing with a couple of middle schoolers last night since you weren't here either."

"Hey, R2," Blank said with a laugh. "Welcome to The Stranded, I guess."

"What up, fam? The fun has just arrived," the new player announced.

I knew that voice, I realized. My heart sank. How was this even possible?

"Who is this joker?" Zoso laughed. "I like him."

"Anas?" I asked. "What the hell?"

I heard him clear his throat. Stephy was still laughing in the background.

"Who is this Anas of which you speak?" he asked, sarcasm dripping from his tone.

I sighed, embarrassed at what I was about to say in front of my friends.

"Jedi Master," I said. "Is that you?"

"Solo!" Anas cried. "So, this is your clan?"

"How did you find me on here?" I asked.

"Oh, I totally peeped your gamertag when I was in your room. You left your screen open," Anas explained. I could see him shrug in my mind's eye like it was no big deal.

"Wait . . . Anas?" rED asked. "As in, your neighbor?"

"Oh, I see what's going on now," Stephy said. "That gamertag though . . ."

"Everyone, this is Anas," I started, but Anas cleared his throat again. "He prefers to be called Jedi Master."

"How's it going?" Anas said.

"Jedi Master, this is rED, Blank, Stephy . . ."

"My, my, my," Anas growled. "A lady player. My kind of woman."

"And Zoso is her husband," I finished.

Anas coughed. "Of course he is."

"It's nice to meet you." Zoso laughed. "Can you shoot?"

"Can I shoot?" Anas huffed. "Solo's got nothing on me."

"Who is Solo?" Blank asked. "I feel like I'm trapped in *Empire Strikes Back*."

"Best movie ever," rED said.

"My man!" Anas shouted.

"I am Solo," I explained. "He's been calling me that from day one."

"Hey, where's Chewbacca?" Zoso laughed. "What is this, *Battlefront*?"

"This is my clan, Anas." I ignored Zoso's chuckle. "In here we go by gamertags only. So, if you want to play with us, then you have to call me Grymm. Got it?"

"Yeah, okay, fine," Anas agreed. "Grymm. I got it."

"And should we continue to call you R2?" Blank asked with a chuckle. "Or would you prefer Deez2?"

"Just call me Nutz?" Anas answered.

Stephy snorted into her mic. rED tried to hold back, but eventually laughed with her.

"All right, Nutz," Zoso said. "Let's see what you've got."

As it turned out, Anas could actually shoot. Before long he was taking point as we cleared the battlefield of alien scum. He bantered with the rest of the clan and held his own against their constant teases. It was after midnight when he sent me a private message.

"*I have a plan for tomorrow,*" he wrote.

"*What's that? You mean for the mailbox?*" I typed back.

"*No, for blowing up the Death Star. OF COURSE I MEAN THE MAILBOX!*"

I stuck my middle finger up to the screen as if he could somehow see it. Then with a sigh I typed my response.

"*What's your big plan?*"

"*I have a GoPro!*" he typed. "*With this new HD card I found, we should be able to record for eight straight hours.*"

"*You're thinking it could watch the mailbox when we can't?*" I asked.

"*Exactly,*" he confirmed. "*We leave it there overnight to see if anyone comes after we're gone.*"

"*I like it,*" I typed.

"*Good,*" he said. "*One other thing . . .*"

"*What?*"

"*Does your mom know?*" he asked. "*About Irsa sneaking out to surf? You swore you'd never tell!*"

"*I had to tell her.*" My fingers pounded the keys. "*I already mentioned seeing her surf before I knew the situation. I had to tell her so she WOULDN'T say anything to your dad.*"

There was a pause before Anas sent another message.

"*Admiring my sister from afar, were you?*"

"*You're stupid,*" I typed. "*I just never saw anyone surf like her before, is all.*"

"*It's never going to happen, man.*"

"*SHUT UP!*" I said it out loud as I typed.

"*So, is your mom going to tell my dad or what?*"

"*I don't think so,*" I typed with a sigh. "*She gave me an earful today, but she's cool.*"

"*Good.*"

"*But . . .*"

"*What?*" he asked.

"*My mom invited you guys for dinner Sunday night. We're going to have to put on the performance of a lifetime for your dad.*"

"*Leave that to me,*" he typed. "*I know how to handle my dad. Just go along with whatever I say.*"

"*Yeah, right!*" I laughed out loud.

"*We'll talk about it tomorrow.*" He clicked out of chat, and I returned my attention to the game. rED was ahead of me as we came upon a barren city.

"Okay, losers, I'm out of here," Anas announced.

"What? We've got to finish this wave," rED said.

"No can do." His avatar fell back. "I've got an early morning tomorrow. Solo, I mean Grymm, this time you're coming with us. Seven a.m. sharp. We have to go check the mail."

And with that, Anas logged off. For a minute, no one said anything as we continued to interact in our digital world. rED was the first to speak up.

"I like him," he said, breaking the silence.

Then everyone started talking at once, giving their genuine approval of Anas.

"Seriously," Zoso said, "that kid is hilarious."

"You have to tell us what happens tomorrow," Stephy said. "You can't leave us hanging. I have to know if someone wrote back again."

"I promise I will," I agreed.

We played out the rest of the wave. Then one by one The Stranded logged off until only rED and I remained.

"Well, I've got to get to bed," I said. "You heard R2Deez2Nutz. I've got an early morning tomorrow."

rED laughed. "I still can't believe that's his gamertag. I really do like that kid, almost more than playing with Biggles."

"Does anyone know where Biggles is?" I asked, trying to sound matter-of-fact. I still held out hope that Biggles would come through for me.

"Nope," rED said. "He hasn't logged on in days."

"Weird."

"Yeah," rED agreed, "but now Anas has an in. It's kind of cool to have him on board, like we get to be a part of your life there. I say we keep him."

"Give it a week." I laughed. "You might change your mind."

"Do you think that guy with the dog really answered your letter?" rED asked.

"We'll find out, I guess." I sighed.

"Grymm?" There was a pause. "You know it can't actually be your dad, right?"

"I know it's crazy," I said. "It's impossible. Still, I can't shake the feeling that this mailbox is special. It's hard to explain."

"I just don't want you to get hurt," rED said. "You know, thinking it might be him and then finding out it's just some weird coincidence. I worry about you."

"I know you do, man," I said. "But things are okay here."

"It's the girl, isn't it?"

"What?" I laughed.

"The way you talk about her," he said. "You've got a thing for her, don't you?"

"I don't know . . ."

"Oh, come on," he probed. "She sounds pretty awesome."

I couldn't deny that I felt something for Irsa. I couldn't hide the fact that everything about her intrigued me and made me want to know more. She was on my mind more often than not, but I wasn't ready to think of her as anything but a new friend. Anything else had so many implications.

Could she even date someone like me? Didn't Islamic women only date Islamic men? I thought I'd read that somewhere. Even if she could date me, I doubted she would be into someone like me. She was so wise and talented. What could I possibly have to offer her? I was nothing but a mess.

"I don't think it's going to happen," I said. "It's complicated."

"Well, do me a favor," rED said. "If you ever do get a chance with her, clutch it, okay?"

I laughed into my mic. "That IS what I always say, isn't it? You've got to clutch it."

"Yeah," rED said. "So, follow your own advice on this. Okay?"

"Okay," I said, "I will."

By the time I logged off it was well after one o'clock. I'd almost forgotten about the email I was waiting on. When I closed my gaming window and pulled up the Internet, I saw that I had a new message. My pulse sped when I saw that it was from my potential new Vicodin source.

I opened the email and was surprised to see that all it said was "*Text me,*" followed by a phone number I'd never seen before. That was it. No greeting, no signature, no explanation.

My hand shook with nerves as I plucked my phone from my desk. This could be it. This could be the answer I was looking for. If this worked out, I could have a steady supply of Vicodin from now on, or at least until I was old enough to get a prescription without my mom knowing about it.

Or this could be another dead end.

Not knowing what to say, I just typed *I got your email* into the text box and sent it to the number. For ten minutes I stared at my phone, willing it to come to life with a response. When it finally chirped in my hand, I jumped. With my heart pounding in my ears, I opened the text. There was a PayPal link, nothing else. I clicked on it, and it took me to a sales page. What was being sold was not specified, but I knew what it was.

The page displayed only a list of prices that choked the breath from my lungs. This person was charging five dollars per unit, or two hundred dollars for a thirty-day supply. I knew what that meant too. I would have to shovel out five dollars per pill or spring for a whole bottle of them for two hundred dollars. I would need at least that many to get through a month, and that was pushing it.

Biggles never charged me that much. I'd always been able to pay him what little I got for trading in video games or mowing the neighbor's lawn. How was I going to come up with two hundred dollars? How was I going to get more after that? Two hundred dollars a month. That was the price for keeping the shadows at bay.

My palms began to sweat and my body ached as my mind raced through possible solutions. If I could just buy a month's supply to keep me going, then I could buy enough time to find another seller who charged less. Maybe Biggles knew of one. I would need to take this one month at a time. I could ask my mom for the money, make up some excuse for why I needed it, but I knew that wouldn't work. She'd be suspicious right away.

I could get a job. That was a thought, but I doubted I would make enough to afford the pills by the time I needed them. Then there was the transportation issue. The job would have to be close enough to bike to. A job could work in the long run, but I needed faster money. There was only one viable solution, I realized.

I had to sell something.

Looking around my room, I took an inventory of what I could part with that would bring in enough funds. Falling to my knees, I rummaged through my game drawer, counting in my head the worth of each game. It was no good. Even if I traded in every game I owned, I wouldn't have near the amount I needed.

Then my eyes fell on my music equipment. The sequencer alone would get me at least half of what I needed. If I threw in the interface, I might just have it. That was crazy, though. My music equipment? How could I live without the means to make music and mix songs? Even when I wasn't creating, I never doubted that I would return to it. Thanks to Anas, I was finally ready. I had just found my passion again. How could I give that away?

I told myself that it was temporary, that as soon as I got a job, I could buy a new sequencer and interface. I told myself that this was a matter of life or death. There was nothing else I had that was worth enough money.

Then I remembered the mostly new hybrid surfboard sitting on the back porch. It was name brand and sturdy. I wondered how much I could get for it. Curious, I searched the type and brand of my board on a local marketplace site. To my surprise, similar boards were listed for almost three hundred dollars. If I listed it for less, it was sure to sell fast.

Exhausted, I sank onto my bed. My mind felt heavy, like the enormity of my choice was literally weighing me down. How could I sell my board? My mom got that board for me because she was excited about my new hobby. She was proud of me for the first time in what felt like forever. Irsa and Anas would never understand either. I'd have lie to them all for this to work. I'd have to tell them it was stolen. I'd be even more of a fraud.

Either way, one of my passions had to go. They would both get me the money I needed. I had to sacrifice something in order to keep up the habit that was ensuring my survival. If I sold my music equipment, I'd lose a part of my soul. My music was everything, and my following was growing, but my board was a part of this new beginning. It was a part of who I was becoming. It was a symbol of hope for both me and my mom.

Something had to give. I had to lose something in order to keep myself ahead of the darkness. It was worth it, I told myself. Digging my tin out of my pocket, I swallowed two more pills to help make the decision less painful. I needed the numbness to see this decision objectively. Time was running out.

By the time the blissful haze had overtaken my mind, I'd made my choice. With fragile resolve, I slunk to my computer where the marketplace site waited. I made my listing, set the price for two hundred dollars, and posted it before I could change my mind.

Then I fell back onto my bed, drew my knees to my chest, and tried not to cry.

Nine

The pounding on my window woke me at exactly seven a.m. It also woke my mom. She bounded into my room, her robe loosely tied and her hair in tangles.

"What in the world is all that ruckus?" she demanded, her eyes only half open.

With a lazy moan, I rolled over and pulled the cord to my blinds. Although the sun was rising into the humid morning sky, there was a full moon once again pressed against the glass of my window.

Anas heard the blinds draw and turned with his usual proud smirk. When he saw my mom gawking back at him, her eyebrow cocked, he fell to the ground for cover.

"Well, there's something you don't see every day," she said.

"Speak for yourself."

"Does he realize it's Saturday morning? Is this going to be a new Saturday morning thing now?" She crossed her arms.

I sat up with a stretch. Outside, Anas was low-crawling across the lawn back to his bike, his backpack bouncing up and down like a turtle shell as he struggled to pull up his pants. Irsa sat on her bike at the curb and watched him, unamused.

"You're an idiot," I heard her say through the glass.

"Their dad works Saturdays," I answered my mom. "So, probably."

My mom staggered toward the kitchen. "Tell Anas it's too early for butt cracks, will you?"

Groaning, I stood and rubbed my eyes. "Is it ever the right time, though?" I yelled after her.

"I don't know!" she yelled back. "I've been single for a while."

"Gross."

Shutting my door behind her, I brought my computer screen to life and checked my listing. There were over fifty views. With any luck I'd have an offer by the end of the day. As good as that news was, my heart ached with the thought of what I was about to lose. I wanted to take more pills to help ease the pain, but knowing that I would have to live on a minimum supply from now on, I went without for now.

It only took a minute to dress and grab my stuff. My mom was finishing up the last sandwich when I came into the kitchen. She handed them to me with a bag of chips and three bananas.

"You don't have to keep doing this for us," I said, stuffing it all into my backpack. "I can pack a lunch."

"I know you." She licked peanut butter from her fingers. "You'd just throw some beef jerky and a box of pop tarts into your bag and call that lunch."

"What's wrong with that?" I kissed her on the cheek. "You sure you don't mind me leaving you on your day off?"

"Are you kidding me? I have three episodes of *General Hospital* to catch up on. I MAY even go shopping for some home décor later. You're the one missing out," she said, patting me on the cheek.

"Clearly." I backed away to the door. "I'll see you later on."

"Don't forget the sunscreen!" she yelled to me as I let the door flop back into place behind me.

"It's in the bag!" I yelled back. Then I tucked my board under my arm and hopped on my bike.

"Bout time," Anas spat when I met them at the curb.

"Sorry. I had to console my mom from the fright you gave her," I lied.

"Oh." Anas lowered his head in shame. "She saw me? What did she say?"

"Well, at first she was completely grossed out, but then she looked out the window and saw your face and realized she'd seen the better half up close." With a loud hoot, I pedaled past him while he processed my joke. Irsa laughed and raced to catch up with me as Anas fumed behind us. By the time he caught up, we were already at the bridge.

"Ha, ha!" He pedaled twice as fast to keep up. "Very funny."

We caught the downward slope of the bridge and looked out at the green of the Intercoastal. It was low tide, and the air was thick with the smell of brine and saltwater. The clouds from the day before had vanished, leaving behind a clear, vibrant sky in their wake.

"Where are you going?" Irsa called when we passed the first street on the island. I looked back to see that she and Anas had stopped at the turn.

"I thought we were going to the mailbox?" I asked, confused.

"You've been going the long way this whole time?" Anas laughed. "No wonder it takes you forever."

"We can't go that way. My father will see us," Irsa added.

"There's another way?"

"Rookie," Anas chided, turning down the residential street. "Follow us."

We weaved our way through backstreets lined with pastel-painted houses and baby palms. Life teemed around us as people walked their dogs or gathered up their morning papers. Above us seagulls announced the start of a new day, and a row of pelicans dipped low in the sky as they approached the sea.

By the time we popped back onto the main street, we were on the far end of the island. I followed behind Irsa as she rode down the planks of a scarcely marked beach access and onto the sand. We all jumped off our bikes to walk them past the fluffy embankment and onto the hard-packed sand by the tide. I looked behind me toward the pier to gather my bearings. It loomed in the far distance. In the other direction the sand bar was close, which meant the Kindred Spirit was even closer.

"Well, I'll be damned," I said with a laugh.

"See?" Irsa smiled. "Short cut."

We were at the mailbox within minutes thanks to this new-to-me shortcut, which gave me little time to mentally prepare for what I might find inside. By the time I dropped my bag and board into the sand, Irsa and Anas were already watching me with anticipation.

"Aren't you guys going to get your boards?" I wiped the sand from my legs.

"No way." Anas still kept a safe distance from the mailbox. "I have to know right now."

"Me too," Irsa agreed. "The anticipation is killing me."

I looked from them to the awaiting mailbox, which stood stoic and regal beneath the shade of the dunes. Taking a deep breath, I tried not to think about how much calmer I would be if I had just taken a couple of pills.

"Here goes nothing." I walked up the beach to the Kindred Spirit alone as they stared after me.

My mind raced with a thousand possibilities and consequences should I find another answer to my letter. I almost chickened out. If I checked the mailbox and there was indeed another letter from my dad, this mystery would only intensify. I thought about what rED said to me the night before: *I just don't want you to get hurt, thinking it might be him and then finding out it's just some weird coincidence.* If there were a response this time, it would be no coincidence.

"Just do it!" Anas yelled, his eyes wide.

With a deep breath, I lowered the lid. Just like the day before, the green notebook was on the top of the pile even though I'd buried it at the bottom. I tried to keep my hand steady as I withdrew it from the opening. With a deep breath, I flipped to my last letter. When I saw the writing below it, my arms failed me. I dropped the notebook into the sand.

"What is it?" Anas squealed. "Is it Zombie hands?"

I could only stare at the notebook lying face-down in the sand. My body was stuck, unable to move until my mind could comprehend the reasons behind what I'd just seen.

Irsa jogged up to me. She laid a cautious hand on my shoulder. "Was there another letter?"

I looked into her sympathetic face. "I don't understand why this is happening."

"We're going to get to the bottom of this," she assured me. "We're in this together."

"Do you think I'm cursed?"

Irsa looked down at the pages in the sand and then back up at me. She gave my shoulder a reassuring squeeze.

"There's only one way to find out," she said to me. Then she turned to Anas. "Let's get the boards."

"But . . ." he tried to argue. "What did it say? I have my camera! We can catch him this time."

Irsa grabbed the collar of his shirt and pulled him toward the dunes. Plucking the notebook from the sand, I took it over to the bench and sat. I peered down the beach in both directions, looking for signs of the man with the dog or of anyone who might have done this. For the most part, the beach was still empty aside from the same joggers and scattered fishermen who were always there. The shore hadn't yet filled with vacationers and locals willing to brave the tourist crowds.

Irsa and Anas emerged with their boards a minute later. Irsa pushed her brother toward the water and smiled at me, assuring me as she always did. Anas attempted to shake free of her long enough to say something to me, but Irsa only pushed him harder whenever he tried.

"Leave him alone," she scolded. "Let Josh read it in private."

When they were in the water and I was alone, I opened the notebook again. The handwriting below my latest letter was the same as before, the words eerily familiar again.

Son,

There is only one explanation for how this is happening. We are being given a chance to make things right between us.

It is the only thing that makes sense. This mailbox is the In-Between. It's the threshold between death and life itself. It is here that we have to make peace with our wrongs. Do you understand?

You have to know that I am proud to be your father. I always have been. Nothing you could ever do could change that. I miss you more than words can say, Son. I miss all those times too. Those hockey games were some of the best days of my life. Days that are forever behind me now.

You never let me down, no matter what I may have said or done in the past. Your heart is too pure. Your mother and I always saw that. I know you still make her proud.

It is my greatest prayer that you can forgive me for leaving you, my son. Please give me this chance to make things right.

I am with you always.

This time the tears flowed, and I could not stop them. Every ounce of my being told me that this was my father speaking to me. The words rang too true to not be his. The words my soul longed to hear from his lips were incarnated on the page, written from an unseen hand and placed in a mailbox in the middle of nowhere. The *In-Between*, he had called it. That described the Kindred Spirit perfectly. When I was here, I felt like I was sitting on the very precipice of life and death. So much of me had died since my father left this world. This is the only place I'd felt him near me since then.

Wiping my eyes, I looked out to the water where Irsa and Anas laughed and struggled to mount their boards atop the lively morning sea. Surfing with them, I realized, was the closest to

Heaven as I had ever been. Living each day without my dad, without having his smile or the comfort of his voice, had been my closest notion of Hell. Only here, in this place, did the two unite and somehow exist as one at the same time. The In-Between.

With shaking hands, I reached into the Kindred Spirit for a pen. I had to write back. This was him. It just had to be. I took a cleansing breath and put it to the paper.

Dad,

I can't believe it's really you. I can't believe this is happening. Are you here? Am I just missing you somehow?

How do we make peace with our wrongs? I ask myself that every day. And what then? What if we do make peace with our wrongs, Dad? Will you leave me again? If you are here with me, then I never want to leave the In-Between.

My heart is not as pure as you think, Dad. I guess that's why I am here. If people could see the real me, if they could see into this soul of mine, they'd run away from me. I'm a time bomb, and even I don't know when I'll explode.

How do you right your wrongs when all you are is wrong?

I love you, Dad.

It was all I could write; all I could muster. There was too much to think about.

I was now convinced that my father was the one writing to me. How could anyone else possibly know just what to say? No, I was sure it was him, and I was determined to prove it once and for all. I had to see him, had to see what happened when my letters were answered.

Drying my eyes, I closed the notebook and tucked it into the bottom of the pile as usual. Then I shut the lid, grabbed my board, and jogged over to Irsa and Anas. They stopped laughing and turned to face me, their smiles falling as they waited for me to say something.

I looked at Anas. "You still have that camera?"

His face lit up. He curled his lips into a mischievous grin. "Hell, yeah," he said. "This is going to be good."

It only took a few minutes to position the camera behind a sprouting of beach grass. Anas had thought of everything. He nestled the camera inside a sandwich bag until only the lens was sticking out, then he buried the covered part in the sand and aimed the lens at the mailbox.

"Okay, we only have eight hours or so of battery life. I'm not going to turn it on until right before we leave. Until then we have to keep our eyes open for people who write in the mailbox."

"Let's surf farther down the beach this time," Irsa suggested, "so we don't spook the dog guy this time."

"It's not the dog guy." I took my board to the water.

"How do you know?" Irsa asked.

"Of course, it's the dog guy," Anas shrugged. "Who the hell else could it be?"

They both followed me into the shallows, and we paddled out past the breakers.

It's my dad," I said. "I'm sure of it."

"Josh . . ." Irsa started, but I wouldn't listen to reason. Some things defied reason.

"His last letter sealed the deal for me. He explained it all. He said that we were both stuck in the 'In-Between.' It all makes sense to me now."

"The 'In-Between'?" Irsa asked.

When we passed the breakers, we straddled our boards, waiting for a big enough wave to come by.

"It's the place between this life and the next," I tried to explain. "He said we were stuck here because of our past sins or something."

"Al-Barzakh," Anas whispered, nodding.

"It can't be." Irsa's brows furrowed.

"What?" I asked.

"In Islam, Al-Barzakh is the barrier that stands between the spiritual world and the physical. The two touch yet never meet," Irsa explained. "It is halfway between reward and punishment."

"Then you understand," I said. "The In-Between."

"Are you saying that the mailbox is some sort of . . . portal? To Al-Barzakh?" Anas's eyes were wide. "No wonder my father forbids us to go near it."

"I'm saying that it's my dad who is writing me." I shrugged. "I don't care how it's possible, but it's him. I know it."

"The camera will tell," Irsa reasoned. "You'll have your answer, Josh. I just hope it is the one you want."

"Man," Anas said, still stunned. "Can you imagine what we're about to capture on that camera if you're right?"

Straddling our boards, we all turned toward the mailbox. Now that the sun was higher in the sky, light reflected off its black surface like a beacon.

"It could be nothing." Irsa was determined to remain rational.

"Or it could be everything," I countered.

"You know what this means, don't you?" Anas asked. "We're going to be YouTube famous."

Irsa and Anas watched the mailbox for another minute and then turned their attention back to the sea. I watched the mailbox a moment longer. I imagined the possibility of seeing my father materialize in front of the camera. Is that how it happened? Did he just appear out of nowhere? Did I barely miss him each time? The In-Between . . . *could it be?*

The breakers crushed the sand with a fury in front of me, rousing me from my reverie. I tried to concentrate on the waves, on riding the great morning surf before the tide came in. Anas and Irsa enjoyed the bigger swells, smiling and whooping with every good ride. Whenever someone approached the mailbox, though, we waited and watched them from the corner of our eyes.

First an elderly woman came to sit on the bench. She reached in, withdrew the top notebook and wrote a short note. Later came a young couple who walked up to the mailbox with joined hands. They read from a few of the notebooks and then replaced them without writing a word. Each time someone approached, Irsa and Anas went on full alert, but not me. I knew who was leaving those letters, and I knew we wouldn't see him while we sat just off shore.

After an hour or so of my trying to focus on the waves and failing, Irsa hopped off her board and waved for Anas to join her at my side.

"You're too distracted to enjoy this good surf," she said.

"I know. I'm sorry," I said. "I just . . . I can't stop thinking about my dad."

"Well, if it's not a good surfing day, then there's always the next best thing. You know what I think today should be, Anas?" Irsa raised an eyebrow at her brother.

Anas looked confused for a minute. Then a slow smile etched across his face.

"Yes." He nodded emphatically. "That's exactly what this day is."

"What are you guys talking about?" I asked. "What day is it?"

"Boardwalk day!" They shouted in unison, looking to me with excitement.

"What's boardwalk day?" I couldn't help but laugh at their excitement. "There's no boardwalk at Sunset."

"The Myrtle Beach boardwalk is only a 45-minute drive away," Irsa explained. "If we leave now, we'll have a few hours to spend before we have to get back."

"Arcade, baby!" Anas was already headed for shore. "They have two of them! I still have my birthday money from last month. If you're nice, I might buy you some tokens. Have you never seen the SkyWheel?"

"No, I've never been to Myrtle." I called after him. "Wait! What about the mailbox?"

"Nothing ever happens while we're watching anyway." Anas shrugged. "We'll start the camera and come back in time to check the mailbox. If there's another response, we'll check the footage. If not, we'll reset it for tonight. We won't miss a thing. I promise."

"You need the distraction," Irsa urged. "It will be fun."

The decision was made before I could think of a way to protest. Within minutes, Irsa and Anas had buried their boards and were hopping on their bikes.

I took one last, long look at the Kindred Spirit before I conceded and followed suit.

"How are we supposed to get there if it's a 45-minute drive?"

Anas rolled his eyes at me as he pedaled out in front.

"Dude," he said, "haven't you ever heard of Uber?"

Ten

The driver let us out beside a sidewalk cluttered with people. The 187-foot SkyWheel loomed above us, the top disappearing into the cloudless sky. Irsa smiled at it. I could feel her excitement as I craned my neck to watch the massive Ferris wheel spin. Its height was astonishing. We'd been able to see it from over a mile away. Standing next to the massive ride filled me with dread rather than excitement. I loathed heights, but I knew Irsa would want to ride it.

"Gets me every time," she said with admiration.

"Arcade first!" Anas jogged toward the boardwalk. "My money, my choice."

"Sounds good to me," I said, happy to take Anas's side on this one.

"Fine," Irsa agreed, "but I call dibs on the crane machine."

The smell of funnel cakes and hot dogs wafted in the air as we walked down the crowded boardwalk. The beach beside us was busy with people frolicking in swimsuits and tank tops. Palm trees and waving American flags lined the planks of the walk as we weaved our way through the crowd. Everything about this place was different from the small town of Sunset Beach. From the shops and beachside bar and grills to the towering waterfront hotels, Myrtle Beach was a tourist's paradise.

It took less than five minutes to walk to the bright blue arcade busting at the seams with small children and playful adults. Anas ran straight for the token machine and started shoving in dollars. I looked around, surprised.

"Where are all the teenagers?" I followed Irsa to the nearest crane machine where she waited her turn. "I thought there'd be more people our age here."

In fact, I'd been so sure of it that I had taken a couple of pills to ward off my anxiety. Now I was down to my last twenty-two pills, which would be worth it if I were going to meet people I would be going to school with next month.

"They all go to the Pavilion up the street," Irsa explained. "It's got more rides and even a teen club."

"Why didn't we go there then?" I laughed. "Don't people from school go there? Don't you want to see people you know? Your friends?"

We watched as a mother-daughter team struggled to position the claw above a fluffy, stuffed heart. They hit the button. When the claw lowered, they'd missed their mark completely.

"Why do you care?" Irsa smirked. "Don't you hate meeting new people?"

"I don't HATE meeting people. I'm just not good at it," I explained. "I guess I just thought I'd get a look at what to expect when school starts."

"You're not missing anything." Irsa positioned herself behind the controls once it was free. "We are better off here. Trust me."

"But . . ." I started to pry when Anas skipped over, his hands filled with shiny, gold coins.

"We each get a dozen," he said. Irsa counted them out and handed me my share before turning back to the crane machine.

Though I was still curious, I dropped the subject for now. I watched as Irsa dropped two tokens into the machine and eyed her target. She maneuvered the crane over a stuffed dolphin and then leaned over to look through the glass at the side of the machine. Moving the crane another centimeter to the left, she pressed the button. The crane came down right onto the dolphin and grabbed it by the tail. It lifted it into the air and started back to the opening. The dolphin was only inches from the drop point when it fell.

Irsa let out a frustrated cry. "Man!"

"So close!" I stood beside her as she dropped two more tokens into the slot.

This time the claw grabbed the dolphin's fin, but dropped it immediately.

"Let me try." I put my own tokens in the slot.

I took my time, aimed the claw to where I thought it would fall directly on the body of the dolphin, and then hit the button. The claw dropped, grabbed the dolphin right below the fins, and lifted it. The dolphin started to slip from the jaws as it made its way to the drop point. We held our breaths. As the crane moved, the claw lost its grip, and the dolphin fell. It bounced off the edge of the opening, and then fell right in.

"You got it!" Irsa jumped up and down with excitement. "I've never gotten anything from one of these things. I've been trying for years. How did you do it?"

"Beginner's luck, I guess." I grabbed the stuffed animal from the prize slot and handed it to Irsa. She clutched it to her chest, her eyes gleaming.

My cheeks flushed with pride. I decided right then and there that making Irsa smile like that was the strongest drug I would ever know. It was intoxicating, exciting, and empowering all at once. I wanted to do it again.

"Let's try to get another one," I said.

"Oh!" Irsa grabbed onto my shoulders. "Let's get that fuzzy heart for the little girl who was just here. She and her mom are over by the Skee-Ball machines."

"Okay." I laughed at her excitement. "I'll try."

The heart proved to be more difficult to capture. We took turns trying to grab it, each time screaming when the claw dropped it closer and closer to the opening. We went through tokens like a drunk through booze, becoming more intoxicated with determination with each turn. By the time we were down to our last two tokens, we had amassed a crowd of small children who cheered and bit their lips beside us.

"Final chance." I held up our last two tokens.

"You do it," Irsa said. "You've got a better chance."

I started to protest when the little girl who'd wanted the heart came over with her mom to see what was going on. Her little blonde curls bounced, and her eyes grew wide when she saw that we had gotten the toy within a half inch from the opening. She pointed it out to her mom through the glass.

Taking a deep breath, I looked at Irsa. She nodded to me, and I dropped in the last two tokens.

"The momentum will knock it in," she assured. "You just have to clutch it."

"Clutch it," I repeated with a smile and then got into position. "Let's do this."

I took the whole time allotted, measuring the distance with my eyes and looking through the side of the machine to gauge my angle. With a second left on the clock, I hit the button. The crane lowered, and the jaws of the claw opened. When the claw shut, it embraced the heart inside and began to lift it. The toy teetered inside the jaws, threatening to fall just short of the opening. When the heart did fall out, there was a collective gasp. Again, the toy bounced off the wall of the opening. Then it fell inside.

The crowd of kids around us erupted, and Irsa bounced with them. "You did it!"

I locked eyes with the little girl as I reached into the machine for my prize. Then I handed it to her just as she started to look sad for having lost it.

"We got this for you," I said. "We saw you trying to win it earlier."

Her eyes widened as she realized I was giving her my hard-earned prize. She reached her tiny hand out and grabbed it from me with a shy smile.

"Thank you," she said.

"You're very welcome."

Her mother thanked us too, smiling at both me and Irsa as her daughter waved goodbye. Irsa turned me to her and wrapped me in an excited hug as the crowd around us disbanded.

"That was awesome," she said. "Did you see how happy she was?"

Her warmth passed straight through my flesh and warmed my heart from the inside. I inhaled her, letting the drug that was Irsa seep into every part of me. Her joy was intoxicating, and knowing that I had caused it was more exhilarating than the sickest wave ride. When she pulled away, our eyes locked. The heat I saw in hers showed me that she was feeling something for me too.

"What's all the commotion over here?" Anas asked, walking up to us with a fist full of paper tickets. "You hit the ticket mother-load or something?"

Irsa and I broke away from each other. I tried my best to look normal.

"No, actually," I said with a cough. "We didn't get any tickets."

"What?" he screeched. "Well, get to it. I've got my eye on a sick Pokemon hat over at the prize counter. If we pool our tickets, we might have enough."

"Pokemon?" I laughed.

"Do NOT judge me."

"We're all out of tokens." I shrugged. "Sorry."

"What?" Anas cried. "You blew through your tokens, and you have nothing to show for it?"

"We have this . . ." Irsa held up her small, stuffed dolphin and smiled.

Anas looked from Irsa to me with disgust.

"You guys are a disgrace to arcade-goers everywhere," he said. "Come on. Let's get in line for the SkyWheel."

I followed them outside and down the boardwalk, too distracted by the spark that had passed between Irsa and me to think about what we were about to do. The line was long but moved quickly. When I finally looked up at the monstrous wheel, my heart bubbled and pooled into the pit of my stomach. I was going to freak out. Irsa would see me freak out and think I was a coward or worse . . . just plain lame.

Irsa and Anas were like jumping beans in front of me, hardly able to contain their excitement. I, on the other hand, was about to throw up.

"Is there a bathroom near here?" I asked, trying my best to look unaffected.

"Are you okay?" Irsa asked, concerned.

"I'm fine," I assured her. "I just have to take a leak before I get on."

"It's right around the corner," Anas pointed. "Hurry up, man."

I jogged around the corner, and when I was out of sight, I leaned against the wall of the ticket booth and tried to catch my breath. Before I even let myself think about it, I grabbed the tin from my pocket and swallowed two pills with one gulp. The chalky tablets stuck to my dry throat, and I had to swallow a few times to get them down.

When I'd caught my breath and assured myself that relief was coming, I straightened my trembling legs and jogged back just as it was our turn to get on. The people in the gondola in front of us evacuated, and we started to get in.

"It's a glass-bottomed one!" Anas shouted ahead of me as he climbed in. "Jackpot!"

I looked inside the gondola. The walls were already transparent, which made things terrifying enough, but when I looked down and saw that the floor beneath Anas's feet was also see-through, I took a step back.

"There's no way." I retreated. "I can't do this."

"Oh, come on, Solo," Anas pleaded. "This is the ultimate thrill right here."

"Yeah, well, it's a little too thrilling." I took another step back.

"Are you all going or not?" The ride's operator was getting impatient.

Irsa followed me out of the gondola and grabbed me by the arm. "He and I will catch the next one."

"Single rider!" the operator yelled. "Anyone else want to ride the glass-bottom?"

We turned to the two college-aged women behind us, clad in cut-off jeans and bikini tops. They looked at each other as they thought about it.

"Come on, ladies," Anas said with a wink. "I promise it will be the ride of your life."

They turned back to one another and laughed. "I think we'll wait for another gondola," one of them said.

"Your loss." Anas shrugged as the operator secured his door. "Just remember, if the gondola's a rockin', don't come a knockin'."

"Gross!" Irsa laughed as Anas's gondola lifted into the air and another came around.

When I looked up, I could no longer see the entire height of the ride and decided that no amount of Vicodin was going to make this okay. From where I was standing on the platform, it looked like we were about to be launched into deep space. I scrambled to come up with an excuse not to ride, but I was out of time. When the gondola emptied, Irsa hopped inside and turned to me.

"Come on," she urged.

I was torn. My heart told me to get into the gondola with her where we would be utterly alone together for the first time, but my survival instincts were running a full-HD slideshow in my mind of the numerous ways in which I was about to end up a permanent stain on the pavement.

"I don't know . . ." I said. "I'm not sure I want to die today."

"Well, then." Irsa held her hand out to me. "I dare you to live."

I looked at her, at her reassuring smile and her outstretched hand, and my heart won. I clung to the numbness that was beginning to spread throughout my body as I took her hand. Before I could even catch my bearings, we were lifted into the air. Irsa laughed as I clung to my seat, hanging on for dear life to the only thing I could. The world outside grew smaller and smaller as we rose higher into the sky. From somewhere above, Anas screamed with delight.

"Do you really think hanging onto the bench will save you?" Irsa smirked.

"It's all I have at the moment," I panted, trying not to look out the window.

"Look at me." She stifled another laugh. "There's nothing to be afraid of. In fact, it's beautiful up here."

"Whenever I get myself into these situations, all I can think about is the numerous ways in which I have tempted fate," I admitted. "The height of this ride might be a little too tempting."

"You're not going to die." Her smile softened.

"How can you be so sure?" I struggled to steady my breath as we rose higher and higher.

Irsa bent her head to look me in the eyes. "Because if you die, I die . . . and I've got too much life still to live."

"I hadn't thought of that," I admitted with a shrug. I had to close my eyes as we were well above the rooflines of the tallest hotels. "You would be going down with me. Usually I think fate is out to get me, but there's no way you're going to die today. So, I might just be safe after all."

The Vicodin was starting to numb the fear that coursed through me. I could feel the blessed calm take over and with it a surge of adrenaline when I chanced a peek through my squinted eyelids. We were now closer to the clouds than the ground. When I looked down, the panic fought back.

"Nope," I croaked. "I'm definitely going to die. It will be a heart attack. Don't worry, you're safe. Fate's been after me for a while."

"No way." She laughed. "If you go, I go. That's the deal."

I felt the warm touch of her hands as she grasped mine and came to sit beside me. Her eyes were warm, understanding, but the spark I'd seen earlier had grown into a flame. My heart thundered just below my shirt. Everything was spinning with us: my body, my head, my heart, and my thoughts. Irsa was so close that I could feel the heat of her against the skin of my arm. I couldn't think straight, couldn't feel the nerves that should have made me anxious. I was sure that the chemicals coursing through my system made me more courageous than the real Josh ever could be.

"No, Irsa," I said, drawing closer to her. "You have to live. You're going to change the world someday."

Her face flushed as it inched closer to mine. "Why do you think that?"

"Because you've already changed mine," I said.

And that was the end of all thinking. My brain shut down, and my heart took over. The fear faded and vanished like the ground below us. All that existed now was Irsa and her chocolate brown eyes, which looked right through to the core of me, to where my heart sputtered and skipped at the sight of her. Somewhere in the far reaches of my mind, I heard rED's voice. *If you ever get a chance with her, you have to clutch it . . .*

"Clutch it," I whispered in agreement to myself.

Irsa looked at me questioningly, then smiled. I leaned into her before she could say anything, our eyes still locked. She bent to meet me. I closed my eyes.

When her lips met mine, it was only for the briefest moment, but it felt as though all time had stopped. Everything around us fell away into nothing. Warmth radiated through me and erupted in my chest in a succession of fragmented explosions. Nothing had ever been as perfect as those few seconds.

My mind flashed inexplicably to the Kindred Spirit. If the war and peace I felt there was really the In-Between, then those seconds with Irsa pressed against me as we were suspended in the clouds was surely Heaven. She pulled away, and her eyes fluttered open. We stared at one another, our breaths coming in quick drags. She opened her mouth to speak when something above us caught her attention. Her eyes widened in terror.

"Oh, boy," she breathed, and I followed her gaze.

Neither of us had noticed that the ride was stopped near the top of the rotation, just before the drop on the other side. Below us, the people on the beach looked like specs of colorful debris that littered the beach. Blue rooftops glistened in the early afternoon sun, and the ocean sprawled out in the distance toward infinity. Above us, the view was much different.

The glass-bottomed gondola was only feet away from ours. Anas's bewildered face was pressed to the glass floor, his lips contorted in smooshed shock. He gawked at us; mouth agape and body sprawled. I felt my face flush as Irsa cleared her throat and moved away to her bench.

"We are never going to hear the end of this," she said shyly.

I watched Anas peel his face from the glass and point at me. He yelled to me, but his voice died on the wind. However, I could read his lips easily.

"So gross!" he yelled over and over until the ride started again.

We moved slowly then, stopping every few seconds to change riders at the bottom. When Anas was below us, we chanced a look at one another. So many questions raced through my mind, and yet I didn't know what to say. I narrowed it down to just one and found the courage to ask it.

"What do we do now?"

Irsa looked at me and smirked. Then she turned in her seat to look out at the ocean.

"Now we don't ruin it with a bunch of questions," she said. "If you don't ask, I won't have to give the answers that I don't want to say and you don't want to hear. So, for now? We just . . . live."

I didn't know what that meant, and something told me that I didn't want to know. After putting myself out there like that, the rejection would kill me. So, I didn't pursue it. Instead, I changed the subject as quickly as I could before things got awkward.

"It's not so bad coming back down." I looked out the window. "You can see up the coast for miles from up here."

"It's magnificent," she agreed, not breaking her gaze from the scenery. "I could stay up here for hours."

I wanted to be close to her again, just to feel her warmth against me. The moment was over. I knew that, but I also knew that we would be back on the ground within minutes. The debate in my mind was brief. I left my bench to sit beside her again so that we were both looking out at the ocean on her side. She didn't flinch or protest, just grinned as we watched the specks on the beach turn back into people, and the ground rise up to meet us.

We were still grinning when the operator opened our door, and we got up to leave. Looking around for Anas, I readied myself to face what was sure to be an overly dramatic rant. I didn't see the group of girls sneering at us as we exited.

"Oh, look," one of them said. "The terrorist has recruited a new troop."

It took me a minute to figure out that she was looking at Irsa when she said it. Irsa froze as soon as she saw the girls waiting to get on. A strange look washed over her usually joyful face. For the first time, fear flashed in Irsa's eyes. She glared at the girls. Then she simply took a calming breath and walked away without saying a word.

"I think I'm too scared to ride this thing now," another girl said, loud enough for Irsa to hear. "She might have put a bomb on it or something."

Irsa froze, her body tense. Yet she said nothing, just collected herself again and walked on. The girls giggled and whispered among themselves as they watched her go. I watched Irsa walk away with her head downcast. Rage bubbled up until I couldn't take it anymore. Without even thinking about it, I walked up to the girls. My anger, coupled with my dose of chemical courage, propelled me to forward. The girls gave me the once-over as I approached.

"You know what?" In my peripheral I saw Irsa turn as I spoke. "You SHOULD be scared to ride. It says in there that the weight capacity is only thirteen hundred pounds. From the look of it, your egos far exceed the weight limit."

They looked stunned, like I'd pistol-whipped them against their made-up cheeks. I turned, my eyes locking with Irsa's. The corner of her mouth lifted in the slightest smile as the girls hissed behind me.

"Excuse me?" one of the girls yelled. "Who do you think you're talking to like that?"

"Don't know. Don't care." I shrugged as I walked to Irsa. I turned to offer them fake concern. "Seriously though, ladies, between the fake tans, the fake lashes and the fake nails, you're all so full of crap you might bring the whole ride down. Please, for goodness sake, think of the children on board."

The ride operator stifled a laugh as he ushered the girls into the gondola while they whined in their high-pitched voices to one another. Irsa's smile beamed brighter than the afternoon sun. She laughed and even waved to the girls as their gondola took off into the sky. Her newfound exuberance was how I was sure that no one had ever stood up for her before. It made me feel both noble and sad.

"I can't believe you just did that!" she said. "Do you have any idea who those girls were?"

"Nope, but I'm guessing they're wondering who I am right about now."

"That was Ashley Brafton and crew." Irsa's eyes were wide. "She's the head cheerleader and was our sophomore class president."

"And I bet she dates the quarterback and was prom queen too," I teased.

"Actually . . ." Irsa stopped walking. "Yes. Ashley's the most popular girl at school."

"Well, if that's the case, it's all good then," I said with a grin.

"You haven't even started school yet, and the most popular crowd hates you because of me," she pointed out. "How is that all good?"

I shrugged. "Because they would have hated me anyway. I'm not exactly the popular type. I mean, can you see me dressed like a Ken doll flexing my biceps for the cheerleaders beside my apple-red Camaro?"

"I'm pretty sure most of them drive a Prius."

"Prius?" I snorted. "See what I mean? We don't need that kind of negativity in our lives."

We walked side by side, laughing as we rounded the corner toward the boardwalk. Our faces fell when we came face to face with a disgusted Anas. His arms were crossed and his hip was thrust out to his side as he glared at us.

"Where have you been?" Irsa asked. "You totally missed Josh sticking it to Ashley Brafton."

"I was trying to wash the sight of you two smooching off my eyeballs. Wait . . . Ashley Brafton? But she's so hot!"

"Let's get out of here." I checked the time on my phone. "It's getting late."

"Yeah, and I don't want to spend any more of my money on you two lovebirds," Anas said. "I'm saving the rest. Just remember that we're coming to your house tomorrow night with my father, and you're going to have to pretend that you don't even know Irsa. That MIGHT be a little harder now."

"It's not a problem," Irsa assured. I tried not to take her cool tone and casual demeanor personally. "This is a non-issue."

They both looked at me.

"Yeah, sure." I shrugged, though it felt as though someone had pulled on the loose threads of my heart. "It's a non-issue."

Eleven

We biked back to the mailbox as the sun reached its highest point in the late afternoon sky. The drugs in my system kept me calm and pleasantly desensitized as I pedaled, but that didn't stop me from analyzing Irsa's cool dismissal of our kiss. I wondered if it really had been a "non-issue" for her.

The beach was loaded with weekenders and locals alike. Even our mostly secluded end of the beach bustled with fishermen who had found a spot to cast their lines away from the swimmers and boogie boarders.

We ditched our bikes in front of the Kindred Spirit. Thankfully, the area around the mailbox was vacant, and I was able to retrieve my notebook as Anas unearthed the camera.

"Is there a response?" Irsa asked as Anas removed the plastic bag from the lens.

"There are a lot of new entries." I flipped through the pages until I found my latest letter. The page below it was empty. "Nothing from my dad."

"Then I'll just rewind the footage and let it go all night. I bet we'll have something good in the morning," Anas said.

Irsa made her way behind the dune to retrieve her board. "We've got just enough time to catch a few waves."

We surfed the rest of the afternoon away as the fishing trolleys and sailboats crossed the sea behind us. I tried not to think about the mailbox, or the kiss, or my market listing that was sure to have a buyer by now. Instead, I rode the Vicodin buzz like a steady wave and kept my eyes to the open ocean until the sun began its descent and it was time to go. After we buried Anas and Irsa's boards, Anas reset his camera and pressed record. Then we mounted our bikes and began the journey home.

"You want to work on some music tonight?" Anas asked, excited.

My mood darkened. "No, I . . . I haven't really been into it lately."

"You'd better stay on your game, or another DJ might steal your thunder," Anas warned, pedaling ahead of us.

Irsa pedaled beside me. "Still thinking about your dad?"

"Do you think we'll see him?" I asked. "On the camera, I mean?"

She shrugged. "I don't know. Either way, though, tomorrow is going to be quite a day."

"Are you worried that your dad will find out?" I asked. "It's going to be hard to pretend we don't know each other."

"What good does worrying do?" she asked as we turned down the beach access. "I'll deal with whatever happens."

When we got home, I waved goodbye as they disappeared into their trailer. My mom was inside finishing up dinner when I walked in. There were shopping bags from all the major home goods stores in the area lined up next to the couch.

"Just in time for pizza," she said, bending to take it from the oven.

I pointed to the bags. "What did you do, buy out the mall?"

She brought the pizza to the table, and I grabbed the plates.

"I just thought we'd spruce the place up a bit before we had our first guests tomorrow."

"Mom, I doubt Mr. Salid cares about what our house looks like," I grabbed the first piece of pepperoni and sausage. "Besides, he's seen the place already."

She grabbed two cans of Mountain Dew and met me at the table. "I know, but it's good to take pride in your home. Also, I got you a new bedspread and some surfing-related wall hangings for your room too."

"I like my room the way it is." I took another bite, the cheese sticking to the roof of my mouth.

"Well, don't you want your room to look nice before Irsa sees it for the first time?" she asked, winking at me.

"Too late," I mumbled with a mouth full of sauce and crust.

"What?"

"Never mind." I swallowed. "Thanks, Mom."

When dinner was over, I plopped down at my desk and brought my computer to life. rED had left a message asking if I was going to be online tonight. Stephy had sent me her weekly animal video, this one featuring a walrus doing sit ups. Still nothing from Biggles. I decided I would have to play with The Stranded another night. Instead, I took a deep breath and checked my marketplace ad.

Two people had expressed interest, but no one had made an offer. A part of me was relieved. I needed the money and I needed it fast, but to part with something that I loved, something that was a part of the very core of me, was devastating. On the other hand, if I didn't find more pills, I was a goner. With a sigh, I withdrew the tin from my pocket and flicked it open with my thumb. I didn't need to count them. I was down to my last twenty.

The only thing keeping me from panicking was the buzz that was still with me and the hope that someone would come through and buy my stuff. It had to happen. I had no choice. Taking a deep breath, I stuck the tin back into my desk drawer. I told myself that if I just did what I had to do, then everything would be all right.

I grabbed the biggest empty box I could find from the ones still piled up on the porch. Then I took it back to my room and locked the door behind me. I let myself go numb as I unplugged my sequencer and interface and wrapped up their cords. I put it all in the box and sealed it with boxing tape.

It was funny how my hopes and dreams, once so grand and achievable, were now easily contained behind a layer of cardboard and boxing tape. It didn't even matter who ended up with my stuff. In the end my addiction had bought me at a bargain, taking hold of my future before I'd even considered its value. Shaking the thought from my mind, I set the box in my closet and shut the door. I couldn't look at it anymore.

It's only temporary, I told myself as I flopped onto my bed. I just needed to figure things out. The Vicodin in my system was beginning to fade like the summer evening heat, but I hung onto the remnants of calm for as long as I could. My body started to throb and I suddenly wanted to just stop moving. More so, to stop thinking. I wanted to take more pills, but I knew that I couldn't. So many questions tumbled and collided inside my mind.

How would I find the money to keep buying pills? Would I ever be free of them? Could I really keep this up? What would my father think if he knew I had picked up the habit that had killed him? Did he already know? Was it my sins that kept us trapped in the In-Between? Was he writing back to me even now? What would the video show in the morning?

How could I pretend not to know Irsa in front of her father tomorrow? What if I messed everything up? What if he found out about her surfing? Would I kill her dreams too?

Irsa. My thoughts always circled back to her.

What exactly happened between us in that gondola today? Did it mean as much to her as it had to me? Why was she acting so cool about it? Why, with everything else going on in my life, could I not stop thinking about her? Was this love? Did love burn like this, like a fever in my chest? Was she thinking about me right now too?

As I lay there in the still of my room, I reached my hand up and parted the blinds. Outside, Irsa's trailer sat quiet under the glow of the streetlight. Though the blinds were drawn in Irsa's window, I could see light escaping between their slats. As I lie there wondering what she was doing, the light went out.

With a sigh, I rolled over. My thoughts settled on the heat of Irsa's lips against mine. As my eyes closed, I saw the mailbox in the distance . . . watching it all.

Twelve

The knock on my window didn't come as early as I thought it would. In fact, it was almost eight by the time it woke me up. I raised my blinds, expecting Anas to have his butt cheeks pressed to the glass as usual. Instead, Irsa stared back at me with a smile and a wave.

Jumping up, I wrestled to straighten my disheveled clothes and tried desperately to flatten my sweat-dried cowlick. She knocked again with a giggle, and I opened the window.

"Do you always sleep in your clothes?" she asked.

"I wish I could say no."

"Well, come on. We don't have much time," she said.

"Where's Anas?" I asked.

Irsa rolled her eyes and stepped aside. Behind her, Anas had his back to us with his arms wrapped around his scrawny body. He moved his hands up and down his back, pretending to make out with himself.

"Oh, Irsa," he mocked, making smooching noises as he caressed his own butt. "I love you so much. Muah, muah, muah."

I grabbed a half-empty can of Mountain Dew from my desk and chucked it at him. It hit him dead-center in the middle of his back, the lime-yellow liquid drenching the top of his pants. He turned with a scream and saw the now empty can lying on the ground. Then he made a circle as he assessed the damage to the back of his clothes.

"Now I have to go back in and change, you jerk!" he cried. "It looks like I pissed up my own back!"

With an angry huff, Anas turned on his heels and stormed back into his trailer.

Irsa turned back to me. "Is that even possible?"

"I don't know," I said with a shrug. "Your brother IS pretty limber."

Irsa laughed, and my heart thundered at the sound. I cleared my throat. "Give me just a minute."

Shutting the window, I searched my floor for a pair of shorts and a clean-ish shirt. My mom was right. I really needed to clean my room before tonight. I wouldn't put it past my mom to give Mr. Salid a grand tour of our place. It felt more imperative than ever to make a good impression on him, if it wasn't already too late with the burnt cookies and all.

I looked into my mom's room on my way out. She was just waking up. "I'm heading to the beach for a bit," I announced.

"Just be back in time to help me clean up and break down all those boxes outside," she said.

"You got it," I agreed. "We won't be out there long."

By the time I grabbed my bike and pulled it to the curb, Anas had emerged from his trailer in a new set of clothes.

"Jerk," he muttered again, and Irsa and I laughed.

The morning was especially humid, and beachgoers were already staking their sandy claims for the day, laying out blankets and setting up shelters along the shore.

The tide was low, leaving ruffled lines on the wet sand from where the sea had slunk farther and farther from the dunes. The dry sand was already hot, scalding the back of my calves as our bike tires tore down the shore.

"I can't wait to see what's on this thing," Anas said, dropping his bike when we reached the mailbox.

"Josh has to check for a response first," Irsa reminded him, "or else we'll be watching hours of tide rotation."

I followed behind, wishing with every bone in my body that I had taken at least one Vicodin before we left. Not knowing what to expect from the footage had made it tempting, but I knew that I would need them for Mr. Salid's visit tonight. I had to conserve.

Now here I was, possibly about to see my dad again on film. Would he look like a ghost? A zombie? I shuddered at the thought.

First thing was first. I had to see if he'd even responded. Taking a deep breath, I reached for the mailbox lid, my hands shaking.

Irsa laid her hand on my shoulder. "No matter what happens, we're here."

"Thanks," I said, unable to smile back.

She stepped away to help Anas locate the camera. I rummaged through the notebooks. At first, I didn't see the green one. For a minute I thought that someone had taken it. Both relief and panic washed over me as I took all the notebooks out and went through them one by one. When I found it, the cover was bent back, its pages ruffled as if someone had shoved it carelessly into the bottom of the pile.

"I don't know how much footage we captured." I turned to see Anas pull the camera from the dune. "The lens was buried beneath two inches of sand. That's weird. It wasn't even windy last night."

I turned back to the notebook in my hands. They shook as I flipped to my latest letter. There was another response just below it. Same writing. Same person.

Son,

I don't know if we're just missing one another, but maybe that's the whole point. We've been separated by time and space, and by sin and waste.

We make peace with our wrongs by owning them. Do you understand? We have to face what we've become. We have to look at ourselves and our sins and realize that our mistakes do not have to define who we are. We have to break the cycle. That's what this is all about.

I made terrible choices in my life that I've had to face. My decisions became your undoing. The only way your soul will ever be free is to face what happened. That is why I keep coming to this place. My soul will be at peace when you are free from the burden of my mistakes. You have to face your fears, and I must face mine. It's the only way either of us will find our peace.

There's a storm on the way, my son. I can feel it in the depths of my soul. It comes for us both. It's up to you whether it breaks us or sets us free.

I am with you, always.

"Did he write you back?" Anas asked, and I jumped. I blinked back the tears and read the letter again, trying to make sense of it.

"Josh?" Irsa stepped closer to me. I cleared my throat. "Yeah, he wrote back."

"Do you still think it's your dad?" Anas asked.

I committed the words to memory. "It's him. I'm sure of it."

"Well, then, let's prove it." Anas kissed the camera lens with glee. "I bet we captured something on this baby that no one has ever witnessed before."

Anas and Irsa took the camera to where the dunes shaded a small patch of sand. I closed the notebook and hugged it to me as I joined them. Irsa cupped her hands over the viewer to make it easier to see beneath the blaring sun. Anas hit play.

"We have twelve hours of footage on here," I said. "We can't sit here and watch the whole thing."

"Don't need to," Anas assured. "We'll just fast forward and stop it if we see anything suspicious. Besides, I don't know how much we actually captured with all that sand covering the lens."

"If you see anyone that looks like your dad, tell him to stop," Irsa said in her gentle voice.

A lump formed in my throat. What exactly was it that I was looking for? Was my dad just going to come strolling up to the beach in the dead of night? Would some invisible force open the mailbox and remove the notebook? My mind raced with possibilities.

We watched the footage in double-time as lines streaked across the tiny screen. People of all sorts had visited the Kindred Spirit and left their mark that evening. Some brought children or lovers. Some wandered up the shore alone. None of them looked like my dad. None of them looked the least bit suspicious.

"See anything?" Anas asked.

I squinted and leaned closer. "Nothing. It's just a bunch of tourists."

"Well, we suspected nothing happened until nighttime anyway." Irsa shrugged. "Keep going."

We kept watching. On the screen, the afternoon faded and the visits to the mailbox became sparse and then stopped altogether. For a long time, there was only stillness. It wasn't until the light had all but faded that we saw movement again.

"What's that?" Anas pressed play. We all leaned in closer.

"Whatever it is, it's just off camera," I said. "You see that? There's something moving around to the left."

"You can barely see anything now, it's so dark," Irsa said. "I can't tell what it is."

My breath caught in my throat as I struggled to see, to make out what was happening in the viewer. Something moved again, this time on the right of the screen.

"There!" Anas said, pointing to it.

A flash of white, a flicker of a dark patch—whatever it was moved quickly, passing back and forth in front of the mailbox as it grew steadily closer.

"What is it?" I strained to make out the figure.

"I don't know," Anas squeaked, "but it's freaking me out."

"Wait!" Irsa shouted, scooting even closer. "I think I know what it is."

Before we could ask, a black and white snout sniffed the camera.

"Aww, man!" Anas sat back on his heels. "It's just a dumb animal."

As we watched, the snout backed away, and a fuzzy face came into view.

"It's a dog," I said, my heart sinking.

"Wait . . . is it THE dog?" Anas asked. "As in 'the man with the dog' dog?"

He leaned back in, and we watched the dog's mouth open. His pink, wet, tongue shot out of its mouth, and it licked the camera lens, leaving slimy streaks behind.

"Gross!" Anas wiped at his lips with the bottom of his shirt.

Irsa put her hand on my shoulder. "It sure looks like the same dog."

"So it WAS that guy all along." Anas shook his head. "I really thought we were going to capture something cool, not some stupid guy with his mutt."

"We're trying to figure out who's leaving those messages, not become YouTube famous," Irsa snapped at him.

"It still doesn't make any sense." My thoughts ran through every possibility for the millionth time. "Why would some random guy leave messages like that? Why?"

"I can't answer that," Irsa said.

"Here's why the lens was covered in sand." Anas nodded back to the viewer. The dog had turned its back on the lens and was now pushing sand over it with his back paws. Only a small corner of screen remained uncovered.

"There you have it, folks," Anas announced. "Bupkis T.V."

He stopped the recording and got up. I grabbed his arm.

"Just keep going," I said.

"There's nothing left to see," Anas argued. "That mutt buried the lens. It's over, Solo. We've got our man."

"No." I shook my head. "It can't be him. It can't be. Please . . . just show the rest. There has to be more."

Anas gaped at me. He looked to Irsa for reason. I turned to her for the same. She studied my face, her eyes seeing straight into the black pit inside of me. Could she see that I was about to be swallowed whole? That this couldn't be the answer?

She sighed and reached out to her brother. "Give me the camera. We're going to keep watching."

"There's nothing to watch," Anas protested.

"Then you have nothing to argue about," she countered.

Anas thought for a minute. Then his shoulders dropped, and he plopped back down beside us and flipped open the viewer. He pressed the fast-forward button.

We all watched, but I was the only one leaning in, holding my breath, hoping beyond all hope that something would pop up in that one clear corner. We watched the screen grow black as night fell in the recording, and then there was nothing else to see, save for the timer in the center of the screen that counted down the hours and then the minutes left of the recording.

Irsa and Anas sat back in the sand. They were there for support, but I could feel their apathy. They thought I was wasting my time. Still I watched, until the minutes ticked down and the black night on the screen lightened a few degrees with the approaching morning. I was about to give up when something on the screen caught my eye.

"Press play!" I cried.

Anas snapped out of his daydream and mashed the button. The recording slowed to real-time as we watched the last minute of film.

"There!" I cried again. "There's a light! Do you see it?"

Irsa leaned in, squinting against the bright sun that hovered just above us.

"There is a light," she agreed, "but it could be anything. A lightning bug, the sunrise off the ocean. It could be a ghost crab for all we know."

"It's probably nothing." Anas leaned in to take a closer look.

"The sun isn't even up yet on the recording," I argued. "And there's no way that's a crab."

We all strained to see the last seconds of the video as the light in the corner of the screen turned brighter and brighter until the footage ended and the viewer paused where it was.

"You saw that, right?" I asked, turning to the both of them. "You saw that light!"

"If only that stupid dog hadn't covered the lens," Anas huffed.

"Rewind it," Irsa said. "Just the last minute."

We watched it again. This time the other two gave it their full attention. Their breaths caught at the same moment mine did when the strange light grew brighter and closer. Then again, the recording stopped.

"No!" Anas cried. "We just needed like, two more minutes!"

"That could have been something though, right?" I pleaded. "It could have been something."

"Yeah, but we totally missed it." Anas stood and brushed off his butt.

I helped Irsa to her feet.

"It could have been something," she said, "but now we're right back to where we were from the beginning."

"I really thought the video thing would work." Anas put the camera in his bag. Then a thought came to him and a smile spread across his lips. "Maybe we should just be here ourselves instead."

"What are you talking about?" I asked.

"We could just spend the night out here," he said, excited. "We could hide back behind the dunes and catch whoever or whatever's been leaving those messages in person. Mystery solved once and for all."

"That's crazy."

"Actually, it could work," Irsa brightened. "I think it's worth a shot."

"What? What about your dad? What if you get caught?" I asked. "You're talking about sneaking out in the middle of the night."

"It's not like we haven't snuck out before," Anas assured. "We'll be back before he even wakes up. We can do this."

"We are doing this." Irsa slapped me on the shoulder. "Tonight."

"Tonight?" I squealed.

"As soon as our parents go to bed." She grabbed her bike. "We're going to get to the bottom of this once and for all."

"I don't know . . ." I started to argue.

"You should stay and write another letter," Irsa interrupted. "Whoever this is has to have something to respond to. Anas and I have to get back. I'm supposed to be getting stuff together to bring over for dinner."

"Crap," I said. "I almost forgot that was tonight."

"Are you ready to put on your game face?" Anas hopped on his bike.

I thought about the pills I would take before they arrived. "I'll be ready by the time you all come over."

"We'll catch you later then." Anas waved.

Irsa turned back to me, empathy in her eyes. "Tonight's the night. We're going to get answers once and for all."

They pedaled away as I stood in the hot sand contemplating what the evening would bring. Finally, I took the notebook to the bench beside the mailbox and opened it. I read the letter over and over again, trying to imagine the strange man with the dog writing those words to me. It just didn't make sense. Who was that guy? Why would he do it? HOW could he do it? How could he know exactly what to say? It just didn't ring true in my heart.

I read the letter again, and this time I imagined my father's rugged face. I imagined him saying those words to me, and it felt right. I could hear his voice as clear as if he were sitting right beside me. *There's a storm on the way . . .*

With a sigh, I grabbed a pen and started writing.

Dad,

I want to see you more than anything. Maybe we don't have to be apart. Maybe in this place we can be together.

A friend of mine once said that a man without faith is a man without hope. Well, I have faith that in this place it's possible. I hope you do too. That's why it's called the Kindred Spirit, because it joins lost souls, right? I've never been more lost.

I don't know how to make peace with my wrongs when my wrongs are all I have left of you. If I let them go, I'll have to let you go too. I can't do that.

Meet me here, Dad. How else can I get over what happened to us? How can I face my fears when my greatest fear is that no one could ever love the person that I've become? Prove me wrong.

I don't know what storm you're talking about, but let it come. As long as we're together, we can face anything.

Please meet me here, Dad.

I could feel the last plea in the darkest depths of my soul as I shut the notebook and placed it back inside the mailbox.

"I'll see you tonight," I whispered, and then I grabbed my bike.

Thirteen

The remaining moving boxes were broken down and in the trash. My mom's new housewares were placed, and the dishes were washed and put away. Even my room was looking good with fresh bedding and wall décor.

I'd had just enough time to fill The Stranded crew in on what was happening with the mailbox. rED was still adamant that the letters could not have come from my father, but his doubt did nothing to shake my faith.

By the time Mr. Salid, Anas, and Irsa knocked on the back door, I was ready.

"It's go-time," my mom whispered to me.

"Just remember," I whispered back. "You can't say anything about surfing."

Though I'd taken two pills an hour earlier, my hands shook at my sides. I shoved them into my pockets so no one would notice. I wondered if Irsa and Anas would be nervous. My mom was. I could tell by the high pitch of her voice as she invited them all in and showed Mr. Salid where in the kitchen to set his covered dish.

When Anas walked in, I had to bite my lip to keep from laughing. His hair was neatly brushed and slicked back away from his forehead. I'd never noticed just how much his ears stuck out from the sides of his head. He wore button-down shirt and pressed slacks. A giggle escaped my throat when I saw the leather loafers on his feet.

"Shut up," he mouthed to me behind his father's back.

"Whatever you brought smells wonderful," my mom said as Irsa walked in, but I barely heard her.

Irsa was dressed from head to toe in sheer fabric the color of a russet sunset. Her sheath-like dress grazed the floor as she walked. I'd never seen her look so beautiful or so feminine before. She met my eyes, her face flushing.

"It's lasagna." Mr. Salid removed the tin-foil cover for my mom. "I got the recipe years ago from a colleague who was from Sicily."

"Italian." My mom chuckled. "What a pleasant surprise. Lasagna is one of our favorites. Isn't it, Josh?"

When I didn't answer, Anas came to stand beside me. He smelled like Old Spice.

"Dude, quit ogling my sister and answer your mom," he whispered. "You're going to ruin us in the first five minutes."

I blinked my eyes away as fast as I could and smiled. "Lasagna? I hope you brought one for everyone else."

Mr. Salid laughed and looked pleased at my joke. For a minute no one spoke, and the room filled with the awkward silence of new acquaintances. Or in our case, pretend new acquaintances. Irsa stepped to her father and smiled at him.

"My goodness, I haven't introduced you, have I? Forgive me," he said, slapping his forehead. "Allow me to introduce you to Irsa, my lovely daughter. Irsa, this is Tina and her son, Josh."

"It's a pleasure to finally meet you." My mom shook her hand.

I wasn't sure if it was custom or not, but I followed suit, grabbing Irsa's hand as soon as my mom let it go.

"It's nice to meet you," I said.

Our eyes locked for only a second, but in that second a thousand words were communicated. The corners of her mouth curled up ever so slightly, as if to tell me that everything was going to be okay. I held onto the calm that radiated from her as I let go of her hand.

"I don't know what I would do without my Irsa," Mr. Salid continued. "She is the backbone of this family, truly. In all honesty, she helped me with the lasagna. She has since she could barely walk. She could probably make it in her sleep."

"It's our favorite too." Irsa smiled.

"Well, Irsa, maybe you could come over sometime and teach me how to make it," my mom said. "I'm afraid the best I can do is unwrap a Stouffer's and throw it in the oven, and I couldn't even do that in my sleep."

Everyone laughed, which helped to break the ice a little. I felt my shoulders ease though the way Anas was standing all prim and proper beside me was freaking me out. I wondered if he would keep the polite act up all evening.

"I can, however, make a mean buffalo chicken dip. Josh, why don't you get it out of the oven while I give Youssef the grand tour." My mom turned to Mr. Salid. "It will give the kids a minute to get to know one another."

"Of course," Mr. Salid smiled, following my mom into the hall as she pointed out where the bathroom was.

Anas turned to me, shedding his façade like a heavy jacket. "Dude, you need to relax."

"I'm trying. This is just so weird," I whispered. "Why are you dressed like a used car salesman?"

"What are you talking about?" Anas ran a hand over his slicked hair. "I look sexy as hell."

"You look like a televangelist."

"We don't have time for this." Irsa looked cautiously into the hall. "Anas and I are ready for later. We packed a bag with flashlights and everything."

"What?" I asked, not following.

"For the stake-out at the mailbox, remember?" Anas smiled. "After the parents go to bed, we're going for it. You're with us, right?"

"Yeah, I'm in," I whispered. "I still think it's crazy though."

"I think you mean crazy awesome." Anas winked. "Be ready to go at midnight."

"Wait . . ." I started to argue, but Anas stood up straight and Irsa casually walked away.

When my mom and Mr. Salid came back down the hall, they were both smiling. I threw on a mitt and retrieved the bubbling dip from the oven.

"Of course, you can't always see the floor in Josh's room," my mom was saying.

"It is the same way with my son." Mr. Salid laughed. "It is good to know that this is a problem even for a boy with such a great mother at home."

"Well, thank you." My mom pressed her hand to her heart. Anas looked at me and rolled his eyes.

"Shall we eat then?" I motioned to the food. The sooner this dinner was over with, the better.

My mom got out the plates and utensils. "Is your son always in a rush to eat too?"

"Every single day," Mr. Salid answered with a laugh.

"Oh, please, let me help you with that." Irsa went into the kitchen to help my mom serve up the food.

"Why thank you, Irsa," my mom said, surprised.

Mr. Salid and Anas had a seat at the table, so I followed. I watched Irsa serve up the food onto the plates with practiced ease. Then she brought us our beverages and poured out tortilla chips into the bowl that my mom handed her. I thought that maybe I should help, but I got my cues from Anas and Mr. Salid who sat there, thankful, as the women served us. To them it was nothing other than usual to let the women serve. It seemed a custom steeped in thousands of years of tradition.

Irsa didn't seem to mind at all either. In fact, she looked happy to do it. She was as focused as a dancer caught up in a routine she'd practiced a lifetime to perform. I marveled at the contradiction that was Irsa Salid as she served me my dinner with a smile.

"I can see why you value your daughter so much, Youssef," my mom mused. "I haven't had this much help since I was a young girl in my grandmother's kitchen."

"Hey, I help," I protested. "Sometimes."

"Yes, you do," my mom agreed with a smirk. "Usually under the threat of violence."

Everyone laughed as I took a swig of water from my glass to hide my embarrassment.

"Yes." Mr. Salid placed his napkin on his lap. "My Irsa will someday make a wonderful wife and mother."

I choked on my water. Setting down the glass, I gulped the air in order to get it out of my throat. A sharp, sudden kick to the shins came from under the table. I looked up with watery eyes to see Anas glaring at me.

"Sorry," I squeaked. "Wrong pipe."

I was sure that my face was as red as the lasagna on my plate. Everyone was staring at me. With a cough, I took another swig of water and focused on my dinner. I didn't dare look at Irsa.

"So, Irsa, what is it you want to do after high school?" My mom rescued me. "You know, before the whole wife and mother thing."

As glad as I was that my mom had taken the focus off of me, I was nervous about where this line of questioning might lead. I knew my mom. She would pry, and prying could lead to Mr. Salid discovering the truth about where Irsa really spent her days.

"Well, I think about it a lot." Irsa came to sit beside my mom. She folded her napkin into her lap. "There are just so many possibilities. Sometimes I think I would like to study marine biology. They have a great program at UNC Wilmington. Then I could still help out at home."

"Oh, I always thought that would be such fascinating work," my mom said.

"Other times I think I might like to be a teacher," Irsa said with a shrug.

My mom nodded in approval as she stabbed at her lasagna. "That's a great idea too. Then if you found a teaching job around here, you'd have holidays and summers off to go sur . . ."

Anas pretended to choke on his food. He coughed loudly, cutting my mom off before she could finish her sentence. Our eyes were wide as we stared at her until she realized what she had almost done.

Mr. Salid raised an eyebrow at Anas.

"Wrong pipe," he said with a shrug.

Mr. Salid turned his focus back to his food, using a chip to scoop some dip from his plate. He was oblivious. We took a collective breath.

My mom cleared her throat, relieved. ". . . Spend with your family."

"Yes," Irsa said, "that's the idea exactly."

Mr. Salid put the chip in his mouth, tasting my mom's buffalo dip for the first time. At first, he looked quizzical, as if trying to figure it out, but then a satisfied smile settled on his face.

"This chicken dip is quite good," he said to my mother.

"I'm pretty sure it's the best thing I've ever eaten," Anas agreed, shoveling it into his mouth.

"And here I've been too busy chatting it up to even taste your lasagna." She took a bite at last.

"It's really good," I said to Mr. Salid. "The sauce is amazing."

"Why, thank you," he said with a nod. "That's the most important part."

"Oh, my goodness." My mom hummed with delight. "Did you make this sauce from scratch?"

"Yes," he said. "It's taken a long time to perfect. I am very glad you like it."

"And is this ground turkey?"

"Yes." He took a swig of water from his glass. "It is so hard to find beef that is *halal* in this area."

"*Halal*?" I asked.

"Yes, in Islam we must only eat meat that has been slaughtered according to Islamic law. Usually I have some *halal* beef in my freezer for such an occasion, but since the busy season started, it's been hard to find time to drive into Wilmington to shop."

"But the chicken dip . . ." My mom's voice raised with panic as if she had just inadvertently fed kryptonite to Superman. Mr. Salid held up his hand to calm her.

"Is perfectly fine," he said. "Please, do not worry."

"He only gets super picky about his beef." Anas smirked. "Really sucks when you're craving a burger."

Mr. Salid shot Anas a cross look, and Anas's smirk fell instantly.

"Like I was saying," Mr. Salid continued, "we've learned to adapt to our environment here and to make some concessions where needed. It's a small price to pay to live in this beautiful town."

"I could not agree with you more," my mom said. "Though I'm sure Josh wishes he still had his Taco Bell and Pizza Hut nearby."

"Actually," I said. "I'm getting used to it here. It's not so bad."

I told myself not to look at Irsa when I said it, but I did see a soft smile form on her lips from the corner of my eye.

"Have you all lived here long?" my mom asked. "Where are you from originally?"

Mr. Salid wiped his mouth with his napkin and then placed it back on his lap.

"We've only lived in Sunset Beach a few years. Originally, we are from a small province in Iran. It was my wife who wanted our children to be raised in the United States," he explained. "She was progressive like that, my Yasmin. She believed that there would be more opportunities for them in this country. Unfortunately, she did not live to see her dream realized."

"I'm so sorry," my mom said. I looked at Anas, who had stopped eating at the mention of his mother.

"A few years after we lost her, a job opportunity opened up for me in Los Angeles. We moved there in 2007," Mr. Salid continued.

"Los Angeles," my mom said, impressed. "What kind of work did you do there?"

Riveted, I leaned in. It dawned on me just how little I knew about Irsa, Anas and their family.

"I was hired as a case manager for a law firm there," Mr. Salid explained. "They were looking for someone fluent in Farsi, my native language, you see."

"What in the world made you all move out here?" I asked. When my mom looked sideways at me, I cleared my throat and continued. "I just mean that Sunset Beach is a big change from L.A."

"They were a bunch of jerks out there is what happened." Anas picked up his fork once again and stabbed at his food.

Mr. Salid held his hand up to quiet him and then tried to explain. "We found that the city was not the best place to be a, well, a . . ."

"A Muslim," Irsa finished for him when he struggled. "Our mosque was defaced many times, and although most people were very accepting of us, Anas and I were targets of some persistent harassment at school."

"Yes," Mr. Salid agreed. "It got to the point where I feared for the safety of my children."

My mom shook her head. "That's horrible."

"They think those people on the news doing all those terrible things in the name of Islam are like us, but that isn't us," Anas said. "It's not us."

"I do not like to complain," Mr. Salid said, humbly. "We are much happier here in this small town. It all worked out for the best."

"The people here are nicer?" I thought about the girls we'd seen at the SkyWheel the day before, and the way they'd talked to Irsa.

"There are still some who don't accept us," Irsa explained, "but this is the first place that's ever really felt like home. We've met some amazing people who are very dear to us."

She looked at me when she said it. My chest filled with warmth, but also sadness. I tried to imagine her and Anas living in a big city where they had to deal with hate like Ashley Brafton's every single day. They'd had to face the anger of people who didn't even know them. It made me nervous just to be in a crowd of strangers without my faith painting a bullseye on my back. I couldn't imagine what it was like for them.

Sure, I'd seen the horrible things going on in the world. I had family in New Jersey who described what it was like to see the Twin Towers fall on the other side of the Hudson on September 11th. I learned about terrorist attacks in school. I felt the fear and confusion watching all the death and destruction on the news. That kind of evil was unfathomable to me, but none of that is what I saw when I looked at the Salids. Even though I had a hard time wrapping my mind around Mr. Salid's strict beliefs, I couldn't understand the rampant hate for Muslims. Not when I looked at the family I'd grown to love who were sharing a meal at my dinner table.

"There's just too much hate in this world." My mom sighed. "What does it all accomplish besides more hate? I wonder what would happen if we chose to love one another instead. What if we chose to embrace the things that make us different and just love each other for them? That's what my faith has taught me anyway."

"Mine as well. I wholeheartedly agree." Mr. Salid raised his glass into the air. "There'd certainly be more occasion for good food and company."

"And lots of lasagna," I said, joining in the toast.

"And friends," Irsa said.

Anas raised his glass too. "And chicken dip!"

We all laughed and clinked our glasses together as the last of the evening's nerves melted away and conversation turned to lighter topics. Irsa told us all about what the schools in our county were like, and Anas filled us in on the different seafood festivals held throughout the year in the area. Mr. Salid educated us about the coastal hurricane season and told us the best evacuation routes.

By the time the Salids left, it was well past ten o'clock. After a warm goodbye, my mom shut the door behind them, and we both plopped down onto the couch, exhausted.

"Well, we pulled it off," I said, relieved.

"I almost gave it away for a second there." My mom slapped her forehead. "I'm a terrible liar, and now I officially feel even guiltier for keeping things from that man. I like Youssef."

"Yeah, I know," I said. "He's actually really nice."

"But that Irsa is something special." She elbowed me in the arm. "And Anas is a riot. I see why keeping this secret is so important to you. I won't ruin it. I promise."

"Thanks, Mom." I leaned into her, and she put her arm around me. "That really means a lot."

"I'm just so proud of you for getting out there and making the most of this move." She hugged me close. "You made some really good friends."

"They are pretty great," I said with a smile, but the guilt of what I was hiding from her squelched any pride I might have felt. I was a fraud and a coward. The tin in my pocket felt heavy again as though it contained all of my mother's hopes and dreams that at any moment could burst free and spill out at her feet.

"Well, I'd better get these dishes in the dishwasher so I can go to bed." She gave me one last squeeze. "Some of us have to make a living."

"I'll do it," I said, looking at the clock. Irsa and Anas would be at my window in a little over an hour. "You've done all the work tonight. I've got this."

"Wow, that Irsa really is rubbing off on you," she teased.

"I guess so."

"Remind me to thank her later," she said, getting to her feet. "I'm going to bed then. Don't stay up too late."

"I won't," I lied.

My mom yawned and started for the hallway. Then she stopped and turned to me with a smile.

"I love you, Joshua," she said.

"I love you too, Mom."

When she turned to leave, I felt the darkness close in on me. I needed her to come back. I needed her to see me for who I really was. More than anything, I needed her to accept me and to tell me that everything was going to be okay.

"Mom?" I called to her, and again, she turned to me.

"What's up?" she asked.

I wanted to tell her. I wanted to tell her about the pills, and the lies, and about everything that was happening with the Kindred Spirit. So badly, I just wanted her to know everything about Me, THIS Me, the real Me—and love me anyway. In that second of weakness, I almost thought it was possible that she could. Then I remembered the looks of disappointment in her eyes all those times I had let her down, and I could no longer find the words.

"Thanks for tonight," I said instead and tried my best to smile. Even with the waning haze of numbness from the last dose of my secret addiction, I didn't have the nerve to let her in.

"You don't have to thank me," she said. "That's what I'm here for. Good night, my sweet boy."

"Good night."

I sat there alone for a second, weighed down by the chains of my failures. I hated myself for lying to her. I hated that I'd become all that she despised. I hated the pills with the same intensity with which I needed them. Plucking the tin from my pocket, I opened it and stared at the handful of pills I had left. I thought about just throwing them away, just dumping them down the drain and letting the water cleanse me of my deepest sins.

It should have been such an easy thing to do, but I couldn't bring myself to do it. As disgusted as I was with them, I needed the pills to keep up this new life that I loved and that my mom was so proud of. So instead, I swallowed another pill to ease the pain of guilt in my chest and to chase away the doubt. I had to focus on tonight. My dad was waiting. He understood who I was, and he would love me anyway.

When the numbness renewed, I stood and rinsed the dishes that Irsa had helped to collect into the sink. By the time I was done loading them into the dishwasher, I had just enough time to see if anyone had made an offer on my music equipment.

Walking down the hall as quietly as I could, I put an ear to my mother's door. The silence on the other end assured me that she was fast asleep, so I went to my room and closed the door behind me. I pulled up the marketplace site and held my breath as it loaded. When it did, I saw that someone had left a message asking if my equipment was still available. They offered to pay full price for it and more if I was willing to take it to the post office where they had a post office box. It happened to be the nearest office.

Stunned, I replied before my emotions could talk me out of it. I accepted their offer and sent them a link to my PayPal account. If this went through, I would have more than enough money sitting in my account by tomorrow to buy another bottle of pills.

I should have felt immense relief. I should have been happy. Instead, sorrow took hold of me as I took the heavy box out of my closet. I hugged my equipment to my chest and reminded myself over and over that this was only temporary. I could always buy more equipment. With a shaky hand, I wrote the P.O. Box number on the top and set it next to my dresser. I would take it to the post office tomorrow.

There was just enough time to stuff a flashlight and a blanket into my backpack before the knock sounded on my window. I turned off my computer screen and lamp. Then I crawled outside.

Fourteen

Anas and Irsa had both changed. They were now clothed in black from their heads to their toes. Anas even had thick, black streaks beneath his eyes.

"Why didn't you dress in black?" Anas whispered.

"I didn't know that was a requirement," I whispered back.

"We're trying to blend in with the night," Anas said. "Don't you watch any movies?"

"Are we going to the beach or robbing a bank?" I asked. "And what's with the black eyes? You going in for a touchdown?"

Anas sighed. "It's camouflage."

"It's my eyeliner," Irsa argued.

"Whatever," Anas spat when I stifled a laugh. "Let's just go already."

We slowly walked our bikes to the corner and paused to look back, each of us holding our breath. When there was no stir from either of our homes, we let out a collective sigh and took to the pedals.

The night was darker than I thought it would be once we passed the safety of our street lamps. The streets, usually alive with cars and walkers, were eerily strange and still. Even the birds had gone to sleep for the night, leaving the crickets and frogs to chirp in their place.

The bridge was drenched in black shadow, making it hard to maneuver. We had to walk our bikes all the way to the other end where the meager street lights from the island made it easier to see. Though we could hear the ocean breakers in front of us, all we could see ahead was a splattering of porch lights and the black abyss beyond them.

We turned down the first street as usual while a lone deer scampered off into the brush beside us. Although it appeared that the whole island was lost to slumber, we didn't dare say a word until we were far from any signs of civilization.

The planks of the beach access were almost pitch black. Anas paused to take out his flashlight, and we followed his lead out onto the beach. A single silver reflection of the crescent moon danced on the waters in front of us, showing us that the tide was low. In the distance, heat lightning illuminated the clouds for a brief second and then faded back to black. The sand beneath us was cool as it hit the back of my legs while we pedaled toward the Kindred Spirit.

The darkness was even more stifling than the humid air. We maneuvered around abandoned sand pits and scampering ghost crabs. I grabbed my own flashlight out of my bag and shone it at the dunes. The farther we traveled from the houses and the street lights, the darker it became and the harder it was to find our destination.

"There!" I yelled when I finally captured the movement of the waving flag in my ray of light.

Ditching our bikes, we made our way up the dunes, the light from our flashlights bobbing in front of us. The Kindred Spirit blended into the blackness surrounding it like a viper among weeds.

"Creepy." Anas slowed his pace.

"You're not changing your mind, are you?" I asked, my own dread threatening to master me.

"No, but I'm not the one who has to touch the thing," he said. "Zombie hands, remember?"

"I think it's kind of peaceful out here." Irsa grabbed the flashlight from her brother and made her way behind the dunes to retrieve her board. "You should see if he wrote you back already."

"Wait for me!" Anas followed Irsa and the light behind the dunes.

I took a deep breath. "Right."

The wind whipped through the beach grass with a low hum as I walked up to the Kindred Spirit. I aimed my light on the bench beside it, half expecting to see my dad there waiting for me. It was empty as usual. I lowered the lid and looked inside.

"Please, no zombie hands," I whispered to myself as I reached in.

My notebook was still buried at the bottom. I dug it out and held my breath as I opened it. The pages fluttered as I turned them to my latest entry. There was no response.

"Nothing yet," I said, relieved. We hadn't missed it.

I put the notebook back on the bottom of the pile and closed the lid. Irsa and Anas were laying their boards side-by-side on the sand just behind the Kindred Spirit when I found them. Then they sat down on them and waved me over. I squeezed between them.

"Now what?" I asked.

"Now we go lights out and wait for whoever or whatever has been writing you to show," Irsa said.

"Lights out?" Anas squeaked. "As in we're going to sit here in the dark?"

"It's the only way," I agreed, clicking my flashlight off.

Irsa did the same. Darkness fell on us like a stage curtain after the final act. Only our night was just beginning. In the silence between the crashing of the waves, I thought I could hear the pounding of my own heartbeat.

"Is anyone else as freaked out as I am right now?" Anas whispered. "I can't see a thing."

"You're the Jedi," I joked, not sure whether I was trying to calm him or myself. "Can't you stretch out with your feelings or something?"

"Yeah, well, I'm definitely sensing a big pile of Bantha fodder coming from this direction." He blindly thrust his hands in my face. I shoved him away.

"You two are a couple of babies." Irsa laughed. "Just close your eyes and listen to the waves and feel the wind on your face. It's relaxing."

I gave Anas one last shove and scooted closer to Irsa before he could retaliate. Her warmth and calming energy spread over me like a security blanket.

"My mother used to say that the darkness was not a thing to be feared," Irsa said, "that it was only there to expose the light. You cannot see the light without first knowing the darkness."

There was silence for a minute while her words sank in. I thought about my own darkness as the remainder of chemicals in my system battled against my nerves. Her mother had it backwards. I was sure of it. My life had been filled with light back in the days when my father was alive and my family was intact. That brightness only cast a darker shadow on what became of my life when it all fell apart. Only the pills kept me from being swallowed by the darkness of it all.

Then again, as I sat there with Irsa listening to the water crash on the shore, with the possibility of being reunited with my father in this magical spot, I thought that perhaps the light was fighting to return.

"Mom said that?" Anas's voice was barely louder than the wind.

"She did," Irsa assured. I felt Anas relax beside me. "Now seriously, close your eyes."

She paused long enough for us to comply. "Now, imagine what it's like here during the day. See the waves around you and the sun in the sky. Hear the seagulls overhead and the wind coming off the sea. This is our place, you guys. It's the same place as it is during the day."

"I can see it," Anas said. "I'm riding a killer tube just in front of us."

"I see it too. You're taking an epic wave to the face," I teased. "She said to imagine what it's actually like."

Anas elbowed me in the arm as I snickered in the dark.

"Okay, now open your eyes," Irsa instructed. "It's not as scary, right?"

I opened my eyes and looked around. Irsa was right. The night sky was speckled with glowing stars in an abundance I'd only seen in paintings and magazines. Ship lights glowed on the horizon, making it look as though a handful of stars had drifted to earth to float atop the blackened sea.

"Oh, wow," Anas said. "You can see the lights of Cherry Grove from here."

I looked to the right where the soft glow of lights from the neighboring beach illuminated the brush behind the dunes. Though we were still drenched in shadow, the night around us was alive with clandestine light.

"I guess it's not so bad out here," I said, my nerves settling.

"See?" Irsa said. "No big deal."

"But what if it's not?" Anas asked.

"What if it's not what?" Irsa asked.

"What if this isn't the same place at night?" Anas pondered. "What if it turns into *Al-Barzakh* at night?"

"The In-Between," I said.

"Yes," Anas agreed.

"I guess that's what we're here to find out," Irsa said.

For a while we all fell silent as we gazed out at the speckled sky. I thought about my last letter and how I had begged for my dad to come. If this place really became the In-Between in the dark of night, then it would be possible. I prayed that it was.

"It's past one o'clock in the morning," Irsa said, breaking the silence. "We have to be back home before daybreak. I say we take shifts sleeping."

"I don't know if I can sleep out here," Anas said. "What if all hell breaks loose while my guard is down?"

"I'll stay up," I said. "There's no chance I'm sleeping tonight. I don't want to miss anything. Go ahead and go to sleep."

Irsa put her hand on my shoulder. "Are you sure you'll be okay if I lie with him for a while?"

"Yeah," I assured her. "I'll be fine."

I scooted off the board so they could both lie down.

"Seriously though," Anas said, "if you hear or see anything, you'd better wake us up. And no matter what happens, do NOT turn to the dark side on me."

"I'll wake you up if I see something," I assured them both. "I won't let anything happen to you."

"Okay," Anas said, somewhat assured.

I reached into my backpack and grabbed my blanket. Then I moved to where I could keep a better eye on the Kindred Spirit. Sitting there behind the dunes, I listened to the waves roar up the beach as I struggled to keep my thoughts calm and the hopes of seeing my father up. When the wind died down to a gentle breeze, I watched as a wispy fog spread over the brush behind the dunes. Anas snored behind me, the rattle louder than the crickets chirping from the beach grass. Irsa had not stirred for a while.

I tried to stay vigilant, but after a couple of hours of being propped up in the sand, the steady rhythm of the waves, combined with the stressful day and the remnants of Vicodin in my system, had me dozing against my will. I caught myself a couple of times, each time rubbing my eyes and readjusting my position. Before I could catch myself a third time though, I'd fallen into a fitful sleep.

I woke an hour later to a strange sensation on my legs. At first my mind didn't register the movement over the tops of my knees and beside my thighs, but when it did, my eyes flew open, and I remembered where I was. The night was still black dark. When I looked down, I could barely make out multiple black specks moving across the lower half of my body.

"What the hell is that?" I shrieked, and Anas and Irsa darted up.

"What? What is it?" Anas said, groggily. "Is it the dog guy?"

"There's something crawling on me." I tried not to panic. "I can't see what it is, and I left my flashlight over there."

"It's probably just a ghost crab." Irsa grabbed her flashlight. "Just brush it off."

"I don't think it's a crab." I didn't dare move until she came over with the light. "It doesn't feel like one. This is . . . floppier. There's a bunch of them. They're all over my legs."

"Oh hell, I knew it," Anas cried, backing away. "Zombie hands all over the place!"

"Get a hold of yourself. There are no zombie hands!" Irsa said, coming closer. "It's just, well, it's . . ."

"Oh, God." I breathed. "What is it?"

For an interminable second, Irsa approached with the light as I tried to make out the small, flapping specks that had commandeered my legs.

"Baby turtles!" Irsa exclaimed. "Oh, wow, look at all of them."

"What?" I followed the beam of light to where Irsa shone it on my lap.

Tiny, squirming sea turtle babies were flapping their miniature fins as they struggled to climb over me. Irsa followed a trail of them with her flashlight as they fought to make their way across the dunes.

"We have to help them," Irsa said. Anas found my flashlight and came over to see for himself.

"Help THEM?" I laughed.

"Woah," Anas gawked. "You must have sat right in front of their nest. Look, they're still coming out of the ground behind you."

"What do I do?" I watched the babies emerge from the sand in a flurry of frantic movement.

"Here." Anas grabbed his surfboard. "Put them on this, and then get up because we have to dig a track."

"A what?" I carefully picked up a baby and placed it on the board. It was softer than I expected, more fragile. Its flippers flapped against my fingers as if on autopilot.

Irsa made quick work of gathering the turtles from my legs and placing them on the board. "Sea turtles are endangered. We have to help them get to the ocean."

When the last turtle was off of me, I stood up slowly and stepped out of the way. Anas dragged the loaded board to the beach while Irsa got on all fours and started to dig a trench in the sand from the nest out of the dunes.

"They're wild animals. Maybe we should just leave them alone to do their thing," I said, not sure what to do. "They might not need our help."

"Turtles don't usually lay their nests this far into the dunes. If we don't help them, they might not all make it," Irsa explained. "If they're still wandering the dunes trying to find the ocean when day breaks, they'll be picked off by the birds and other animals."

Through the light of the flashlight, I saw her pause to look me in the eye.

"Plus, everyone needs help at some point," she said. "The hard part is letting help come."

She was talking about me. I knew the instant she looked at me that she could see some of my broken pieces. I just didn't know what parts she saw. Before I could say anything, Anas ran up the dune with his now empty board.

"They all made it out to sea," he said, excited. "The tide just picked them up and swept them away."

When Anas got on all fours to help with the path, I followed suit, using my hands to dig and flatten a track that led right past the Kindred Spirit and onto the shore. We worked fast, trying to stay ahead of the exuberant babies that floundered and flopped behind us.

"How do they know where to go like that?" Anas asked, amazed. "They've never even seen the ocean, but they know to go toward it."

"It's just their instinct, I guess," I said as a few strayed from the path. We had to pick them up and gingerly place them back on track. "Some of them are getting lost though."

"Then it's a good thing we are here to help them find their way." Irsa kissed one on the top of its tiny head before placing it back on the path.

It wasn't until the last turtle made it down our path to the shore that we stopped to appreciate our accomplishment. Dozens upon dozens of baby turtles squirmed to the water's edge and got swept up in the tide as we watched and cheered them on.

In the end, we counted over sixty hatchlings, all of them eager and charging toward the sea. When the last one was swept away by the tide, we stood at the water's edge and watched them disappear into their destiny.

"I wonder what will happen to them now," I mused as we stared out into the darkness.

"Unfortunately, only like one in a thousand babies will survive to adulthood," Anas said.

"What?" I asked. "Why? What happens to them?"

Irsa shrugged beside me. "You saw how tiny and fragile they are. They get picked off by all kinds of things."

I couldn't stand to think of how many of the little ones we'd just helped would not live. "That's terrible. What's even the point then? Why were they so eager to get out there if most of them aren't even going to make it?"

"Because they can't stay stuck on the shore," Irsa explained. "They'd die for sure. No, they were meant for more."

"The ones who do live get to be over a hundred years old," Anas said. "It's a crap shoot, but the ones who make it get to live a long, happy life."

"Those babies don't know what the odds are against them," Irsa said. "They only know how to fight to survive. Their home is out there. They know it, and it might be a hard fight to get there, but they won't give up."

"I mean, did you see how eager they were to get out there?" Anas said. "That was crazy."

"Yeah, it was incredible," I agreed. "They were really going for it. Talk about clutching it!"

"They're the definition of perseverance." Irsa reached for my hand as she gazed out to the sea. "That was the most glorious thing I've ever seen."

I looked down at her hand in mine. It felt so natural there, as if our hands were always meant to be joined. Her joy and energy radiated from her like a beacon of hope, and the warmth of her hand filled me with instant peace.

"I know what you mean," I said. Her eyes, as dark and vast as the ocean surrounding us, locked on mine.

"Do you think any of them will get washed back?" Anas asked, but Irsa and I were too lost in one another to hear him. "Guys?"

When Anas turned around and saw our joined hands and the way we looked at one another, his smile fell. "Man, not again! You guys are so gross. I'm going back up there."

He took his flashlight and stalked back up to the dunes where he walked a wide circle around the Kindred Spirit before disappearing behind it. We watched him go until his flashlight was a soft glow among the sands. Then we turned back to each other.

Irsa smiled and gave my hand a squeeze. She seemed to look right into me, into the core of my being. I wondered what she saw among the devastation that made her step closer and raise her face to meet mine.

As our lips met again, I wondered if there would ever be a drug as powerful and addictive as Irsa Salid. I knew all about gateway drugs and about trading out one addiction for another. As she pressed her body against mine, I thought that maybe the pills had just been a gateway to this new kind of drug. In that moment, I would have traded the pills, the lies, my very soul, for an eternity of this kind of high.

This time Irsa did not pull away. We melted into one another while the waves crashed around us and the tide embraced our ankles. I wrapped my arms around her and pulled her closer, breathing her in. She smelled of lavender and sea spray. The sheer fabric of her hijab caught the wind and wound around us, enveloping us in our own private world where the only thing that mattered was the two of us. My mind flashed to that first moment on the waves. I felt just as free. I was flying.

When Irsa started to giggle, I came back to myself.

"What's so funny?" I breathed, keeping her close.

She looked up at me with glassy, far-away eyes. "Are those mints in your pocket, or are you just happy to see me?"

I looked down to where she was pressed against my right pocket where I kept my tin.

"Oh!" I stepped back. "Yeah, that's my mints. Not that I'm not happy to see you."

"You really do love those things." She raised an eyebrow.

"Yes, I do."

"Let me have one." She made it sound like a question, but the way she was staring at me made it feel like more of a demand.

"I . . . I only have a few left," I said.

"You can always get more," she argued. "You can spare one, can't you?"

"I don't know." I faked a laugh, but panic grabbed hold of my throat. "You haven't experienced my morning breath yet. I might just need the rest of them."

"Why won't you give me one?" she persisted. "You know I don't care about that."

"I . . . can't."

"Why not?" She crossed her arms, waiting for me to explain myself. I had no answers.

"I just can't," I pleaded. "Okay?"

"You know, I've noticed something about you, Josh Hurley," she said. "I've noticed how some days you look so serious, like you have the weight of the world on your shoulders. Then there are other times when your eyes glaze over and you talk faster and smile easier. You almost seem happy for a while, but it's not real happiness. There's still that sadness in your eyes."

"That's crazy." My hands started to shake. "What are you talking about? I'm a teenager. I'm just moody. It's normal. I'm normal."

"What's really in the tin, Josh?"

"Irsa, it's just mints." I could feel the sweat start to bead on my forehead. "You're making this into something that it's not."

"Then just let me have one." She held out her hand.

"Maybe later." I grabbed hold of her hand. "Your brother is probably scared to death over there by himself, and we still have a mystery to solve."

Irsa didn't say another word. She just watched me as I pulled her back toward the Kindred Spirit. I turned on my flashlight to light our way back and prayed that my diversion had worked. She was too close to discovering the truth about me. She was too smart not to. I had to get rid of my tin before she asked about it again.

When the light of my flashlight caught the mailbox as we approached, I saw my reflection in its glossy surface. My face looked morphed and disjointed. I looked like a monster. Shaking the image from my mind, we found our spot behind the dune. Anas was lying on his board beside our hand-dug turtle track. His backpack was propped beneath his head, and he was sound asleep.

"Yeah, he looks terrified." Irsa snickered.

"Well, it is only an hour or two before dawn. You should probably get some sleep too." I tried not to sound too eager.

"I'll stay up with you this time." Irsa scooted her board over.

I was hoping that she would go to sleep so I'd be able to hide my tin in the bottom of my backpack. What was I going to do if she asked about them again? I was out of excuses. I had to get rid of them. Then an idea came to me.

"I should check the mailbox again," I said. "You know, just in case we missed something during all the excitement."

"We would have seen something." Irsa had a seat on the board.

"Maybe, but we shouldn't take any chances."

"I guess . . ." Irsa started to say, but I was already making my way around the dune and out of sight.

"I'll be right back."

Frantic, I opened the lid of the mailbox. When I saw that my notebook was still buried at the bottom of the pile, I knew that it had remained untouched. Checking to make sure Irsa hadn't followed me, I slid the tin from my pocket.

I was desperate to take another dose. I needed it to calm my nerves again, but I didn't dare take the chance of Irsa hearing the tin open or close. So, with a shaking hand, I placed it in the back of the mailbox where I knew Irsa would never look. If she asked me about it again, I could tell her it fell out somewhere. She would think I'd lost it in the sand. I could retrieve it from the box in the morning before we made our way home.

Shutting the mailbox, I tried to breathe normally as I walked back behind the dune. Irsa was waiting for me, the blanket spread across her shoulders. She opened her arms to me, and I went to her with a nervous smile.

"You were right." I sat down beside her. "Nothing yet."

"The sun should be up in a couple of hours." She wrapped the blanket around my shoulders. "It won't be long now."

"Thanks for being here with me," I said.

"I told you. I'm here for you no matter what you're going through. We both are," she said as Anas let out a loud snort before rolling over to continue his slumber. We both laughed. "In our own ways."

"I don't know what I'd do without you guys," I said.

"I'm not going anywhere," she said. "I care about you, Josh. Please, know that."

"I care about you too." I kissed the top of her head as she leaned into me. "Lights out?"

"Lights out," she agreed.

We both clicked off our flashlights and let the darkness consume us. I held Irsa to me as we stared out into the star-dusted sky and waited for the unknown to make an appearance. She never mentioned the mints again, but I knew she would eventually. I would have to be ready with yet another lie.

Irsa could never discover the darkest part of me. I could no longer deny that I needed her in my life. I needed her more than surfing, or my music, or even the pills. She could never know what I really was, just like my mom could never know.

My secret was getting harder and harder to hide, and yet it was becoming more and more imperative that I hide it. I didn't know what to do. I wanted the lies to end, but I had to lie to protect the ones I loved. I wished I could talk to someone who would understand. My dad would know what to do.

An hour passed as I watched and waited for the impossible. I felt Irsa relax. Her head on my shoulder grew heavy, and I knew I had lost her to sleep. As I sat there alone, I stared out at the Kindred Spirit and willed it to hear the deepest cry of my heart:

Bring me my dad. I need him so much. Please, let it be possible . . .

Fifteen

The sound of something vibrating brought me back to alertness. The incessant noise repeated over and over again until I was completely roused. I'd been staring out at the Kindred Spirit for so long that my mind was wading in the shallow space between sleep and consciousness.

It was still dark though the sun's rays were beginning to crest just above the horizon. A soft orange glow, barely discernable, was beginning to spread across the sea. In the distance, a bird called out and was answered by another. Soon the rest of the world would come back to life.

Irsa stirred beside me as I scooted out from under her in search of the source of the noise. Stumbling around in the sand, I found my backpack beside a snoring Anas. My phone vibrated in the bottom of it. By the time I retrieved it, I had missed the call. I squinted at the bright screen. My heart sank when I saw that the call had been from my mom. Worse than that, I had missed six calls from her in the last half hour.

"Oh, no," I mumbled. My mom had discovered my absence and was probably freaking out. I was in so much trouble. I had to call her back before she called the cops.

As my groggy mind scrambled to come up with a good excuse for why I'd snuck out, something caught my eye, and I froze. I stared out at the dunes, not sure of what I'd seen. When I saw it again, I darted back to my spot behind the Kindred Spirit, now fully alert.

"What's going on?" Irsa asked, groggily. "What is it?"

"Ssshhhh." I put a finger to my lips. "Something's happening."

Irsa pulled the blanket off of her. We crept on our knees, getting as close to the dune and the mailbox as possible while still remaining concealed. We watched, breathless, as a faint ray of light surrounded the Kindred Spirit and made it glow from the sand at its base to the tip of its raised flag.

"What is that?" Irsa's eyes were wide.

"I don't know," I whispered.

"Okay, now I'm starting to freak out," she said.

Behind us, Anas let out a loud snort, and we jumped. When he did it again, I chucked my flashlight at him. It hit him in the gut, and he awoke with a start, rolling off his board and into the sand.

He scrambled to his feet and searched for us in the darkness. "What's happening?"

"Get down!" I pointed to the light surrounding the mailbox.

His eyes grew wide when he saw what I was talking about, and he threw himself to the ground. In a panic, he low-crawled to where we were and clung to our shoulders.

"What is that?" he whispered. "Why is the mailbox glowing like that?"

As we watched, the unearthly glow grew larger and larger as my heart beat faster and louder in my ears. This had to be it. This had to be what we were waiting for. The In-Between was opening right in front of us. We were finally going to find out how it was possible for my dad to write me back. I was terrified and excited all at once.

Then a strange sound traveled in on the wind. It was barely audible above the crashing of the waves. Something crunched in the sand in a steady rhythm. The sound grew louder as it got steadily closer. Footsteps, I realized, and my breath caught in my throat. Someone was coming out from the midst of the light.

"There's something out there." Anas clawed at my arm.

"Not something. Someone." I shook him off. "It's my dad."

"Josh, you don't know that . . ." Irsa reached for me, but I was already on my feet.

"Remember the curse!" Anas whisper-shouted after me. "Don't let it get you!"

My phone vibrated again, but I ignored everything as I stared into the mysterious light. On unsteady legs, I made my way around the dune. All of the pain and anguish of the last months bubbled up to the surface. This was it. He had come. My dad had come back to me. I couldn't wait to see him again, no matter what that might mean. The Kindred Spirit had heard the deepest cry of my heart and brought him to me. I wiped my tears and jogged the last few steps to the mailbox.

"I can't believe it." I squinted into the light.

When my eyes adjusted, I saw a dark figure standing in front of me. For what felt like an eternity, we stood staring at one another as I struggled to blink back the tears. When the figure took a step forward, I reached out my hand. I just wanted to touch my dad again.

Before we connected, Anas busted out from behind the dunes. He ran toward the figure wielding his surfboard above his head, ready to strike.

"Release Solo or die!" he screamed, racing to my aid. I caught him by the arm and pulled him back.

"Anas, no!" Irsa yelled as she too charged out of the dunes, her surfboard at the ready.

She stopped dead in her tracks when she got to us and came face to face with the dark figure behind the light.

"Anas!" a deep voice called out. "Irsa!"

"Oh crap, it knows our names!" Anas cried.

The light grew bigger as the figure approached us. It shone right into our eyes, and we had to turn our heads against the brightness. Then it lowered from our faces to our feet. When I turned back, I saw that the light came from a handheld lantern. The figure had been shining it right at us before setting it down in the sand. When the figure stepped closer, I was filled with dread. Mr. Salid stood before us. His brow furrowed as he took in the sight of his children.

"What are you two doing all the way out here?" he shouted. "Do you know what you have done to me?"

"Father, let me explain . . ." Irsa stammered, but he ignored her, his rage building.

"I work day in and day out to provide for you two, and this is how you repay me? By sneaking out of the house in the middle of the night?" His anger was overwhelming.

"Father . . ." Irsa pleaded.

"Do not father me!" Mr. Salid continued. "And what is this? A surfboard? Is this what you have been doing? This is what is worth betraying your father's trust?"

"It was my idea to come out here, Father." Anas came forward to stand in front of his sister. "She was only trying to stop me. I am the one you should be mad at."

"No," I argued. "No, this was neither of their faults. This is all on me. They're only here because of me."

"You stay out of this!" Mr. Salid snapped. "You've done enough already."

Irsa walked up to me, her head hung in resignation. She put her hand on my shoulder and looked into my face.

"It's okay," she said, with tears in her eyes. "No more lies."

Then she turned to her father, her surfboard in her arms. "I have been surfing. Anas and I come out here almost every day. I love it, Father, and I am really good. This is who I am. Please, you have to understand."

"Understand?" Mr. Salid's nostrils flared as he glared at her. He looked from her to the surfboard in her arms. "You want me to understand that my only daughter is out here every day like some heathen instead of tending to her home? You have deceived me!"

"Yes, I have disobeyed you, and I've lied to you, but I only did it because this is what I love," Irsa said calmly. "I can tend to the home and still pursue my passions, Father. I can do both."

Mr. Salid shook his head. "It is immodest, indecent and unacceptable!"

"Why, because that is how things were in Iran? Things are different now, Father. Why can you not understand that?" Irsa's voice was rising.

"I understand now that you are not the person that I thought you were," Mr. Salid said. "I thought you understood the ways of our people, but instead you sneak away from your home in the middle of the night like some kind of homeless tramp? It is you who does not understand your place!"

"My place, Father?" Irsa stood firm. "You would have me wither away in our home all summer rather than allow me to follow what is in my heart?"

"Your heart should be for your faith, for your god!"

Something broke in Irsa then. The normal calm she radiated fractured with her resolve. She squared her shoulders, heat flashing in her eyes.

"The god I believe in would not keep me from what I love!" she screamed, her soul pouring out with her words. "That is YOUR god! It is not mine!"

Mr. Salid looked stricken, as if her words had slapped him in his face. He shook his head from side to side, his anguish making his voice tremble.

"I sacrificed everything I've ever known so that my children could grow up in a country where they are free to practice their faith unprosecuted. It was your mother's greatest wish that our daughter have the chance to get an education without restriction or question." His voice rose with every word. "She never would have wanted this. Praise Allah that she did not live to see that the ways of this country are stealing our children from us!"

"Mother would have understood! Why can't you? It is you who have pushed your children away with your narrow-mindedness!" Irsa shouted. "If you could have just accepted him, he never would have . . ."

"Do not speak to me of my sins while you stand before me having lied and deceived me over . . . this!" With a growl, he snatched the surfboard away from Irsa. "You have lost who you are to this!"

"Father, no!" she cried as he took the board over to the hard-packed sand.

"I will not allow dishonor to come to this family again," he yelled. "Have we not lost enough?"

He raised the board above his head.

"Don't!" I ran toward him, but it was too late. Mr. Salid brought the board down on the hard sand with enough force to shatter the nose.

Irsa fell to her knees and wept as her father smashed the board over and over again until it was splintered and fractured beyond repair. When the fins broke off into the surf, he threw the board down with one final blow. Then he stood there, breathing heavily, as the tide swallowed the shattered pieces.

The three of us stared, shocked, as the weight of what just happened sunk in. It was all over. Our surfing days, our entire way of living, was gone just like that. Irsa covered her face with her hands. Her grief was devastating. I went to her.

"You stay away from my daughter," Mr. Salid said between panting breaths. "She is not to see you again. I have a feeling you are the cause of this."

I couldn't deny it. Everything was ruined now because of me. Irsa and Anas would have been better off if they had never met me, it was true. If I had never written in that mailbox, none of this would have happened. I looked up the beach to where the Kindred Spirit stood. This time when I looked at it, I felt betrayed.

Mr. Salid followed my gaze and then glared back at his children. "Why here? Have I not told you to stay away from that thing? Have I not told you the mailbox is cursed? And yet I find you here, ignoring all that I have told you."

"It is because of what you told us," Anas squeaked, tears rolling down his cheeks. "We knew you would never come here. I'm sorry, Father."

Mr. Salid was silent for a moment, his disappointment palpable. Tears welled in his eyes as he looked at Anas. "You. You are supposed to be the man of the house in my absence now. You are supposed to watch over your sister. Instead, you lie to me?"

"Father, I . . ." Anas stammered.

Mr. Salid spoke to him in Farsi. I couldn't understand the words, but I didn't need to. Anas bowed his head in shame at whatever he said and dropped his board in the sand. Then he helped Irsa to her feet as she continued to weep.

"Now, you get on those bikes and go straight home." Mr. Salid straightened his shirt and ran his hand through his disheveled hair. "I will be there directly."

Anas and Irsa grabbed their bikes as the sun's rays clawed their way into the skyline. Irsa chanced a look at me over her shoulder as she pedaled away. Her eyes, always so full of hope and life, were hollow and lifeless.

"I'm so sorry," I mouthed to her before she turned away.

As their father watched, Anas and Irsa pedaled down the beach and out of sight. Mr. Salid took a deep breath and wiped his eyes with the backs of his hands. Then he turned to me. I couldn't move. The gravity of the moment cemented me where I stood in the heavy sand.

"You will have nothing to do with my daughter." His voice was filled with despair. "She is not of your world."

"What happened to embracing our differences?" I asked as he began to walk away.

His shoulders fell as he turned back. "I guess some differences cannot be overcome."

Then he turned to follow his children down the beach. For a while, all I could do was stare after them as my body trembled. So much had happened in so little time that my mind scrambled to process it all. The air felt thick and toxic. I struggled to breathe.

Though the sky was filling with the light of a new day, the shadows were swallowing me whole. They extinguished the last of my hope and any remainder of happiness within me. I thought I might shrivel and die right there in the sand where the sea could drag me into its blackened depths. I hoped I would. For the second time in my life, my whole world had been ripped away from me. Only this time, it was my fault. I was free-falling out of control.

Then I remembered that I still had my parachute. My pills were still in the mailbox. They were the only thing that could make the pain in my heart stop. I couldn't stand to feel this way. My legs were like dense weights beneath me as I staggered forward. My vision clouded over as the tears poured from my eyes. I tripped over the surfboard that Anas left lying in the sand.

Without knowing what else to do, I picked it up and dragged it to the dunes. I buried it in the usual spot. I just couldn't leave it lying on the beach for some stranger or the tide to claim. A low cry escaped from my throat with the stinging realization that it may never be unearthed by Anas or Irsa again.

When I was done smoothing the sand, I grabbed the flashlights and my backpack. Wiping my eyes, I stumbled down the dunes to the Kindred Spirit. Anger took hold of my heart like a vice.

"You called me here that day. I know you did." I spat. "What the hell do you want from me? WHAT DO YOU WANT?"

When it gave me no response, I let out a jagged breath and opened the lid. There was only one thing that could help me now. The thought crossed my mind that I should just go ahead and swallow every pill left in my tin. I wasn't sure if it would be enough to kill me, but it might, and that thought didn't bother me at all. In fact, it was a relief. Even if I didn't die, at least I could stop feeling this pain for a while. I could just slip away into the chemical oblivion and make it like this year never happened. I could wipe the sound Irsa's weeping and the look in her eyes from my existence. I could forget how much living hurts. Nothing was ever going to get better.

The Kindred Spirit had let me down. It didn't want to reunite me with my father. Anas was right. It had cursed me. It was clear now that the only way for me to be with my dad again was to go to where he was. I didn't need the mailbox for that, I decided. I could do that on my own. Resigned to my decision, I opened the mailbox and reached inside.

I felt around inside until my fingers hit the back of the box, but I couldn't find my tin. When I tried again with no luck, I took out the stack of notebooks and set them on the bench. I reached into the mailbox again and felt nothing. In a panic, I shone my flashlight inside the box, throwing aside the pens in my way. My tin was not inside.

"NO!" I cried, "No, this can't be happening."

I went to the notebooks and shuffled through them, throwing them to the ground one by one. Getting on all fours, I dug through the sand around the base. My tin was nowhere to be found.

"WHAT DID YOU DO?" I screamed at the Kindred Spirit. "You did this, didn't you?"

I kicked the driftwood pole and hit the box as hard as I could. It vibrated from the impact.

"Give them back!" I screamed, kicking it again. "You can't do this to me!"

"Hey!" Someone behind me shouted. "Cut that out!"

I turned to see a jogger who had stopped to watch me. Behind him fishermen and beach walkers were starting to fill the shoreline. In a fury, I collected the notebooks and threw them back into the mailbox. Satisfied, the concerned jogger moved on down the shore. When everything was back in the mailbox, I grabbed my bike and pedaled as fast as I could toward home.

Sixteen

"What the hell were you thinking, Josh?" My mom berated me as I sat on the couch with my head in my hands. "Sneaking out of the house in the middle of the night to surf? Are you serious?"

The lecture had started as soon as I entered the house. My mom was pacing back and forth in her robe, phone in hand, when I walked in. At first, she was so relieved that she just hugged me close, but once the relief subsided, the lecture began. I didn't tell her the real reason why we'd spent the night at the Kindred Spirit. Even if she did understand, it didn't matter anymore. Nothing mattered anymore. It was all over anyway. There was no explaining this away.

How could I tell her that we'd risked everything to spend the night at the mailbox in hopes that my dad would return to me, if even for a moment, from beyond the grave. Now that everything had fallen apart, it didn't just seem crazy, it was downright pathetic. The mailbox was never going to unite me with my father. All that talk about the In-Between and magic was nothing more than a desperate attempt for some kind of closure. I knew now that there was only one way that closure would ever come, only one way to escape from the pain I'd shared with the Kindred Spirit.

So, my mom assumed we'd been out all night surfing, and I didn't bother to correct her. I just sat and waited for the scolding to be over. I sat and focused on breathing. There was nothing I could say, nothing I could do to make the disappointment on her face go away for long. It always returned. It always would as long as I was around. I let myself go completely numb and told myself that this was the last time that I would ever disappoint her again.

"Do you know how worried I was?" my mom continued. "I was about to call the police! What do you have to say for yourself?"

"Nothing," I mumbled.

"Nothing?" she shrieked. "You're not even going to try to explain what you were thinking?"

Defeated, I fumbled for an acceptable answer. Too many thoughts swirled around in my head. It was hard to focus on just one. "I was thinking that I wanted to see what it was like to surf at night."

"Then why didn't you just ask me?" she yelled. "Instead, you sneak out of your window in the middle of the night? That's ridiculous!"

"If I did ask you, would you have even let me?"

That seemed to make her angrier, and I immediately regretted asking. Nothing I could say would be right. There was no way to make her understand.

"That's beside the point," she spat. "It doesn't mean you can just sneak off and do it anyway! I won't let you drink or do drugs either. Does that mean you're going to start doing those too?"

Her words struck me in the chest as if she had jabbed me with a cattle prod. If it hadn't stung so much, I might have laughed at the irony of it all. Instead, I sat there and let the shame and guilt take their jabs at me too. I was helpless to stop it. I didn't like the thoughts that spun in my head. They scared me. I just wanted the old Me back. Where was he? Why couldn't I find him now when I needed him more than ever? I was so tired of pretending.

The need for my pills was the strongest I'd ever felt. I needed the calm that they could produce more than I needed to breathe. I needed them to help me pretend. Without them, the shadows had latched onto my shoulders like a vice, making it hard to even move. My pretenses were shattering. Soon it would be impossible to hide this Me from my mom. I couldn't let that happen. I couldn't let her see this Me, ever.

I was convinced that the Kindred Spirit had taken my tin from me. That was the only explanation for how it vanished like that. I didn't know how it had done it, but I thought I knew why. It was like Irsa said. I'd put my greatest fears into that mailbox. I'd written about my brokenness and about how life without my father had been a nightmare. When the mailbox failed me last night, when my dad didn't come, maybe it was because the Kindred Spirit was forcing me to face those fears.

Then I'd put my pills into the mailbox. I'd given it the very thing that I feared the most. Those pills had stolen everything from me: my dad, my freedom, my very resolve. As much as I needed them right now, as much as my body craved them, I knew that they were responsible for the monster I'd become. I realized with sudden clarity that they'd never been my parachute. From the time I picked up that first bottle, it was already too late to pull the cord. I'd been going down on a fiery jet all along, and now all I could do was brace for impact.

The money for my music equipment should be sitting in my PayPal account by now. If it was, I had enough money to buy another bottle of pills. I just had to make it until they got here. It would be hard to keep Me hidden until then, but soon I would be able to end this pain and misery for everyone. That's what I had to do. Soon I wouldn't have to hide anymore. I wouldn't have to ache anymore.

"I just don't understand. You've never done anything like this before," my mom continued. "Do you know how worried I was?"

"Worried enough to tell Mr. Salid," I said under my breath.

My mom sighed and came to where I was sitting. I chanced a look at her. Dark circles hung from her eyes, letting me know that she'd been crying. I had to look away. It was too much.

"Yes, I went over there," she said. "I had to see if you were there. What else was I supposed to do?"

"You could have left them out of it," I said.

"You weren't answering your phone. I was scared to death! You didn't even have the decency to leave me a note. You could have been kidnapped for all I knew."

"You're right." I couldn't stop the tears that formed in my eyes. "I'm sorry, Mom. This is all my fault. Everything is my fault."

My whole body trembled, and my mind was wired with hopelessness and the lack of sleep. I wanted to be angry with her. It was easier to be mad at her. She'd promised just the night before that she would keep Irsa's secret safe, but she hadn't. She'd gone over there and alerted Mr. Salid. She'd sent him after us.

As much as I wanted to be angry at her for that, I knew that it wasn't her fault. It was mine alone. I'd given her no choice when I snuck out to the mailbox. Everything that happened was my doing. I'd let her down yet again. I always would. She deserved so much better than me.

So did Irsa. It was because of me that she and Anas snuck out of their home too. She was just trying to help me. I should have known that it was only a matter of time before I ruined things for her too. I should never have let her get so close. Mr. Salid was right about me, and he was right about the mailbox. It was cursed, and so was I.

I wished more than anything that we could all just go back to previous night, when the Salids sat at our table, when the feeling of warmth and friendship had filled the air and my heart. Instead the crippling disappointment that I knew so well had found its way back. It opened its arms to me like an old friend, and I succumbed to its familiar embrace. My mind was filled with more black than the ocean last night.

My mom studied me a second. The anger on her face melted into concern, which was so much worse. When she sat down beside me, I couldn't hold my brokenness back from her. I didn't have the strength to. I wiped the moisture from my eyes as she put her arm around me and held me tight against her.

"Well, I did say I wanted you to get out of the house more." She sighed.

"This isn't funny, Mom."

"No, it's not," she said. "But we all make mistakes, Josh. It's whether or not we learn from them that matters. We aren't defined by our poor choices."

"Tell that to Mr. Salid."

"Why, what happened out there? I saw them when they got home." Her voice was full of regret. "Irsa looked really upset. I take it he knows about her surfing now?"

This time when I looked back up at my mom, I couldn't stop the tears from falling onto my face. "She tried to explain everything, but he wouldn't even listen to her. He was so angry. He destroyed her board, Mom. He smashed it to pieces right there on the beach in front of her."

"Oh, Josh . . . oh, honey." Her voice broke as she pulled me close. "I'm so sorry it came out this way. Maybe I can go over there and talk to him once things boil over. He was probably just caught up in the moment. It's got to be hard to find out that your child has been lying to you for such a long time."

Just when I thought I couldn't feel any worse, the shame tightened its grip. My own lies and deceit slammed into me with enough power to force the air from my lungs. Shaking off my mom's embrace, I stood up. I couldn't take the pressure of the guilt any more.

"I don't need your help, Mom," I said. "Nothing can fix this."

I needed to get away from her, away from the weight of all these things I could no longer carry. Soon my broken pieces were going to spill right out onto the floor. Then she would see the mess I really was and try to put me back together, but that was impossible. I knew she would spend a lifetime trying. She would kill herself attempting to make me right again. I couldn't do that to her, I couldn't. The sooner she left for work, the better. Wiping my eyes again, I started for the hall.

"Josh," she called after me, and I turned back to her, not looking her in the eyes. "I'm so sorry this happened, but it was bound to come out eventually. Lies always do. You can't blame yourself for that."

"I know they do." I prayed that my own lies would stay hidden for just a while longer. "Am I grounded?"

"Oh, you'd better believe it," she said with an exaggerated nod. "No gaming for two weeks. Let the Grounded Gang . . ."

"The Stranded," I corrected.

"Right, you let them know you won't be online for a while," she said. "When I get home, I expect you to hand over your headset and controllers."

"Fine." I lowered my head. "I'll tell them my goodbyes."

"Good. Now, why don't you try to get some sleep? You look terrible."

"I might lie down for a minute." I attempted a weak smile. My mom came over and embraced me again. I tensed in her arms.

"Josh, I know things look bad right now, but you'll feel a lot better after you've gotten some rest." She looked into my face. "We can figure all of this out when I get home. You may not want my help, but that's what I'm here for."

"Thanks, Mom," I said, breaking away. "You're right. Everything will be better."

"That's the spirit." She smiled.

I gave her a forced grin and then dragged myself to my room. I held it together long enough to shut the door behind me. Then I sank to the floor a trembling mess. For a while I just sat there, trying to find the strength to catch my breath. I didn't know what to do with myself. My mind was reeling, and my body throbbed. My stomach ached, but the thought of food was sickening. Everything hurt. Worse than all of that, though, was the weight on my chest. Every part of me screamed out for an escape from the sadness that was so far beyond despair. I just wanted it to stop. I wanted Me to stop. I needed so badly to just be gone.

The only thing worse than my mother finding out about everything would be living life like this forever. This pain was never going to go away on its own. The need to end it was acute and instinctual. I was as desperate for relief as a starving man was for food. I needed those pills.

Staggering to my desk, I brought my computer to life. Several messages from rED flashed across my screen, but I ignored them all. With my heart pounding, I pulled up my PayPal account, typed in my password, and held my breath.

"Please be there," I whispered as it loaded.

When it did, I saw that the money for my equipment had been transferred over. Two hundred and fifty dollars now sat in my account. Frantic now, I switched over to my source's sales page. I selected the thirty-day supply and transferred every last dollar from my account into theirs. In the notes section I typed: *I gave you extra. Please, have it here tomorrow!* Then I clicked the send button.

A calm came over me then, almost as if I'd taken another dose. There was light at the end of this excruciating tunnel at last. Now that I knew it was just a matter of time, the desperation yielded, and the weight eased a bit. Again, I wondered how many pills it had taken to kill my dad. Ten? Twenty? Ultimately, it didn't really matter. This new bottle would have enough to do the job. With that thought, came reassurance.

I was about to turn off my computer when another message from rED popped up.

"Need to talk to you, ASAP! It's important," it read.

It wasn't like him to message me this early. Something was wrong. I yanked my headphones over my head and logged in.

"What's up?" I asked as soon as we were connected.

"Dude! Where have you been?" rED asked.

"Sorry, man," I said. "Things have been crazy the last couple of days."

"Are you okay?"

Tears welled up in my eyes, but I forced them back. I wanted so badly to tell him everything and to say a proper goodbye. He'd been nothing but the best of friends to me for so long, but I couldn't let him in. I couldn't let myself be a burden on anyone else.

"I'm fine," I lied, trying my best to sound normal. "What's going on with you?"

"Man, I've been trying to get a hold of you. You haven't logged on for days."

"What's the matter?"

"It's Biggles," he said. "He's in serious trouble."

My pulse quickened at the sound of Biggles's name. He'd been missing from the gang for a while now.

"What kind of trouble?"

"He got arrested," rED informed me. "He's in jail right now. That's why he hasn't been online."

"What? . . . Why?" My throat tightened. "What happened?"

"You won't believe this," rED continued. "He was caught trying to buy a controlled substance online. Apparently, he got hooked on the pain meds they gave him after his accident last year. He's been scoring them online ever since. They finally caught onto him. Can you believe that?"

"Oh, no." My mind reeled out of control. I had just committed the same crime minutes ago.

"I know," he said. "None of us had a clue. Did you? He always talked to you the most."

"No . . . no, I didn't know." The guilt returned with renewed force. I knew that Biggles had been scoring the Vicodin for himself, but he was also helping me out. He was going down for the both of us. I'd ruined yet another life.

"I didn't think so," he said. "It's just such a shame."

"A shame . . ." I repeated in a daze.

"I wish he would have talked to us about it before it got to be this big of a deal. We're his best friends. We could have helped him through it, you know?"

I did know. I knew exactly why Biggles didn't say anything. They were the same reasons I couldn't either.

"Maybe he was scared of what everyone would think," I said. "Maybe he was too ashamed to let us in. Maybe he thought we would tell on him."

"I guess you could be right," rED agreed, "but he should have known better. He should have trusted us enough to let us in. I hate that he's been dealing with this alone."

You don't know what you're asking, I thought. *You don't want to deal with this. Maybe he was protecting you, just like I'm protecting you now.*

"What's he going to do?" I asked.

"Well, the gang's trying to come up with his bail. Then he'll have to worry about a lawyer," he said. "Do you have any money to help out?"

"No." I thought about the money I'd just given away for more pills and sank into my chair. "I don't have any more."

"That's okay," he said. "I'm sure he knows you would help out if you could."

"I would." I could barely breathe. "I would."

"Hey, are you sure you're okay?"

"Yeah," I said, wiping my eyes. I tried to sound normal. "I just feel so bad."

"We all do," rED agreed.

You guys have no idea, I thought. *You're so much better than all of this. You don't deserve to know this kind of pain.*

"Keep me posted, okay? I have to get going," I said. "There's something I have to take care of."

"Yeah, okay," rED said. He sounded disappointed. "Are you going to be online later tonight? Zoso has been looking for you too. He says he has a great song idea."

Despair slammed into me again. What I wouldn't give to be able to go back to the days when my music was all that weighed on my mind. Life had been so simple then, so full of hope and promise. All of that was gone now.

"Actually, I'm not going to be online for a while," I said. "I got grounded for two weeks. It's a long story."

"Man," he said, "no wonder you sound bummed out. What did you do? Stay out past curfew?"

"Something like that."

"Well, if you talk to R2Deez2Nutz, tell him to log on," he said with a chuckle. "We could all use a good laugh, especially if you're not going to be here for a while."

"I will," I said, struggling to keep it together. "Will you tell the gang that I said I love them and that I am really sorry?"

"Yeah, man," rED said. "Don't sweat it. Two weeks will go by before you know it. Don't worry about it, okay? We'll talk to you soon, right?"

This was the last time I was going to hear his voice, I thought. It was the last time he would hear mine. I knew that it would take a long time for rED to understand what I had to do, but eventually he would. Just like my mom, he would see that they were better off without having to worry about me all the time.

"Right," I lied to him for the last time. "I'll talk to you soon."

"Stay out of trouble."

"You know me," I said with a forced laugh, knowing these were my last words to him. "Thanks for always being there for me. You know, with filling me in on Biggles and stuff."

"Of course. I'm always here for you. Bye, brother," he said, and then he clicked off.

"Goodbye, rED," I whispered back to the broken connection.

I shut off my computer and struggled to stop the tears that overwhelmed me. It was too much. Everything was too much. I wanted to get rED back on the line. I wanted to keep talking so that it never had to be the last time, but it was better this way. I'd already ruined too many lives. I couldn't ruin his too. Biggles was in trouble because of me. When he'd first offered me the pills, I never thought that things would turn out this way. I was looking for an escape. He was looking to be a friend. Now both of our lives were in shambles.

Collapsing onto my bed, I waited for my mom to leave for work so I could get my music equipment to the post office. I didn't know how I would find the strength to get there, but I had to go. It was only fair. Thanks to whoever had bought my equipment, I only had to survive the pain a little bit longer.

With a shaking hand, I lifted the blinds and looked across the street to the Salids' trailer. A part of me thought that if I could just get a glimpse of Irsa, if I could just see that she was okay, it might not feel like the world was closing in around me. If there was just one fragment of hope that I hadn't ruined her entire life, then I could be all right until the pills arrived.

Outside, the sun hovered just above the horizon as if it, too, was reluctant to move. Birds filled the skies with their morning songs, and neighbors were beginning to stir. It was the start of a new day, but the Salid trailer was eerily still. Mr. Salid's car was in the drive, but the blinds were drawn tight. I couldn't even detect movement in the slivers of space between the slats. All was quiet.

Letting the blinds fall back into place, I rolled over and tried to breathe normally. Tension coursed through my entire body, tightening every muscle. There wasn't a place on me that didn't hurt. I was afraid to close my eyes, afraid of the collage of images that were swirling around inside my head. Irsa's devastated face, her splintered board, all those messages from Biggles, the mailbox, and all of my dad's letters flashed and spun in my mind like a dizzying kaleidoscope.

I thought about the way my dad's face had looked when I walked into his room that day and found him on the floor. I remembered his bluish-grey skin and vacant eyes. Soon that would be my face. That thought was both terrifying and calming all at once. My dad had found peace that day. Now I could too.

In the other room, my mom showered for work. I focused on the sound of the water running through the pipes as I curled myself into a ball and waited. A new day had started, but I was stuck in a nightmare of regret and despair. My thoughts swirled in my head like a deadly vortex, sucking me deeper and deeper into the darkness. I stopped trying to claw my way out. I was too tired to fight anymore. Instead I drifted, helpless, as it swallowed me whole.

When my mom came in to check on me before she left the house, I pretended to be asleep. She ran a gentle hand across my cheek and kissed my forehead before tiptoeing out of my room. I heard the truck back out of the drive and forced myself to get up. My body felt stiff, and I was cold even though the heat from the summer sun was penetrating the thin glass of my window. I looked at the clock. The post office would be open in a minute. It was time to go.

My hands were still shaking when I picked up the cardboard box. I checked to make sure the tape was secure and the address was right before I stumbled outside. I grabbed my bike and looked over again at the Salid trailer. Mr. Salid's car was no longer in the driveway. I thought about going to the door, just to see if Irsa and Anas were all right, but then Irsa's devastated face flashed back into my mind, and I decided it would be a bad idea. She was better off without me, I reminded myself with renewed resolve. Everyone was.

The morning sun blazed down on me as I pedaled down the street toward the post office. The cloudless day looked out of place. The way the lush green trees lined the street and accented the brilliant blue sky seemed wrong. Even the sounds of the seagulls in the distance were all wrong to me. I was still stuck in the darkness of the night before. The way life flourished around me only made me feel more alone. Any part of me that had once felt alive was now dead.

I was soaked with sweat by the time I got to the post office, but I still felt chilled to the bone. The line was long when I went inside. It seemed like every able body in Sunset Beach had a package to mail out before work. I struggled to act normal, as if this was just another day. The people around me smiled and chatted with each other about the heat or the upcoming hurricane season. Their words felt fast, their movements hurried, as if everyone was stuck on fast-forward, but it was me who had slowed down.

I had a hard time handing the box over to the smiling woman behind the counter. A small voice in the back of my mind screamed for me not to give up my equipment. It felt wrong, like I was betraying a life I was never going to get to live. When the woman grew impatient, I forced the box onto the counter. She looked at the address, slapped a sticker on top, and took the box away. I watched for a minute until the next person in line stepped up to take my place.

The people coming into the post office looked twice at me as I stumbled back into the heat. Without my pills it was getting harder and harder to appear okay. I knew I had to get it together before my mom came home that afternoon. She was already worried about me. I couldn't give her any more reason for concern. I didn't want her to remember me like this.

The ride home was a blur. I was lost in my thoughts. When I staggered into my kitchen, my clothes were totally soaked. I was so thirsty that I drank straight from the faucet, splashing the water on my face when my stomach could take no more. The thought of food still made me nauseous, so I went to my room and changed into dry clothes. Then I wrapped a blanket around me as I sat at my computer. I pulled up my marketplace listing and marked it as sold.

I reached to turn off my monitor when a message alert stopped me. It was from my new source.

After I read it, relief flooded through me like the rain after a relentless drought. I fell into my bed and wrapped myself in the covers until the shivering subsided. Tears wet my pillow as I closed my eyes and prayed that sleep would take me away fast. I tried not to think of anything else besides this feeling of reassurance. The message had been short, but it was what I needed to be able to drift away into unconsciousness at last.

"In the mail. Arrives tomorrow," was all it had said.

Seventeen

It was late in the afternoon when I finally woke up. At first, I was disoriented. I couldn't understand why the sun was streaming into my room. For a brief moment, I thought that I was late meeting Irsa and Anas on the beach. It wasn't until I sat up that the throbbing in my head brought back all the memories of the morning. The heaviness of them made me long to close my eyes again and forget about waking up. I wanted to just sleep until my pills arrived, but I couldn't.

When I saw that my mom was going to be home within the hour, I dragged my body out of bed. It was the last thing I wanted to do, but I had to clean myself up. She had to believe that everything was okay. Tonight, would be my last and greatest performance.

I opened the blinds and looked across the street again. Mr. Salid's car still wasn't there. The house was still quiet. I wondered if I would ever see Irsa again. Stumbling to the shower, I let the hot water revive me and wash away some of the sting from all that had happened. I took in deep breaths of steam and gathered up all the strength I could muster to get through the evening. The anxiety and fear had subsided with those few hours of sleep. Everything was all so clear now, so simple.

Killing myself was no longer a choice, it was a necessity. Knowing that it was out of my hands made everything, even the waiting, easier. On the roadmap of existence, I saw death as simply my next destination, nothing more and nothing less. I was blissfully numb, void of all other emotion besides tremendous relief and a new sense of purpose. I felt . . . happy.

This was the final night, these the final hours, in which I had to hide myself from my mom and the rest of the world. Tomorrow the secrets, the lies, and the letdowns were over for good. My mom would be at work when the package arrived. She wouldn't be here to stop me from swallowing every last pill in the bottle. She couldn't stop me from locking my bedroom door and lying peacefully in my bed while death came to take me to my dad.

By the time I was dressed, I felt steadier and more focused on what I had to do. The weight on my chest was still there, but I had renewed strength knowing I only had to carry it for one more night. I took my headset and controller into the living room just as my mom walked through the door. She balanced a large pizza box in her hands and used her foot to kick the door shut behind her. She looked relieved to see me up and dressed.

"Well, you're looking much better," she mused.

"I feel much better." I set my controller and headset on the counter and then took the pizza box from her. The smell of sauce and melted cheese made my stomach ache. I finally felt like I could eat.

"I told you sleep would do you good." She patted my face.

"You were right, as usual," I said, setting the pizza on the table.

My mom threw her purse and keys on the counter and kicked off her heels. She picked up my gaming stuff.

"I thought I was going to have to call in the SWAT team to pry these away from you."

"As much fun as that would be, I thought I'd save you the drama." I smiled.

"Oh, but you know how much I like a good drama. You hungry?" She took my things down the hall to her room.

"Starving," I said, getting plates down from the cabinet.

When my mom returned, she was dressed in her favorite pair of loose-fitting sweats. Her hair was pulled back in a messy bun. I took in the sight of her: the way her eyes glittered beneath her thick lashes and the way the tip of her nose turned up when she smiled. I hoped she knew how much I truly loved her.

"I ordered your favorite," she said, opening the pizza box. "Extra pepperoni."

"Wow, thanks," I said. "What's the occasion? I thought you were mad at me."

She shrugged. "I'm your mother, getting mad happens. Good thing for you it never lasts long, even if you did scare the living hell out of me this morning."

"I'm sorry about all of that," I said.

"I know you are." She nodded. "I also know that you had a rough morning too. I thought we could both use some pizza and a movie."

"More than you even know." I grabbed two Mountain Dews from the fridge.

We sat at the table as if it were any other night, as if nothing bad had ever touched our lives. My mom plopped a steaming slice of pizza on my plate.

"So, have you heard anything from Irsa or Anas?"

"Nothing yet." I took a bite and savored the taste of the garlicky sauce.

"Give it time," she said, grabbing her own slice. "You know, I've been thinking about this whole mess all day. I really do think I can talk to Youssef, you know, single parent to single parent. I'm not saying he'll listen to me or let Irsa keep surfing, but I think it's worth a shot. I really do."

She looked at me, waiting for me to object.

"Actually," I said instead, "I think that's a good idea."

"What?" she asked, raising an eyebrow. "That was too easy. Usually you don't want my help. You said so this morning."

"I was upset this morning." I shrugged. "Now I think you're right. You guys really hit it off. I bet he would listen to you. Anything to help Irsa."

"You know, that girl really is a good influence on you." My mom smirked at me. "I hope I can help."

"I hope so too."

"Okay then." She looked so happy to help. "I'll go over there this weekend and see what I can do."

"Thanks, Mom."

After that, the tension from the morning was gone. We didn't talk about it again. Instead, I ate two more slices as I listened to my mom talk about her day. I took in her excitement about her new job, reassured that she would be just fine once I was gone. Seeing her joy only affirmed that I'd made the right decision. With me out of her way, she could live a normal life. She would finally be free from all of her concerns and apprehensions. She'd never have to hide her disappointment from me again.

We finished dinner, and I offered to do the dishes while she picked out a movie. Then we plopped down on the couch to watch *Austin Powers* for the billionth time. It had always been our favorite. Tonight though, the jokes seemed funnier, and my mother's company was more enjoyable than ever. We even made a run to the store for ice cream and sprinkles before watching the sequel.

Never once did she notice the trembling of my hands or the sweat that beaded on my forehead as my body cried out for more of the drug it was dependent on. I hid it all well, and though my head ached, we were having too much fun trying to impersonate our favorite characters for anything else to matter. We didn't call it a night until we had laughed our way through the third movie. It was past eleven when my mom finally rose to go to bed.

"Oh, man, I don't know how Mike Myers is able to play all those characters. That Fat Bastard character is too much." She stretched her arms above her head. "But I think Goldmember will always be my favorite."

"I know. I love the way he talks with that Dutch accent. The part when he's trying to say father, but it comes out as *Fasha*?" I laughed. "Classic."

"I think that's the best part of the whole movie," she agreed. "Instead of mother, you should just call me *Masha* from now on."

"Yes, *Masha*," I teased.

We both laughed as she turned off the television and straightened the couch cushions. I watched her, committing every part of her to memory. This is what I wanted to remember the most tomorrow as I waited to leave this world. I wanted the smile on her face to last forever.

"Well, I've got to get to bed," she said. "What are you going to do with yourself tomorrow now that you don't have your games? You're not going to go surfing alone, are you?"

I shrugged innocently. "No. I'll probably just hang out."

"Good," she said, relieved. "I didn't want to have to worry about you out there by yourself."

Just like in those last moments with rED, I thought about what I wanted my last words to her to be. This was the last time she was going to hear my voice. This was my last chance to let her know how much I loved her. Walking over to her, I looked her in the eyes and gave her a genuine smile.

"You don't have to worry about me anymore, Mom," I said. "Everything's going to be okay."

She smiled back and patted my cheek again. "Oh, honey, I'm always going to worry about you. That's my job."

"I know." I put my arm around her. "You do a good job."

I wanted to tell her that she could stand down now, that there would be no more worrying about me. She needed to know that she'd done everything she possibly could and that it was okay for her to let me go now.

"I'll never stop worrying about you, Josh, because I'll never stop loving you," she said, hugging me back.

"I know," I said. "I love you, Mom."

"I love you too, my boy. We should do this more often." She kissed me on the cheek before pulling away. "Don't stay up all night working on your music, okay? Get some sleep tonight. You had a long night last night."

"I'll try," I said as she started to walk away.

When she reached her bedroom door, she looked at me one more time. "See you tomorrow."

"I'll see you," I said, and then she went inside and shut the door.

For a minute, all I could do was stare at the shut door. I didn't want that to be it. The scared little boy in me wanted to call her back to hold me until it was over, but I couldn't. I had to do this alone. I thought about my last day with my dad. It had been just a normal day like this one. We ate dinner and watched a hockey game together like any other night. I couldn't remember what his last words to me were. At least I got to say goodbye to my mom.

Going to my room, I didn't even bother turning on the light. My body and mind were exhausted. I sunk onto my bed and pulled the covers over me to stop the shivering. How easy it would be just to sleep until the package arrived, I thought. I was so tired, but there was just one last thing I needed to do. So, I set my alarm and rolled over. I let my mind replay the evening. It was a good last night. The look of joy and contentment on my mom's face ensured me that I was doing the right thing. Everything really was going to be okay.

Sleep took me easily, and soon I was lost to blissful unconsciousness. It felt like only minutes had passed when the knock at my window woke me. At first it was quiet, but the longer it took me to react, the louder the noise got. Finally, I rolled over and pulled the blinds. My groggy mind expected butt cheeks to be pressed against the glass as usual. When Anas's sullen face grinned at me instead, I jumped up.

"Anas, what are you doing here?" I asked when I opened the window. "Your dad is going to kill you if he catches you out of the house again."

"No kidding. So, let me in."

When I moved out of the way, he attempted to throw himself inside in a panic, but his feet slipped, and he dangled halfway through. I grabbed onto his pants and yanked him the rest of the way inside. Then I shut the window and the blinds.

"Dude, now my boxers are so far up my crack I'll need pliers to dig them out," he said, getting to his feet and adjusting himself.

"What's going on?" I asked. "Are you guys all right?"

"I'm actually here to check up on you. You haven't logged onto your Xbox," he said.

"I'm grounded," I explained. "No games for two weeks."

He looked around my room, his eyes landing on my empty desk. "No music either? Your equipment is gone."

"Oh . . . yeah," I stammered. "That too."

"Bummer." Anas had a seat on my bed. "You look like crap, by the way."

"Thanks," I said, sitting beside him. "How are you guys? What happened when you got home? Is Irsa all right?"

"Oh, man, everything is so screwed. We're not allowed to surf anymore." Disappointment hung on his face. "My dad says it's a waste of time for me and is forbidden for Irsa. So lame."

"That's it though? You're not grounded or anything?"

"Worse," he said. "I have to go to work with my dad and help with the shop until school starts. This was supposed to be my last summer of freedom, you know?"

"What about Irsa?" I asked. "What's going to happen to her?"

Anas bowed his head. "My dad is sending her to live with one of her school friends for the rest of the summer, where her mother can keep an eye on the two of them all day. He says she needs to spend some time with a proper Muslim woman so she can have a good mother figure or whatever."

"He's sending her away?"

"Yeah," Anas said. "She leaves tomorrow."

"Man," I said, stunned. I'd messed things up for them worse than I thought. Shame and guilt clawed their way back into my mind. I really had ruined Irsa's life.

"I hate him." Anas stared down at his feet dangling off the bed.

"No . . . no, don't say that. He's your dad." I tried to comfort him, but for the life of me I couldn't understand why Mr. Salid would keep Irsa away from her passion, her natural gift. "I'm sure he thinks that he's doing what's best for you guys."

"I know, but he won't even listen," he said. "I just wish he would understand."

"I know," was all I could think to say.

"I tried to get Irsa to come over and say goodbye, but she wouldn't," Anas said. "I don't think she wants to risk letting my father down anymore. She hasn't said much. She just looks guilty all the time."

"I'm so sorry," I whispered. "Will you tell her that I am so, so sorry?"

"What are you sorry about?" Anas nudged my arm. "It was our idea to sneak out, remember?"

"Yeah, but you guys were just trying to help me figure out who was writing those letters," I said.

"That is true, but what an adventure we had. Am I right?" He smiled wide. "I mean, it was almost better than that part in *A New Hope* when Leia, Luke Skywalker and the real Solo get stuck in that garbage compactor. You remember that part? They had to find a way out before they got flattened?"

"Yeah, I guess . . ."

"We just didn't make it out before it was too late, is all." He shrugged. "But surfing with you and trying to figure out how to break the mailbox curse was the most fun I've had in my whole life."

"Mine too." I realized it was true as I said it. "But none of that matters anymore. It's all over now."

"That's what everyone thinks when things come to an end." Anas got to his feet. "Everyone's sad at first because they can't see how the story could possibly continue, but then there's always a sequel or two, maybe even a few prequels. Then years later, some more sequels and even a few character stand-alone stories."

"You do know that life isn't actually like *Star Wars*, right?" I asked. "Please tell me you get that."

"My point is, it's never really over," he said. "You just have to wait for the next part of the story to start."

"What if there is no next part?" I asked. "Sometimes the dark side wins. The End."

"Maybe for a little while, sure, but the good guys always come back even stronger. It's never really over." Anas walked over to the window and lifted the glass. "It's all about perspective, Solo."

"I guess." I shrugged. "That's just never been my experience."

"Yeah, well, that's why I'm so much cooler," he said with a wink.

"I'm sorry you have to go work for your dad the rest of the summer."

"Don't be. At least I'm getting paid," he said, "and I can still play my Xbox, so you should really be jealous."

Anas climbed down and hit the ground with a thud. He turned to me before he ran back to his house.

"I'll see you later, Solo."

I watched his scrawny legs pound the sandy grass of my yard as he ran toward his trailer. This was the last time I would ever see the little weirdo who had become one of my dearest friends.

"Hey!" I called out to him in a loud whisper. He stopped and turned. "May the Force be with you."

Anas smiled, his white teeth shining under the street lamp.

"And also with you," he said with a bow. Then he ran to the back of his trailer and out of sight.

I was about to shut the window when a flicker of light caught my eye. The lamp in Irsa's window turned on. As I watched, the blinds parted, and she peered out into the night. For the first time since I'd met her, she wasn't wearing her hijab. Her long, dark hair flowed around her face in black ocean waves. She was the most beautiful thing I'd ever seen.

Our eyes locked. A thousand words were communicated between us the second our eyes met. The sadness in the warm depths of hers was almost too much to bear, but I couldn't look away. She put her hand up against the glass of her window as a tear ran down her delicate cheek. I put my palm to my own window, wishing more than anything that I could embrace her one last time.

"*I'm sorry*," she mouthed to me from across the dimly lit street.

I didn't understand. What could she possibly have to be sorry about? How could she blame herself for anything that happened? I wanted to run over there, to tell her that none of this was her fault. She had nothing to be sorry for.

I wanted my last words to her to be an explanation of all the things that she meant to me. I wanted her to know how I truly felt about her.

But I had ruined her life.

She stared at me as she removed her hand and lowered the blinds. I prayed that she would find her way back to the sea someday. I prayed that she would rise from the ashes I had made of her life.

"I love you," I whispered into the darkness as the light in her room went out. "I'm so sorry."

Eighteen

I left the house the next morning as soon as my mom left for work. There was one last end to tie up. My stomach was still in knots as I pedaled over the bridge under the heat of the glaring sun. I'd barely made it to the bathroom this morning before I threw up every bit of pizza left in my stomach. The withdrawal symptoms were getting progressively worse. My head pounded, and I couldn't keep myself warm even though I was sweating through my clothes. I didn't let it bother me though. I knew I wouldn't have to suffer any of it much longer.

When I reached the beach, a crowd of people blanketed the shore with their colorful umbrellas and vacation smiles. The crashing of the waves was all but drowned out by their music and laughter. It all seemed apart from me, as if I no longer shared the same reality as the rest of the world. I pedaled as fast as my unsteady body could past all the movement and the noise until only a splattering of people walked beside me on the remote coastline of Bird Island. I spotted the American flag as it rippled against the ocean breeze just ahead. Below it, the Kindred Spirit sat waiting in the dunes as it always had.

I remembered the day I'd first found it and the way it had called to me. It felt like so long ago now. I remembered how angry I was then when I had written that first letter on the pages inside. As horribly as things had turned out, though, I was no longer mad. I didn't see myself as a victim of misfortune or tragedy anymore. Instead, I'd embodied those things. I'd embraced them as who I was now, and it was up to me to destroy them. Ditching my bike, I slowly ascended the dunes toward the mailbox.

"I get it." I stared into the black surface of the Kindred Spirit. "I know why you brought me here now. You never intended to bring my dad back to me, did you? All along, you were bringing me to him. I was always meant to join him. I see that now. You win."

Retrieving my notebook from inside, I took it to the wooden bench. I gathered my thoughts as I stared out at the crystal blue waves. My words mattered more now than ever before. These would be my last words in this world. I was glad they were to my dad. My hand shook when I touched the pen to the page. I lifted it up and took a deep breath to steady myself. Then I tried again.

Dad,

You never came to me the other night. At first, I couldn't understand why, but I think I do now. This is the way it was always meant to be. I still have faith that we can be together on the other side of this life.

I will find you there.

This is the way I make peace with my wrongs. This is how I face my fears.

You were right about the storm, Dad. It's coming. It's on its way to take me away from here.

We will be together again soon.

J.

Satisfied, I shut the notebook and took a deep breath of ocean air. I felt at complete peace. I'd done everything I needed to do. If my dad really had been the one writing to me all this time, then he knew I was coming. I prayed that he would be on the other side waiting for me.

For the last time, I placed my notebook at the bottom of the pile and shut the lid of the mailbox. Then I looked at the Kindred Spirit. I marveled at the fact that something so unremarkable had become the very cusp of my existence. It really was a gateway from this world to the next after all. In the end, it truly was the In-Between.

While I was still marveling, I felt something cold and wet run up the back of my leg. It was followed by a loud snort. Startled, I spun around. A shaggy, black and white dog was attempting to sniff my butt. The tips of his fur were caked with wet sand, and he licked my hand when I bent down to pet him. I realized that this was the same dog that we'd seen on the beach and in our hidden video. His owner was just behind him. The man jogged up the dunes to retrieve him.

"Wilbur!" he shouted. "Wilbur, leave him alone."

"It's okay," I said as he came up and clipped a leash to the dog's collar. This was the closest I'd ever been to the man that had once been our prime suspect. I stared at his rugged, worn face.

"Sorry about that," he said. "I should have kept his leash on. I wasn't expecting anyone to be out here."

"Really, it's fine." I studied him. The man had a sad look about him, but I was sure I'd never met him before.

"I didn't mean to interrupt." He started to walk away. "I'll give you your privacy."

"Wait. I'm already done," I called, and he turned around. "I was wondering, do . . . do you write in the mailbox a lot? I mean, do you ever respond to anyone in there?"

The man looked surprised by my question. He thought about it for a minute before answering.

"I try to come here every day if I can." He patted the dog's head. "This used to be my wife's favorite spot."

"Oh, I'm sorry," I said. "I didn't mean to pry or anything."

"I've seen you out here before, haven't I?" he squinted at me. "You're usually with those other kids out in the water. The girl's got the . . . thing." He swirled a finger around his head, trying to think of the word.

"It's a hijab. Yeah, those are my friends."

"Yeah, that's it," he said. "You kids seem awfully interested in the Kindred Spirit."

I scrambled to think of how to explain why we'd watched him. I decided that I had nothing to lose by just being honest. What did it matter now anyway?

"Someone's been answering my letters in there. We thought that maybe it was you since we see you here all the time."

"Oh, I see." He ran a hand through his wiry hair. "I'm sorry, but it's not me. I've tried to find the words to write something in those pages. I just can't seem to figure out what to say, let alone how to respond to anyone. Usually I just flip through the letters."

"You read them?" I asked.

He looked embarrassed. "I know it's strange, maybe even rude to read other people's thoughts. It's just that it's been only me and Wilbur for so long. It's a comfort, I guess, to know that so many people out there are going through the same things."

Though in my heart I had always known it wasn't this man writing to me in the mailbox, it was good to know for sure. It meant that my dad was still out there, and he was waiting for me.

"I understand that completely," I said as I grabbed my bike. "I'm sorry I bothered you."

"It was no bother," he said. "I hope you find who it is you're looking for."

"I do too," I said as I hopped on.

I took in the warmth of sunlight on my face as I pedaled down the beach. Dipping down into the surf, I let the water splash against my legs. The warm saltwater seeped into my shoes, but I didn't care. Not caring was the best feeling in the world. It was the freedom of letting go that I'd only ever found on the waves, or in Irsa's embrace. This time the freedom would last forever, and no one could take it from me.

Pedaling past the throngs of beachgoers, I looked into the faces of countless strangers. For once, I pitied everyone else. They were all still battling their own demons and fighting for that fleeting feeling of joy in their lives. Some of them waited all year, working day in and day out in a job they hated, just to have a week or two of peace. Sure, they were happy now, but they still faced ceaseless conflict. I'd already raised my white flag. I didn't have to fight anymore. I wanted to tell them all how much better it was to just surrender.

Mr. Salid's car was parked in the lot of the bike rental shop. I chanced a look in the window as I rode by. Inside, Anas stood behind the counter, his dad at his side. Mr. Salid looked to be explaining how to use the cash register. As I passed, Anas punched in buttons, and the cash drawer opened. He smiled up at his dad as Mr. Salid looked on proudly. I turned away before they saw me, assured that Anas was going to be okay. If only I could be as sure about Irsa.

By the time I reached the bridge, the sun was high overhead. I looked out at the shallow pools of the Intercoastal, knowing that my package was probably waiting for me on the front stoop. The end was finally here. My body completely relaxed as I rode the decline of the bridge, taking in my last glimpse of the water. The relief was intoxicating. I took two laps around the roundabout at the base of the bridge, just to prolong my final minutes in the humid summer air. By the time I pulled onto my street, I was ready.

As soon as I turned the corner, I looked over at the Salid trailer for the final time. As usual, the blinds were closed, and all was still. I wondered if Irsa was already gone. It was just as well if she was. I'd already made peace with the fact that I would never see her again.

When I turned into my drive, I almost ran head-first into my mom's truck. Bewildered and confused, my pulse quickened. My mom was home. I yanked my phone from my pocket and checked the time. It was just after ten o'clock. She shouldn't be here. I'd watched her leave the house before I did. This didn't make sense.

I assured myself that she probably just forgot something or she was taking an early lunch. Either way, I had to play it cool until she left. I wasn't prepared to put on another performance for her, so I took a minute to collect myself.

Walking around to the front stoop, I looked to see if my package had been delivered. There was nothing there. I walked to the back door and checked the top of the porch. Still no package. My pills must not have been delivered yet. With any luck, they wouldn't come until my mom went back to work. I knew I had to get inside. She might be worried that I wasn't home. I didn't want her mad at me. So, taking a deep breath, I opened the door and walked in.

It took my eyes a minute to adjust to the indoors after being outside for so long. When they finally did, I saw that my mom was sitting on the couch. Irsa sat beside her. Both of them had tears in their eyes.

When she saw me, Irsa jumped up and ran to me. She threw her arms around me. I was so happy to see her that I pulled her close. She was shaking.

"Are you okay?" I asked her. "Anas told me everything. Are you here to say goodbye?"

"I'm leaving within the hour," she cried. "I'm so sorry."

I held her at arm's length and looked into her tear-filled eyes. "You have nothing to be sorry about. Do you understand? This was all my fault. I'm the one who is sorry."

"Josh?" my mom called out. The anguish in her voice startled me. I let go of Irsa long enough to turn to where my mom sat on the couch. Mascara ran down her face. She looked at me with wide, vacant eyes.

Then I saw my package on the coffee table in front of her. It was open. A prescription bottle dangled from my mom's fingers.

"What's going on?" I looked from Irsa to my mom. It felt like the air had been sucked from my lungs. She'd opened my package. She knew about the pills. I scrambled to think of a way to lie my way out of it.

"You tell me, Josh." She set the pills on the table. "What are these?"

"I don't know," I said, not knowing what else to do. "What is it?"

"Don't lie to me." Fresh tears streamed down her face. I had to do something. She couldn't know the truth, not now.

"Mom, I'm not lying," I pleaded. "What are those?"

My only hope was to play dumb. The walls were closing in around me. I couldn't think. I could barely keep my legs beneath me.

"These are the same pills, aren't they?" My mom got to her feet. "They're the same pills that killed your father. Did he get you addicted to them?"

"WHAT?" I shouted. "No! What are you talking about? He would never do that. I don't know where those came from!"

"They're addressed to you, Josh! They came to the house!" My mom was hysterical now. I couldn't take that look on her face. I couldn't stand her tears. It couldn't end like this. This isn't how things were supposed to go.

"I . . . I only ordered my mints, Mom." I tried to convince her. "This has to be some kind of a mistake. They messed up my order last time . . ."

"This is no mistake," my mom said. "I know about the mints, Josh."

Desperate, I turned to Irsa. If only she believed me. She could help me convince my mom. Maybe she could help me get that look off of her face.

"You believe me, don't you?" I asked. "Tell her this is a mistake."

When Irsa looked up at me, a single tear ran down her face. She shook her head from side to side and stretched out her arm. Something was clasped in her hand.

"No more lies, remember?" she whispered.

When she opened her fingers, my tin shook in her palm.

"You . . ." My heart sank into the pit of my stomach. "You took it? When?"

"You fell asleep," was all she said as more tears fell onto her cheek.

I looked back at my mom. She crossed her arms, her eyes boring into me. Suddenly it all made sense. I turned back to Irsa, knowing I was defeated.

"You came over here to tell on me?" I asked as tears formed in my own eyes. "Why would you do that? Do you know what you're doing to me?"

"I'm saving your life," she said.

I stepped back from her, my head reeling. There was no way out of this. It was hopeless. The shame and guilt dug into my core. It slashed at me, robbing me of my voice and my very breath.

"Don't be mad at her. She did the right thing," my mom said. "I decided to take the rest of the day off to be with you. Something didn't feel right last night. I didn't want you to have to spend the day alone. Irsa caught me coming in."

The more my mom explained, the less I heard. My heart pounded in my ears like the strum of a death march. My whole body shook. I couldn't think straight. The sting of betrayal was even worse than seeing the devastation on my mom's face.

"Can't . . . breathe." I stumbled backwards, the room spinning. Panic overwhelmed me.

My mom ran to me, bracing me up in her arms. Behind me, I could hear Irsa crying.

"It's going to be okay, Josh," my mom said. "We're going to get you help."

"No . . ." I didn't want help. I wanted an end now more than ever. I wanted the room to stop spinning. I wanted to wipe the way my mom looked at me from my mind. I couldn't live like this. This couldn't be my life! I was worthless. Worthless!

"Everything is going to be okay," my mom kept saying. She was trying to embrace me, but her arms felt like a snare around me.

I was trapped. Trapped.

I had to escape this hell. I couldn't be here anymore.

I couldn't do this.

With a desperate cry, I broke free of my mom and dove for the table. I clutched the bottle of pills in my hand as my mom screamed behind me. Then I forced my legs back under me as she and Irsa tried to grab the bottle from my hand. It took all the strength I had left in my feeble body, but I wrenched free of them both. Stumbling, I raced to my room while they shouted behind me.

"Josh, no!" my mom screamed, as I shut my door and locked it behind me.

I threw everything off of my dresser, frantic. The picture of my dad fell to the floor and shattered. Heaving all of my bodyweight against it, I pushed the dresser in front of the door. Then I stepped back, my breaths coming in a labored rattle.

My mom and Irsa pounded on the other side of the door.

"Josh, open the door," my mom pleaded. "Open the door, Josh. We can figure this out together."

It was too late for that. It was too late for all of it. It wasn't supposed to be this way.

"Please, Josh," Irsa cried. "Don't do this!"

It took three tries to pry the cap off of the bottle. My hand shook so badly that many of the pills spilled onto the carpet, but there were plenty left inside. I tried to take a deep breath.

Closing my eyes, I imagined my dad waiting for me on the bench of that lonely stretch of beach. I put myself there. I imagined the warm ocean breeze and heard the call of seagulls overhead. In my mind, the pounding and shouts from the other side of the door faded away until all I could hear was the steady crashing of the waves on the shore. My dad smiled at me and patted the seat beside him. *Come, Josh. Come to me.*

"I'm coming, Dad," I whispered as I wiped the tears from my face.

Tilting my head back, I poured as many pills as I could into my mouth. Then I swallowed. At first, I choked on the chalky thickness of them, but I kept swallowing until they all went down. Then I poured in more and choked them down again. My stomach heaved, but I forced the pills back down. It was the only way. This was the only way.

When the bottle was empty, I went to my bed and lay down. All there was left to do now was to wait.

The pounding on the door turned frantic. My mom screamed for Irsa to call the police. I could hear their panicked shuffling in the hall and felt the last pangs of guilt on my chest. It wouldn't be long now, I told myself as my body shivered violently.

I was doing this for them. All the lies, all the hiding, had been for them. Soon they would see that. Soon they wouldn't have to worry about me anymore. Soon we would all be free.

I lay still and watched the sun stream in through my window, and I concentrated on taking deep breaths. Soon the breaths came easier. It didn't take long for the shivering to stop. A warm glow came over my limbs, and my muscles relaxed. I grew tired . . . so, so tired.

"Hang in there, Josh," my mom shouted to me from the other side of the door. "Help is coming!"

Yes, it is, I thought. *Finally, it is.*

I closed my eyes for the last time as the exhaustion took my body over. Sweet relief flooded my senses. I swam in and out of consciousness. As the sirens sounded down the street, I let it all go.

Irsa's voice was the last thing I heard before I let the darkness swallow me for good.

"Not again," she was crying. "Please, not again!"

Nineteen

I drifted on a sea of shadow and light. Surrounded by darkness, I felt nothing. I was nothing. My mind wandered there, on the other side of consciousness, where there was no sorrow or worry. There was no want or need. Only the darkness. Only silence.

Here and there a white-hot flash brought me to myself. Then back to nothing. Somewhere in my mind I registered movement. I heard my mother's voice. It faded the farther into the black I drifted.

My thoughts lingered on my dad. I needed to find him. Though I tried to call out his name, only echoes responded back from the dark. I didn't understand. He was supposed to be there. He was supposed to be waiting for me on the other side, but I was alone in the blackness. I was alone in my confusion.

Suddenly, I didn't want to be there anymore. My emotions returned. All of them, all at once. I was angry and scared, ashamed and unbelievably sad. Brightness startled me when I tried to open my eyes. I couldn't tell if I was awake or asleep, dead or alive. I shut them again. The nothingness around me fractured. I didn't know if I could cling to the emptiness anymore. I didn't want to, but I didn't know if I could find my way out of it. What was going on? What had I done? What had I done?

Then I heard a familiar voice beside me.

"*Josh, come,*" it whispered. "*Come to me . . .*"

My eyelids flew open. The light was so harsh, so blinding that it took a while for the jumble of images to make any sense. Nothing looked familiar in the windowless room. Behind me, a shrill beeping kept tempo with my racing pulse. There were needles in my arm, an oxygen tube in my nose. It was hard to move. I started to panic. My god, what had I done?

When I felt a warm hand close around mine, I turned. My mom was sitting beside me, tears in her eyes. She smiled at me and ran her fingers down my face.

"Shhh, it's okay," she whispered. "Everything's okay now."

My eyes filled with tears. "Mom? What happened? Am I going to be okay?"

"You're going to be just fine." She squeezed my hand. "Thank God."

"I don't remember how I got here . . ."

"The police came," she explained. "They broke down the door so the paramedics could get to you. They rushed you here to the hospital. You had your stomach pumped. You've been in and out of consciousness. They're giving you some activated charcoal now to get rid of the rest of the drugs in your system. They don't think there's any liver damage."

The memories of what happened that morning returned in a flood of remorse and shock. It all felt like so long ago. The last few days were a haze of emotion and confusion. All of those things that I'd felt, all those thoughts . . . they didn't make any sense to me now. All those feelings of worthlessness and desperation had faded like a bad dream. All that remained was bitter sadness and overwhelming fear.

"I'm so sorry, Mom." I blinked back the tears. "I can't believe I did that. What is wrong with me? What have I done? I almost . . . I almost ended up like Dad."

My mom shook her head as tears rolled down her cheek. "It's all going to be okay now, Josh. We're going to get you the help you need. Now that I know about the pills . . ."

She couldn't finish. She struggled to keep herself together. When she looked at me, there was so much warmth and pain in her eyes. I couldn't lie to her any longer. I didn't want to. It didn't feel like the right thing to do anymore. She needed to know everything. She was the only one who could make this okay.

"I'm so sorry." The words rushed out. "I picked up Dad's pills the day I found him. I don't know why, Mom. I . . . I just didn't know what else to do. It was the only part of him that I had left. I'm so sorry I did this to you. I tried so hard to make you proud. I'm so sorry."

"No, baby." My mom scooted into the bed beside me, her tears flowing now. She gathered me up in her arms. "I'm the one who is sorry. I failed you, Josh. I should have seen what you were going through. I should have forced you to talk to me. I should have known that losing your dad was harder on you than you let on."

"I didn't want you to have to worry about me," I said. "I didn't want to be a burden on you like Dad was."

"You could never be a burden; do you understand me?" she cried. "I am always here, no matter what's going on with you. Wherever I am, whatever I am doing, it does not matter. Whenever you need me, I will forever be here for you. It's okay to need someone. I need YOU, Josh. You are my baby, a part of me, a piece of my heart, my soul. We are connected. Can't you see that?"

"But you left Dad because he couldn't stop the pills." I looked into her gentle face. "I've turned out just like him, Mom. You deserved better than him. You deserve better than me."

"You are not your father, Josh." She squeezed me tighter. "You don't have to make his same choices. You will not end up like him because I won't let that happen. We BOTH deserve better than that. You are so much stronger than your demons."

"I miss him so much." I didn't try to stop the tears from falling onto my cheeks.

"I know you do," my mom whispered. "I do too. It's okay to grieve for your dad. You don't have to be strong for me or anyone else anymore. You have to let the feelings come. It's the only way you'll ever be able to let him go. It's the only way we both will."

Something finally broke free inside me then. There was no holding back the sorrow any longer. My dad's smiling face, our hockey nights, and his unconditional acceptance overwhelmed my memory. I didn't want to let any of it go. I was afraid that if I did, I would forget all of who he was.

"I don't know how to let him go," I cried. "Why did he leave me, Mom? Why wasn't I enough to make him stay?"

She squeezed me tight, and we cried together. "Baby, you will always be enough. Your dad loved you so much. He would never have left you if he could have helped it. He just got lost is all. He just got lost."

"I want him back." I sobbed against her shoulder as she held me tight. "I just want everything to go back to how it was."

"I know you do," she whispered against my ear as she rocked me back and forth. "I do too."

We held onto one another and cried. All of my broken pieces fell from the places I'd been hiding them. They scattered around us like shattered glass. I held onto my mom and let out all of the pain that I'd stuffed down for so long. The floodgates had finally broken, and I lay a whimpering shell in my mother's arms. She held me tight against her without so much as flinching. This was Me, the fractured Me, the REAL Me. She embraced all of it.

"I love you so much, Josh," she said. "Nothing you could do could ever change that. You hear me? You are my whole heart."

All I could do was nod my head against her shoulder. The tears rocked me to my core.

"You matter, Joshua." I let her gentle rocking calm me. "Your feelings matter. Your health matters. You have people who love you unconditionally and would do anything just to make sure you are okay. You could never be a burden. I just don't know what I would do without you. You can't leave me too. You can't."

"I won't," I vowed as we both wept. "I don't want to be lost anymore, but I don't know how not to be. I'm so scared."

"I know you are, but we're going to get through this," she assured me, wiping her tears with the back of her hand. "Maybe we should move back to Pittsburgh, or somewhere new. We can move somewhere you feel comfortable. We can find you peace somewhere. Anywhere."

"No, I don't want to move." I sat up, looking her in the eye. "I want to stay in Sunset Beach."

"Okay." She nodded. "Then we'll fight right here."

"What's going to happen to me now?"

"The doctor wants to discharge you to an inpatient mental care facility when you are strong enough. They're going to help you rid your system of the Vicodin once and for all," she explained. "They think withdrawal might worsen your depression, so they're going to take it slowly."

I thought about the last time I'd tried to wean myself off the pills. I had thoughts about taking my life then when I thought that Anas and Irsa had written that first response. This morning, though, I'd actually gone through with it. I could be dead right now. That thought sent a wave of panic throughout my whole body. What if I only felt better now because the drug was in my system again? What would happen to me the next time I tried to break free?

"They're right. I went days without it until this morning," I said. "I almost . . . I don't think I can do this, Mom."

My mom turned my head to face her. "I know you can. You have to. Those pills have taken enough away from us."

"I know," I pleaded, "but what if I just end up like Dad? I'm scared of what I might do if I go into withdrawal again."

"That's why you have to go," she said. "You have to fight to get your life back."

I didn't want to go to an inpatient facility. I just wanted everything to go back to the way it was before this year ever happened. It felt like a chunk of time was missing from my life. I didn't know how to cope with that. More than anything, I just wanted to have the strength to deal with this on my own. I felt so helpless, and this time the feeling terrified me.

"I don't want to leave you, Mom," I said. "I don't think I can go."

"I know you're scared, but you have to let these people help you," she said. "We all need help sometimes. This is just your time. You have to let them help you, okay?"

I thought about that night on the beach when we'd helped those baby turtles. I remembered how defenseless and fragile they had been. Many of them would have died on the dunes if we hadn't shown them the way out. There was no shame, no judgement. We saw their need, and we responded. Now they were free to face the obstacles ahead of them.

Irsa's words came back to me from that night. *Everyone needs help at some point. The hard part is letting help come.*

Maybe it was time for me to let help come. Trying to do this on my own wasn't working. I was a floundering turtle stuck on the dunes. I needed someone to help me dig my way out so I could face my own obstacles. I would never be able to cope with my dad's death until I shed the habit that had taken him away from me. Only then would I be free.

I clung to my mother's warm embrace and nodded.

"Okay," I said. "I'm ready. I need help."

Twenty

"I know why I did it now," I explained to the attentive faces around me. "It's taken these past few weeks to realize it, but now that my mind is finally clear, I can see it."

I looked around the room at the people who had encouraged me on my worst days. There were a lot of bad days in the beginning of my stay at the Wilmington Rehabilitation Center. Every day, though, good or bad, our therapy group gathered in the conference room to share our progress and our struggles. At first it was hard to open up. It was scary to be away from my mom and everything I knew. Ultimately though, having a break from my "normal" had been exactly what I needed. It was easier to take a long, hard look at your life when you could see it from a distance.

Though I still missed home, the people sitting in the circle with me had become friends. Among us was a single mom, a middle schooler and a businessman. There was a teacher, a veteran and a widow. We were sons, daughters, parents and spouses, all fighting the same battle, all struggling to free ourselves of our addictions. We were kindred spirits.

"I was using the Vicodin to cope with my dad's death," I continued. "I didn't want to feel the pain of losing him."

"I know you've been struggling with being able to let go of your father, Josh. How are you feeling today?" Dr. Brenner asked from where he sat at the head of our circle.

Though I'd talked to my mom every day and she had come to every family session, it was Dr. Brenner who'd been my rock through this process. He was the one who helped me open up about my dad. My daily sessions with him taught me that it was okay to not be okay. I didn't have to pretend. He listened to all of my fears and sorrows and helped me find coping strategies to deal with them. Even now, as he grinned encouragingly at me from behind his black-rimmed glasses, he gave me time to think.

"It's still hard. I don't know if I'll ever be ready to let him go. My dad was everything to me, and he left too soon," I confessed to the group. "But I know that I don't have to make his mistakes in order to remember him. Everything that was good about him is who I already am. Since I've realized that, I've been able to grieve. I mean, you've all seen me. There have been days when I didn't think I would ever stop crying. Today feels better, though. Today I'm okay, and tomorrow I'll be even better."

The circle clapped for me as I took my seat among them. For the first time in a long time, I felt proud. As I looked around at my new friends, my fellow warriors, I knew that I was getting my life back day by day. This was the only way to make everything truly okay, and I was doing it.

When the session ended, we disbanded for lunch. Dr. Brenner stopped me on the way to the cafeteria.

"Hey, Josh," he said, jogging to catch up to me. "What you said back there was nothing short of inspiring. I'm proud of you, kid."

My smile came easily. "I was just saying what I felt, like you taught me. No more hiding."

"That's right. You've come such a long way," he said, patting me on the back as we walked down the hall. "How are you feeling about being discharged next week?"

Running my hand through my hair, I stopped to face him. "I'd be lying if I said I wasn't nervous. I'm still not sure how I feel about a lot of things that happened."

The Kindred Spirit weighed on my mind. It was the only thing I hadn't confided in Dr. Brenner about. I didn't know where to even start to talk about it. There was still so much I didn't understand. How much of what happened had been real, and how much had been a Vicodin-induced overreaction? I wasn't sure.

"You still feeling guilty about what happened the day you overdosed?" he asked. "Are you still worried about Irsa?"

"There's definitely that," I confirmed. There wasn't a day that went by that I didn't see Irsa's tear-streaked face, when I didn't hear her cries from the other side of my bedroom door. "I just wish I could go back and change everything."

Dr. Brenner put his hand on my shoulder and looked me in the eye. "We've talked about this. You can't go back and change what happened. You have to work with what you have going for you now."

"I know," I said, tracing the block tile with the toe of my shoe. "I just wish I could get everything straight in my mind before I go home. I can't stop thinking about it all, you know?"

Dr. Brenner considered for a minute. Then he turned to continue our walk toward the cafeteria, and I followed.

"I know what will help you," he said as we walked. "You need to write it all down. Everything that happened, everything you still feel about it, write it down somewhere. It's a great way to work through things."

I was unsure. The last time I poured my thoughts onto the page, I'd invited nothing but heartache. It was easy to think that my problems had all started with a simple letter in a mailbox though I knew that wasn't the truth. My problems started the day my dad died and I picked up his pills.

"You really think it will help?" I asked.

Dr. Brenner nodded. "So much so that I'm canceling our afternoon sessions for the rest of the week. I want you to take that time to write. Can you do that for me?"

I thought about it and then nodded. "I'll get started right after lunch."

We turned the corner, and Dr. Brenner ducked into his office.

"Let's see if I have something for you to write on." He rummaged through his desk drawers. Then with a satisfied smile, he plucked out a crisp, green notebook and handed it to me. "Here, how is this?"

I stared down at the fresh green cover and the spiral binding and almost laughed at the coincidence. "It's perfect."

"I'll see you tomorrow then," he said as I continued on to the cafeteria. "This is going to make all the difference. You'll see."

It was hard to focus on my lunch with this new assignment to consider. The more I thought about it though, the more I liked the idea. Taking only a few bites of my sloppy joe, I dumped the tray into the trash and rushed back to my room. Luckily, my roommate was still at lunch or in his afternoon sessions. I had the whole afternoon to myself.

I plopped onto my bed with the fresh green notebook. Then plucking the pen from my bedside table, I opened it to the first page. I didn't know where to start. So much had happened. It reminded me of a time not so long ago when I first opened another green notebook. I took myself back there. In my mind the ocean crashed in front of me while pelicans passed overhead. The bench beside the Kindred Spirit was warm from the early summer sun. I remembered not knowing what to write back then. I had just followed what so many before me had done.

That thought gave me an idea. I took to the page with a sense of purpose as I began to write:

Dear Kindred Spirit,

That's you, if you're reading this.

I can see you now, flipping through these pages in search of something you didn't know you were looking for. Perhaps, like me, you'll discover something that will change your life forever. You may stumble upon your own mystery in the In-Between. Maybe you'll recover all your missing pieces. At the very least, I hope you'll recognize your own story in mine. That's why I'm writing this. My story, I mean.

Dr. Brenner says it's important to get things out on paper. It was his idea to write down everything that happened and how I feel about it. It was my idea to write to you. If you're still reading this, you could be the reason for everything, you know? Maybe you're meant to learn from my mistakes. Then one day you can return to this spot with your own story and someone else can learn from you. That's the whole point of the Kindred Spirit, you know. To unite lost souls.

That's why you're here, isn't it? The mailbox called to you too, just like it called to me last summer. That's how you found your way so far down the shore. It's why you're sitting on the bench beside the mailbox with my notebook in your hands.

This is the place where my story, our story, begins . . .

Twenty-One

I walked away from the facility with my green notebook tucked beneath my arm. Dr. Brenner had been right. Writing down my story helped to make sense of the summer and of everything that happened. I felt stronger and better equipped to face whatever lay ahead. For the first time in almost a year, I was truly free. This liberation was better than catching the biggest of waves — a greater feeling even, than basking in Irsa's embrace. There were no more secrets, no more hiding. This was who I was now. This was Me, the real Me, the always-was Me that had just gotten lost for a little while.

My mom hugged me close before we got into her truck to go home. I was nervous, but excited. For the first time in a long time, I was optimistic about the future. It lay before me like an endless stretch of beach just waiting to be explored. The whole way back to Sunset Beach, neither of us could stop smiling. We knew we were finally getting our lives back.

I couldn't help but to look over at the Salid trailer when we pulled onto our street. As usual, it was quiet. The blinds were drawn. I knew that Irsa was not inside. There was still another week before school started. It gave me comfort to imagine her there, and to pretend that she was close by. I'd thought about writing her while I was in rehab, but I decided it would be better to give her time. I wondered if she hated me for lying to her, for scaring her, and for letting her down. I couldn't blame her if she did.

As we pulled into our drive, I looked up at my mom. She had that look on her face again, the one that let me know she was up to something. She was barely able to contain her excitement as we got out of the truck.

"What are you up to?" I asked. "You look like a kid about to get an ice cream cone."

"I have a surprise for you," she beamed.

I grabbed my bag and we headed up the stairs to the door. "What is it?"

She shrugged innocently. "I guess you'll just have to go in and find out."

I stared at her sideways, suspicious, then turned the knob and stepped inside.

"Surprise!" a familiar voice yelled.

The living room was decorated with colorful balloons and streamers. A huge *Welcome Home* sign hung above the kitchen. Someone I didn't recognize stood beside the couch; his smile wide.

"Welcome home, Grymm," he said.

"rED?" I asked, with sudden realization. "Is that you?"

"In the flesh."

As soon as the shock wore off, I rushed to greet him. "What are you doing here?" I couldn't believe he was standing right in front of me.

"I told you I would always be here for you, so here I am." He laughed. "You know, you're much uglier in person."

"And you're shorter." We laughed and wrapped each other up in a hug.

I'd thought about rED, too, over the past four weeks. When Dr. Brenner had asked me to identify people in my life who were my biggest supporters, rED was second only to my mom.

"I'm so glad that you're here." I slung my arm around his shoulder. "How long can you stay?"

"Your mom talked my mom into letting me stay the rest of the week."

I turned to my mom who stood by the door, tears brimming in her eyes.

"Thank you," I mouthed.

She didn't say anything, only smiled and watched as rED sat me down and caught me up on life. He never asked about the pills. He never mentioned what happened. He didn't look down on me or feel sorry for me. Everything between us was blissfully normal, only in the flesh and not on screen.

We spent the entire day gaming with The Stranded. The whole gang was supportive. Stephy was so happy to hear from me that she actually cried into her mic. Zoso and Blank caught me up on everything I'd missed. I learned that Biggles was sent to rehab after his trial. He, too, was finally getting the help he needed. I knew that when he got back, I'd be there for him, just like rED was here for me now. The Stranded gang would rally behind him like they had around me because that's what being a friend really was.

When we finally logged off for bed, we talked for hours. Really talked. Never once did rED judge me or criticize. When I finally let him in, he proved to be the best friend I always knew he was.

"You could have told me, you now," rED said from his make-shift bed on the floor beside mine. "I would have helped you."

"I know you would have," I said as I stared at the moonlight dancing off the ceiling. "I guess that's why I didn't say anything. I wasn't ready for help yet."

rED thought about that for a minute. "I'm really glad you're okay now. It all turned out okay in the end, I guess."

"Almost," I said, parting the blinds to glance across the street.

rED sat up onto his elbows. "She's going to understand. If she's as amazing as you say she is, she'll see that you were sick."

I sighed and let the blinds fall back into place. "I hope so."

"Give it time," rED said. Then he lay back down, and all was quiet.

The rest of the week flew by while we played with the gang or just got to know one another better. On the last night of rED's visit, there was a knock at the door.

"I'll get it," I said, pausing the movie and pushing myself off the couch.

When I opened the door, Anas stood just outside, a large cardboard box in his hands.

He smiled wide. "Welcome back, Solo."

"Anas!" I was overjoyed at the sight of him. "Man, am I glad to see you."

"I would have been by earlier, but we've been staying late at the shop balancing the books." He shrugged. "It's the end of the season."

"I'm just glad you're here now," I said.

"Were you really in the loony bin?"

"What? No." I laughed. "I was in a rehab."

Anas nodded his head, contemplating. "Well, that's one way to break a curse."

"I guess it is," I agreed.

"So, can I come in or what?"

"Of course, you can." I yanked him inside and motioned to the couch. "This is my friend, rED. He's part of The Stranded gang, remember? rED, this is Anas."

"R2Deez2Nutz!" rED laughed. "At last we meet. Join us. We're watching a movie."

Anas looked at the screen, and his eyes lit up. "You're watching *Return of the Jedi*?"

"What can I say? I missed having a Jedi Master around," I said with a shrug. "We're at the part when Han Solo is freed from being frozen in carbonite. Can you stay for the rest?"

"And you said real life wasn't like Star Wars." Anas nudged me with his elbow. "Yeah, I can stay."

"How is Irsa?" I asked.

"I haven't talked to her much," he said, lowering his eyes. "She comes home tomorrow night, though."

My heart skipped. I only had to wait one more day to see her.

"That's good." I motioned to his box. "Why don't you put your stuff down?"

"Actually, this is your stuff," he said.

"What are you talking about?" I tried to remember if I'd let him borrow anything.

Anas set the box down on the kitchen table. He pulled out my sequencer and interface and set them on the table in front of me.

"You're the one who bought these?" I asked, stunned.

"I didn't know they were yours until I saw this." Anas turned over the sequencer. Written in black marker on the back was the name of my music channel. I'd written *Cosmic Cloud* on it the day I'd thought of the name. That was years ago. I'd completely forgotten about it.

"But the P.O. Box . . ."

"Please, like my dad would ever let me spend my savings on music equipment," Anas snickered. "I had to be slick."

I didn't know what to say.

"Anyways, I wanted you to have these," he continued. "Your fans need Cosmic Cloud to keep making music."

"No, I can't take these back from you." I started to put them back in the box. "I don't have your money anymore. It wouldn't be right."

Anas stopped me.

"I'd pay even more to be able to make music with my best friend again," he said. Then cleared his throat. "Besides, I'm rolling in that money now that I work for my dad."

"I . . . I don't know what to say," I said.

"Good, then shut up, and press play." He skipped into the living room. "We're about to see Princess Leia in her golden bikini."

"Yes!" rED clapped. "Best part ever."

"My man!" Anas gave him a high five and plopped down on the couch beside him.

I stood there, stunned, looking at my music equipment on the table. My heart filled with appreciation and newfound joy. Everything I'd thought I'd lost to my addiction was returning to me one by one.

"Hurry up, Josh." My mom smiled up at me from the couch. "You don't want to miss the golden bikini."

"No, I don't," I said with a smile as I joined them. "I don't want to miss one more thing."

We took rED to the airport the next day. It was hard to say goodbye, but our friendship was now stronger than ever. I promised that I would keep in touch with how things were going, and this time I knew that I could keep that promise.

School was starting tomorrow. I spent the rest of the day getting ready, all the while checking my window to see if Irsa was back. It wasn't until nightfall that she returned. I was gaming with the gang when I heard a car pull up. Scrambling to my window, I peeked through the blinds.

A shiny, white blazer pulled into the Salids' vacant driveway. My pulse quickened as one of the back doors opened and Irsa stepped out. She was every bit as radiant as she was in my dodgy memory. Getting her bag from the trunk, she waved goodbye to her friends as they backed out of the drive.

The urge to talk to her was too much. Her father wasn't home yet, so there was time. I decided that it would be better to talk to her now than on a crowded school bus in the morning. Throwing on a hoodie and shoes, I rushed out the back door.

"Irsa!" I called to her just as she was about to go inside.

She turned, dropping her bag when she saw me jogging up the drive. Her face lit up with a smile. Then she seemed to catch herself, and it fell.

"Josh, what are you doing here?"

"I had to see you," I panted. "I had to tell you that I'm so sorry, and I'm not mad that you told my mom about the pills. I'm glad you did it. You saved my life, Irsa."

"I just did what I had to do." She looked to the ground. I didn't understand why she looked so sad. I climbed the steps to be by her side.

"I am so sorry that I lied to you," I pleaded. "I'm sorry for everything I did. I wasn't thinking straight. You helped put a stop to all of that. Please, don't hate me. I'm better now."

Irsa looked up at me at last. "I could never hate you, Josh."

"Oh, thank God." I breathed. "I thought for a minute . . ."

"But we can't see each other anymore," she cut me off.

"What?" I tried to grab her hand, but she moved it away. My heart sank. "Why?"

"We're no good for one another," she tried to explain, but her words didn't make sense to me. "My father doesn't want me anywhere near you. This will never work."

"We can figure something out."

"No." She shook her head. I thought I saw her blink back tears. "I have to try to be better at the life I've been given. I can't sneak around anymore. No more lies, remember?"

I shook my head. There had to be a way that we could be together. I could see her feelings for me in the warmth of her teary eyes.

"What about at school?" I pleaded. "We can see one another there."

"No, this is just the way it has to be." She backed away. "I can't pretend that my life will ever be more than what it is anymore. I have to accept that there are just some things that can never happen for me. Please, don't make this any harder than it has to be."

"But . . ." I started to argue, but the trailer door opened behind her, and Anas stuck his head out.

"Solo?" He looked panicked. "My father will be home any second. You can't be here."

"Please, Josh." A single tear escaped onto Irsa's cheek. "You have to go."

Staring into her weary face for a second longer, I tried to think of something to say. This couldn't be it for us. It couldn't be. As I took in the defeat in her eyes, I realized that I was never the only one of us trapped in the shadows. I didn't know how to make this right for her.

"Just go," she said again.

Anas came closer. He put a hand on my shoulder.

"Sometimes all you can do is wait for the sequel," he whispered, giving my shoulder a squeeze.

He was right. Right now, there was nothing I could say, nothing I could do to change the way things were for her. I was just going to have to hope that this wasn't over. Someday Irsa would have another chance at the life I knew she wanted, just like I had. Today was just not that day. Nodding, I tore myself away.

When I got to the street, I turned back to her. "What did you mean that day? The day I locked myself in my room. You kept yelling, 'not again.' What did that mean?"

Irsa shook her head. "I can't talk to you about that. There are some things you just won't understand."

Then she turned and disappeared inside as headlights flashed at the top of the street.

"See you at school tomorrow," Anas said, ducking into their trailer and closing the door.

I made it back inside my house just as Mr. Salid turned the street corner. Through the living room blinds, I watched him heave himself out of his car. He looked even more tired than he had the first time I'd seen him.

He stood at the bottom of his steps and braced himself against the railing as if he were waiting for life to slow down. Then he staggered up his steps and into the trailer.

"That didn't go as well as you hoped it would, did it?" My mom startled me. She was standing in the kitchen when I turned.

"You watched the whole thing from the window, didn't you?"

"You know I did," she shrugged. "Are you okay?"

"It's not me I'm worried about." I sighed.

"I know." She came over and put her arm around my shoulder. "Irsa just needs some time."

"No," I said, as we walked back down the hall. "She needs a miracle."

Twenty-Two

Hurricane season started in August but by September had been so uneventful that we'd forgotten all about it. The school year was in full swing, and I was busy navigating a new schedule and new classmates. It turned out that being the new kid made me instantly popular in our rural school district where everyone grew up together. For the first time ever, I was intriguing to the masses.

Everyone in my third period class wanted to sit with me at lunch. Everyone that is, except for Ashley Brafton and her crew. They stuck their noses in the air whenever they passed by. I only laughed when they did, remembering our exchange at the SkyWheel. No matter how big the lunch crowd was, though, I always saved a seat at our table for Anas. He ate up being the only freshman at a table filled with upperclassmen.

I only ever saw Irsa in the hallway, or surrounded by her friends in the back of the cafeteria. She smiled and laughed with them, but I couldn't shake the feeling that she was just going through the motions. The familiar warmth in her eyes was still missing. I wanted more than anything to go to her, to tell her that we would figure everything out, but I knew that I couldn't. I would only make things worse. All I could do was wait for the sequel.

The humid temperatures turned cooler, and the bright summer sunrises were replaced with hazy mornings. Fall was in the air. The streets, once crowded with tourists and vacationers, were now barren by comparison. The locals had all settled into their normal flow of life after another bustling summer. So, we were caught off guard the day we heard that Hurricane Matthew could be headed our way.

At first no one seemed to think much of it, though my mom and I were nervous. We'd never been through a hurricane before and had no idea what to do. News reports showed possible tracks bringing the storm to us, but my mom's colleagues and my classmates assured us that it was too soon to panic. So, we went about our lives and kept an eye on the news.

By the second week of September, though, forecasters were certain that Matthew would make landfall on our breadth of coast. By Tuesday morning, school was cancelled for the rest of the week, and all residents living in mobile homes were urged by the city to evacuate. Things had gotten serious fast. I paced the living room early Thursday afternoon, waiting for my mom to be released from work.

"What should we do?" I asked as soon as she walked in the door.

She tossed her purse onto the counter and shook the rain from her hair. "I guess we have to leave. Go ahead and pack up anything in your room that's valuable. There are black yard bags under the sink. I have a tarp in the closet somewhere. Hopefully those will keep everything dry in the back of the truck. It's already coming down out there."

I looked at her in shock. "This is really happening, isn't it?"

"Looks like it," she said with a sigh. "I figure we can head back up to Pittsburgh and stay with your grandparents until this thing blows over. They're not sure where exactly it's going to hit."

"What about Irsa and Anas? Are they still here?" Running to the window, I checked to see if Mr. Salid's car was in the drive. The wind was picking up, making the rain fall at strange angles.

"Their car is gone," I said. "I'm going to check on them just in case."

I didn't take the time to grab a jacket or umbrella. My clothes were drenched by the time I made it up the Salids' steps. Knocking on the door, I tried to listen for movement inside. The pounding rain made it impossible to hear anything. I knocked a second time and tried to see between the slats in the blinds. There was no movement, no answer.

When I ran back across the street, I saw that my surfboard was blowing around in the yard. I caught it and secured it under the porch.

"They're not home," I said once I got back inside. "I haven't seen them all day. They probably left already."

My mom pointed to the television. "The highways out are bumper to bumper. I'm not even sure we can find gas at this point."

We watched as footage showed thousands of cars lined up in rows on all the major highways. The roads looked like a parking lot.

My mom bit her lip. "We should have closed the bank sooner."

"All the routes out of here are gridlocked." I wiped water off my face. "What happens if we get caught in the storm out there? Is it better just to stay here rather than chance getting stranded in the middle of the highway?" I couldn't help but to think of the Salids. What if they were already stuck out there?

"I don't know," my mom said, biting her nails. "I've never done this before."

"Well, let's think it through," I reasoned. "If we leave now, we're not going to get anywhere. They're saying some of the roads are starting to flood. We could try waiting until morning for a route to clear out. If there isn't one, we can always go to a shelter or something. It's better than being stranded on the highway with all of our valuables in the back of the truck."

My mom paced the floor as she weighed our options. Finally, she nodded. "You're right. We're not going to get anywhere tonight. Let's just pack everything up and be ready to leave first thing in the morning."

The news said that it was best to take cover away from all windows. Our options were limited, so my mom dragged every blanket, pillow, and towel out to make us a nest in the hallway. Then she dragged the television away from the windows and positioned it where we could see it. Our valuables lay strewn across the dining room floor in black plastic bags like victims of a crime scene.

As we watched hurricane coverage from our makeshift bed in the hall, the wind outside vibrated the trailer. Rain pelted the vinyl siding and the roof. I wished there were a way to board up the windows, but it was too late for that now. We'd delayed too long, and Matthew had taken a turn right for us. Too afraid to turn it off, we slept with the television on. Most of the night I was in and out of consciousness. The wind and rain made it impossible to stay asleep for long. It was after 4 a.m. when I finally dozed off.

A couple of hours later, the sound of banging startled me awake again. I sat up, my senses on the full-alert. Feeble morning light shone through the cracks in the blinds. My mom was asleep beside me. Outside, rain continued to bounce off the roof. When the banging sound came again, I realized that it was coming from the back porch. This time my mom heard it too. She darted up.

"What is that?"

The wind had picked up speed, shaking the trailer now with its force. When the pounding came again, this time it came with a muffled shout.

"Someone's at the door," I said, jumping up.

Throwing on my shoes, I ran to open it. When I did, the wind caught the door. It slammed into Mr. Salid who was standing, drenched, on our porch.

"Are you okay?" I shouted over the wind and rain.

"I'm fine!" he yelled, straightening back up. "Please, can I come in?"

I offered him my hand, and when he grabbed it, I helped him inside and struggled to shut the door.

"Youssef?" My mom grabbed a towel from our pile and took it to him. "We thought you guys had gone already."

He took the towel and wiped his face. Then he handed it back.

"Then they are not here?" The panic on Mr. Salid's face filled me with dread.

"You mean Irsa and Anas?" my mom asked. "No, they're not here. What's going on?"

His words came out fast, frantic. "By the time we boarded up the shop yesterday, it was too late to leave. The roads were blocked. I decided it would be best to wait until daybreak, but when I went to wake my children this morning, they were gone."

"Gone?" I asked.

"Josh went to your place last night, and no one was home. Could they have evacuated with a friend?" my mom asked.

"No," he cried, "they were helping me on the island. We didn't get home until late. Now they are gone. Their bikes are missing."

"They took off on their bikes?" my mom gasped. "In this weather?"

Mr. Salid put his hands on my shoulders. He looked me in the eyes.

"Please, Josh," he pleaded. "Do you have any idea where they could have gone?"

I tried to remember if Anas had said anything to me about sneaking out again, but I was sure he'd never mentioned anything like that to me. Wracking my brain, I tried to put myself in their shoes. What were they doing? Where could they possibly want to go during a storm like this?

My mind flashed to that gloomy summer morning on the water when a thunderstorm loomed on the horizon. The memory was foggy. I'd been under the influence of the pills. I remembered Irsa's explanation for why they had to leave early when it stormed. She'd told me that she never wanted to go. My breath caught in my chest when I remembered what else she'd said. *One day I'm going to come out here during a storm and surf the biggest swell this beach has ever seen!*

"Oh, no." I mumbled.

"What is it?" Mr. Salid cried. "Please, you must tell me."

I tried to rationalize. There was no way Irsa and Anas had gone to our spot. That was insane. It would be impossible to surf this storm. Besides, Irsa didn't even have a board anymore.

Then a thought struck me. I felt the blood drain from my face.

"No, no, no," I mumbled, running to the back door. The rain pelted my arms as I jumped down the steps and checked beneath the porch. My surfboard was gone.

Mr. Salid and my mom followed me out into the rain.

"What is it?" my mom shouted. "What's going on, Josh?"

I looked into Mr. Salid's panicked face.

"They're at the beach!" I yelled up to them. "Irsa's going to try to surf the storm. She took my board."

My mom put a shaky hand to her mouth. "I'm going to call the police."

She ran inside. Mr. Salid met me at the bottom of the steps.

"My Irsa would not do that," he shouted over the wind. "She knows how I feel about her surfing. And if that does not matter, then surely, she knows it's too dangerous. She would never put her brother in danger that way."

Wiping the rain from my eyes, I shook my head. I remembered how only months ago I'd been willing end my life to finally be free of my pain. Now Irsa was risking hers for another taste of her greatest passion. When I looked at Mr. Salid, I felt sorry for him. He just couldn't see it.

"You'd be surprised what people will do when they're tired of hiding," I said.

A gust of wind made us stumble. Mr. Salid grabbed me and steadied me. "Please, you must tell me where on the beach they would go."

I thought about the night when he'd found his children out by the mailbox. It was one of the worst nights of my life. It had to have been even worse for Irsa. I remembered how angry Mr. Salid had been when he discovered her secret. The look of devastation on her face when her dad crushed her board and her dreams still played in my mind whenever I closed my eyes. How could I let him do that to her again?

"Please, Josh!" His face was a mask of unadulterated panic. "They'll be killed out there."

My mom stormed back out of the house with the phone to her ear.

"Where do I tell the police to go, Josh?" she yelled.

There was no more time to think, no more time to consider the consequences. I had to do the right thing. I had to do it for Irsa.

"The Kindred Spirit," I shouted. "They're out by the Kindred Spirit."

Mr. Salid looked shocked. "The mailbox? She'd go there? After everything that happened?"

"She's there BECAUSE of everything that happened," I tried to explain.

Mr. Salid turned to my mom and shouted up to her. "They're out past the 40Th Street access! Bird Island! Please, tell them to hurry!"

My mom relayed the message. I found my bike in a mud puddle beside the house and pulled it to the drive.

"What do you think you are doing?" Mr. Salid asked.

"I have to get to them," I yelled. "I can't let her do this."

"It is far too dangerous!" Mr. Salid insisted, but I ignored him.

"Joshua Hurley, there is no way you are going out there!" my mom screamed from the stairs as I mounted the pedals. "You won't make it to the bridge in this weather!"

I looked into her eyes through the sheets of rain. "I'm the only one who can stop them. Irsa will listen to me. I have to do this, Mom. I couldn't save Dad, but I can save them!"

To my surprise she didn't argue, didn't order me into the house. Instead, she looked from me to Mr. Salid. Then she reached into the house and grabbed her keys. She locked the door behind her.

"Not without me, you're not!" she yelled, motioning to the truck. "Throw the bike in the back."

Not hesitating for a second, I accepted her help and threw my bike into the bed of the truck. I squeezed in beside her and Mr. Salid as my mom backed out of the drive.

Rain pelted the windshield faster than the wipers could clear it. We could barely see two feet in front of us. Luckily, because of the thick cloud cover, it wasn't yet bright enough outside for the streetlights to have shut off. She followed them out to the main road. As the wind jerked the truck from side to side, my mom maneuvered us to the bridge.

We made it to the top before the tires struggled to keep traction against the wind. They screeched and spun out, throwing us across the lane. My mom fought to gain control until the tread grabbed hold of the road again at last. She stomped the gas, and we made it to the decline.

Water covered the causeway in front of us. The Intercoastal was already flooding and spilling out into the road.

"I don't think it's that deep." My mom gauged the situation. "I think we can make it."

Mr. Salid shook his head. "I cannot ask you to risk yourselves."

I looked at the road and then to my mom. "Friends don't have to ask," I said, nodding to her. "Let's go for it."

My mom put more weight on the gas. The truck lurched forward. Mr. Salid and I clung to the dash as the truck hydroplaned across the water. The back end began to fishtail, sending us into a spin. Just before we went off the side of the road, the front tires found solid ground. My mom jerked the wheel and threw us back onto the road.

"Holy crap!" I yelled. "Go, Mom!"

"Yes." Mr. Salid wiped the sweat from his brow. "Go, Mom."

The island was deserted. Everyone had either evacuated or remained boarded up inside of their beach houses. Palm trees bent at awkward angles as the wind battered against them. Unearthed brush whipped down the empty streets as rain pooled in parking lots.

"Turn down this road. It's a shortcut," I said, pointing to the first road on the right.

"No, go to my shop," Mr. Salid argued. "We can grab two more bikes."

We stopped at the corner in front of the bike rental. Mr. Salid shielded his face with his arm as he got out of the truck and unlocked the front door. He disappeared inside. When he came back out, he had a bike under each arm. I ran out and grabbed them from him, and he locked the shop back up. Then we threw the bikes beside mine in the back of the truck and hopped back in.

"All the way down," I said once we turned the corner.

We sped down the street, swerving around overturned garbage cans and runaway yard furniture. My mom pulled the truck into a sheltered driveway beside the beach access. I jumped out of the truck before she could even put it into park. Then I grabbed my bike from the back and hopped on.

"Wait for us," my mom said when she got out.

"There isn't time," I pleaded. "I have the best chance of reaching them first. I have to go."

"It's too dangerous to go alone," she argued.

"You have to trust me," I urged. "I can do this."

She thought for a minute as the rain fell on us in sheets. Then she walked over and clutched me to her. "Go get your friends. We'll be right behind you."

I kissed her on the cheek. Then I dragged my bike to the planks. Wiping the rain from my eyes, I took off down the beach access.

The haze of rain and wind made it harder to see now than it had been in the dark of night. I pedaled as fast as I could until my wheels hit wet sand. The tide was the highest I had ever seen. The water was almost to the dunes. Sand whipped through the air, stinging my face and arms.

I looked out at the angry ocean. Huge waves battered the shore in rapid succession. The breakers crashed down with enough force to shake the ground. The sound of their impact made me flinch. I'd only ever seen anything like it in movies. It was hard not to stare, but every second I delayed was another second that Irsa and Anas could be out in it.

It took all the strength I had to pedal against the wind. When my legs burnt out, I ran my bike down the shore as both the rain and the sea battered against me. I thought about what it had been like to fight back against the darkness of my depression. Battling my way down the shore wasn't much different from my struggle. Only this time Irsa was the one desperate to get her life back. She was the one I was fighting for now.

It was impossible to gauge where I was. When I looked behind me, the tide was too high, the waves too steep to see the pier. Ahead, the rain and whipping sand made it difficult to see more than a few feet in front of me. As close as I was to the dunes, I couldn't see their tops. I scanned the horizon for the American flag, but it was no use.

I didn't see the Kindred Spirit until it was right beside me. I'd almost passed it. The lid was broken. It flapped in the wind, leaving the notebooks inside exposed to the rain and wind. The flagpole rolled on the ground beside the mailbox. The wind had ripped it from the sand and tossed it like a piece of scrap metal. The American flag was missing.

Dumping my bike, I searched the waters for Irsa and Anas, but I couldn't see anyone. I screamed out their names over and over again. I was starting to panic when I heard a voice shout back above the howling wind. I followed it down the shore until I saw movement in the distance. Anas was at the shoreline, his scrawny legs getting thrashed by the tide.

"Anas!" I grabbed him and pulled him away from the harsh waters.

He turned to me, frantic. "Solo! She won't listen to me. I tried to stop her, but she won't listen. She just snapped or something!"

I followed his gaze out to sea, but I couldn't see Irsa. "Anas, where is she?"

"She's out there!" He pointed out to the violent ocean.

The sea churned and spat sea spray into the air at least eight feet. The wind threw the waves in every direction. Finally, when one wave crashed down and another one rose, I spotted her.

Irsa struggled to get her feet beneath her on my board. Once she did though, she stood and found her stance. The white fabric of her hijab whipped around her as she caught her ride.

"Wooohooo!" she hollered as her board glided atop the choppy waters.

I yelled out to her, but she couldn't hear me. She was too caught up in the moment to see the danger all around her. Maybe she didn't care. When the ride came to an abrupt stop, she bailed, landing in the violent waters. I lost sight of her again.

"Irsa!" I called.

Behind me, Mr. Salid cried out. Anas and I turned as he and my mom dumped their bikes and ran up the shore.

"Anas, are you all right?" He scrambled over to his son and looked him over.

"I'm fine, Father," Anas yelled over the thrashing waves.

Mr. Salid embraced him, then he held Anas at arm's length. "Where is your sister?"

Anas pointed toward the sea, and we all looked out in terror.

"We have to get her out of there!" my mom screamed.

For a second, Irsa was nowhere to be found. I jogged forward into the surf, searching the breakers for her. I spotted her paddling out. "There!"

"Irsa!" Mr. Salid shouted, but she couldn't hear any of us from where she was.

All we could do was watch as Irsa poised herself for the next wave. Behind her, a massive swell formed. The water was sucked out from beneath our feet as the wave gathered its strength.

"She's not going to go for it, is she?" Anas grabbed onto my shirt. "She'll never make that wave."

To our horror, Irsa turned the board and paddled as she waited for the monster wave to lift her. When the crest reached a terrifying height, it caught her board. She struggled to stand, but when she did, she took command of the ride. Outstretching her arms, she glided across the water. The fabric around her shoulders flowed behind her like gossamer wings. The grey skies seemed to lighten with the brightness of her smile. Her eyes were ablaze.

"My god," Mr. Salid exclaimed, as struck as I'd been the first time I'd watched her fly atop the ocean. "She looks like an angel."

I turned back to the sea and watched as the wave pushed Irsa closer to the shore. "Irsa!"

Startled, she searched the coastline until our eyes met. She smiled from ear to ear.

"Josh!" she cried happily. "I'm finally doing it!"

"You have to come back in!" I cried.

Irsa's smile fell when she noticed that her father stood behind me.

"Why is he here, Josh?" She struggled to keep the board beneath her now. "Why did you bring him here? What are you doing to me?"

"I'm saving your life!"

Irsa started to lose her balance. "I'm not going to stop, not this time! I can't pretend to be something I'm not anymore! I need this, Josh!"

"We can figure it out together!" I yelled, but she was already bailing.

She jumped into the water. The wave crashed down on top of her.

"No!" Mr. Salid cried.

I held my breath and waited for her to resurface. The board came up first, and then Irsa broke through the water, gasping for air. She clung to the board as the sea threw her from side to side. I started to go in after her, but once she caught her breath, Irsa climbed back onto her board.

"Irsa, no!" I screamed as she turned to paddle back out.

"What should we do?" Anas asked.

"The police will be here any minute," my mom yelled.

"They'll never get to her in time." I said, kicking my shoes into the sand.

"What are you doing, Solo?" Anas shouted.

"I'm going after her." I ran back to the Kindred Spirit. "Please let it still be here."

The wind whipped against me as I dragged myself up the dunes behind the mailbox. I had to close my eyes while I dug. The sand and rain stung my face as it whipped by. When I felt solid foam beneath my fingers, I heaved Anas's board from where it was buried. Then I charged the shore after Irsa.

"My board!" Anas cried as I secured the leash to my ankle.

"Josh, no!" my mom screamed behind me, but I couldn't let her stop me.

The ocean pounded against my body as soon as I entered the water. The chill and force of it startled me. Fear gripped my throat. I looked out to sea at the ferocious waves bearing down on me, and I took a deep breath. I couldn't let fear stop me as it had so many times in the past. I knew that if I could just get out as far as Irsa, I could bring her back.

When I had her in my sights, I used the board to dive straight into the waves. The first one rolled me, churning me like butter. I recovered, breaking the surface to catch another breath. I rolled with the next wave and recovered again. Paddling as fast as I could, I kept my eyes on Irsa. When she was just ahead, I reached out, but the water propelled her forward and out of my grasp.

Ahead of us another monster wave began to form. It looked as if the swell were rising seven stories into the air. Irsa turned her board to ready herself. She spotted me in the water in front of her.

"Don't do this!" I screamed to her. "It's too dangerous!"

"Josh, get out of here!"

"I'm not leaving you!" I screamed.

Her eyes pleaded to me. "You have to go. You have to let me do this. I may never get another chance."

"You won't live to get another chance!"

"You have to let me do this, Josh!" she cried. "Go back to shore. I can do this!""

I shook my head. "I'm not going anywhere without you!"

She looked behind her as the water lifted us into the air. "Go now! The wave is coming!"

I turned my board. "Then we'll ride it in together!"

It was too late for her to argue. The water scooped us up as the swell built beneath us. When the wave caught our boards, she stood up. I followed her lead, my legs shaking beneath me. The ride propelled us forward as we moved into position.

Then we were flying.

Our boards cut through the water side by side as we glided along the giant wave. It was a feeling of utter and complete loss of control. My heart pounded as I looked out at the beach that seemed a million feet below. The speed was exhilarating and terrifying all at once.

I chanced a look at Irsa, who hooted and laughed beside me. The look on her face was that of pure, unadulterated joy. She'd never before looked so free. I could almost reach her outstretched hand. She reached for me too.

Just before our hands touched, another wave rose up out of nowhere beside us. I watched in terror as it knocked Irsa off her feet. Her board flew into her face, cracking against her skull with a nauseating thud. The wave slammed into her as she fell.

I didn't have time to react. I was knocked from my own board with the force of a freight train. There wasn't enough time to even take a breath before I was thrown into the water. My body was tossed about like a rag doll in a rinse cycle. I didn't know which way was up. My lungs screamed for air. When the churning subsided, my board began to float to the surface. I grabbed the leash and followed it up, clawing my way through the water until I broke free.

I gasped for air. My head spun. The water around me moved so fast, so forceful that I could scarcely move. I heaved myself onto my board and tried to get my bearings. My mom, Anas and Mr. Salid were all screaming from the shore behind me. I searched the building whitecaps in front of me for Irsa as the ocean began to swell again.

When the water rose, I saw her floating a few yards away. The leash to her board had snapped off at her ankle. The board was lost to the sea.

Frantic, I swam to her as fast as I could. I got to her as a new wave built behind us.

"Irsa!" I yelled. "Irsa, wake up!"

She was bleeding from a large welt forming just above her right eye. In a panic, I rolled off my board. I grabbed her by the arm and pulled her onto it, making sure her head was secure.

"Josh," she mumbled. "I don't want to die."

I threw my body across the top of hers. My legs dangled over the side. I held her and the board as close to me as I could.

"Then I dare you to live, Irsa." I repeated the words that she'd said to me in the SkyWheel as the wave picked us up. "I dare you to live."

I struggled to keep us upright as another wave barreled down. We were tossed about as the ocean threatened to swallow us whole. Kicking my legs as hard as I could, we inched toward the beach.

Irsa lost consciousness as wave after wave thrashed us from all sides. I just kept kicking, praying that we'd make it to shore before we both drowned. In the distance, red flashing lights sped down the beach. Sirens traveled on the wind. Help was coming.

When I didn't know if I could kick any longer, another massive wave picked us up. It took all the strength I had left to keep us afloat. I squeezed Irsa tight against me as the water hurled us toward the beach. When we got close, my left leg smashed into the shore with brute force. Something cracked. White-hot pain shot up my right side. I cried out as we tumbled onto the beach and came to an abrupt stop.

Within seconds, my mom, Mr. Salid and Anas were at our sides, dragging us to safety beside the mailbox. The world began to spin and ebb as pain and exhaustion overtook me. The red flashing lights got brighter and brighter as help approached. With blurred vision, I looked over at Irsa. Miraculously, she was still on top of the board. Her father grabbed her hand and spoke to her, but his words were lost to the throbbing in my head.

A loud crack startled us. We watched as a gust of wind blew the back out of the Kindred Spirit. Everything inside was thrown out and scattered into the rain. My notebook, filled with letters written by a mysterious hand, was the last to fall. It flapped in the wind and tumbled across the sand. I reached for it as paramedics flocked to my side and began to secure my leg. As I watched, the tide swept my notebook up and dragged it out to sea. With tears in my eyes, I looked back over to Irsa. I grabbed hold of her hand as we were lifted into the ambulance.

Twenty-Three

My mom smiled to me as we pulled out of the hospital parking lot.

"I told you Irsa would like the daisies."

"You were right as usual," I said. "I hope they last until she comes home."

"The doctor said she would be discharged by Monday." My mom pulled out onto the highway toward home. "I think they'll be fine."

"I know," I said," but she's been in there a week already. It feels like forever."

The skies were clear and blue, but the devastation from the storm lingered like a dark cloud. Downed trees and uprooted shrubbery still littered yards and driveways. The floodwaters still filled neighborhoods and blocked out roads. Everything was a soggy mess.

By the time we pulled into our driveway, the sun was hovering just above the horizon. I looked down our street. We were one of the lucky ones. The winds from the storm blew a section off our roof. Water had leaked into the bathroom and drenched the carpets in the hallway, but otherwise our home remained intact. Many of our neighbors had sustained major water damage to their trailers. Some even lost whole rooms when trees toppled over onto their homes.

I looked over at the Salid trailer where Anas was securing new white skirting around their porch stairs. Their old, rusted one had been ripped off in the storm.

I hobbled out of the truck. "Looking good!"

"So does this new skirting." Anas winked. "I'm just trying to get this place together before Irsa comes back home. Didn't I tell you she was feeling better today, Gimpy?"

Gimpy was my temporary nickname now that my left shin was broken in two places. I was immobilized from the knee down. Anas had even written my new nickname in big, black letters down the side of my cast.

"She's almost back to her normal self," I agreed.

"Is your dad still cleaning up the shop?" my mom asked. We hadn't seen much of Mr. Salid since the floodwaters had receded enough to get back onto the island.

Anas nodded. "Yeah, the place is a mess. Aside from our visits to the hospital, he's been down there from dawn to dusk working on it."

"Let us know if we can help with anything," I said.

"No offense, Gimpy, but you're in no shape to help," he teased. "You can just continue to keep my sister company and give the rest of us a chance to play hero."

"I won't argue with that," I laughed as I grabbed my crutches from the back of the truck and followed my mom inside.

I spent the evening gaming with The Stranded gang and talking to rED. It was the wee hours of the morning before I stumbled to bed. My body was still sore from where the ocean had pounded me. I was also exhausted. It had been hard to sleep all week. There was just so much to think about.

At first, I had been worried about Irsa. She'd suffered a major concussion and had some swelling in her brain. Now that I knew she was going to be okay, sleep evaded because I replayed the events of the storm. I couldn't stop thinking about how my notebook had been swept out to sea. I was just never ready to face the Kindred Spirit and what was happening out there. Now I would never know if my dad had written me back. So many questions would never be answered. The mystery behind the letters would always remain just that, a mystery.

Then a thought struck me, and I sat up and turned on my lamp. The notebook that Dr. Brenner gave me sat on my desk beside my sequencer. Grabbing my crutches, I picked up the notebook and hobbled down the hall. To my surprise, my mom was sitting on the couch with a book.

"You couldn't sleep either?" I asked.

My mom looked up from the pages and patted the seat beside her. "Nope. Too much on my mind."

"Same here." I plopped down next to her. "So much has happened this year."

"I know." She draped her arm around me. "Good and bad."

I looked up at her. "Do you think the good things will outweigh all the bad someday?"

"I think they already have," she said, squeezing me tight. She motioned to the notebook in my lap. "What have you got there?"

"It's for the Kindred Spirit," I said with a shrug. "I want to go out there once the sun comes up and see if it's been restored."

"You're going to hobble all the way down to the beach?"

"I might be able to pedal my bike, or you can drop me off if you don't mind waiting a while."

My mom thought about it and then put her head on mine. "Why don't you take my truck? It's going to be yours soon anyway. Think you can manage that?"

"Yeah," I said with a smile. "Thanks, Mom."

For a minute we just sat there in the comfortable silence of one another's company. I thought about how much my mom had been there for me through all the good and all the bad of this year. She had never once let me down.

"I understand why you did it now," I said, breaking the silence.

"Did what?"

"I understand why you told Mr. Salid where to find us that morning," I explained. "It was hard for me to tell him where to find Irsa during the storm. I felt like I was betraying her, but if I hadn't said anything, she might have died. So, I get why you had to break your promise."

My mom sat up and turned to me, her brow furrowed. "I never broke my promise. I mean, I would have, but . . ."

"I thought you said you went over there to find me," I interrupted.

"Yeah, I went over there," she explained, "but no one answered the door. Why do you think I was such a mess? I didn't even know you guys were out there until he pulled up with Irsa and Anas. I never told him where to look."

"You never talked to him?" I tried to put the pieces of that morning together. "If you didn't tell him where we were, then how did he know where to find us?"

My mom shrugged. "Maybe he was already out there."

I shook my head. None of this made sense. "Why would he be out by the mailbox at the crack of dawn? How did he . . . ?"

A thought stopped me mid-sentence. My mind raced through the possibilities. I remembered how shocked Mr. Salid had been when he saw Anas and Irsa standing there in the weak light of that summer morning. My mom's voice repeated in my head. *Maybe he was already out there.*

Shocked, I looked at the clock. Daylight would break soon.

"I need to get to the mailbox." I rose onto my good leg and grabbed my crutches.

"What?" she asked. "It's barely light outside."

"Exactly," I said, going to the door. "Can I still borrow the truck?"

My mom got up and tossed me the keys from the counter. "Do you want me to go with you so you won't be alone out there?"

"I won't be alone," I said, catching the keys. I shoved the notebook under my arm. "Thanks, Mom."

I hobbled down the back steps and heaved my casted leg into the truck. It was awkward, but I was able to get my body behind the wheel and my good leg to the pedals. I looked over at the Salid trailer as I passed. Mr. Salid's car was not in the drive. I knew it wouldn't be.

Feeble morning light began to glow around the edges of the water as I crossed over the bridge toward the ocean. There was still no power to much of the island. The streets were dark and wet. The vacation home windows were still boarded up, and debris littered driveways. When I got to the 40th Street beach access, I parked behind the only other car on the island. It was Mr. Salid's.

It took what seemed like an eternity to hobble down the beach with my crutches, but I went as fast as I could. The tide was low and calm. A crisp breeze caressed my back while I struggled to get across the hard-packed sand. Here and there a seagull laughed in the distance.

Ghost crabs scurried back to their holes as sunlight spread in orange and red ribbons across the sky. I looked ahead at the rocky sandbar that jutted out into the ocean and knew that I was getting close. My arms ached as I heaved myself forward.

When I got there, I saw that the driftwood base of the mailbox still stood in the damp sand. As I hobbled closer, I realized that the original black mailbox had been replaced entirely. A shiny white box now sat atop the driftwood base. It shocked me at first. The white box didn't feel right. Then I saw the familiar letters on the side that read *Kindred Spirit*, and I knew that it was different, yet the same.

The wooden bench still rested beside the mailbox. It remained untouched by the storm. Mr. Salid sat on it with his head in his hands.

"Mr. Salid," I said, coming closer.

When he looked up at me, tears ran down his face.

"Joshua?" he asked, as he wiped his cheeks with his fingers. "What are you doing here?"

I didn't know what to say. "I . . . I came to see if the Kindred Spirit was still here."

"You should not have come." He lowered his head again. "This mailbox is cursed."

"I know that's what you think," I said. "Is that why you're here?"

For a second he said nothing. Then he looked at me, his eyes full of sorrow.

"Tell me, Josh," he said. "Does your god allow you to speak with people you have lost?"

I felt tears well up in my own eyes. I blinked them back. "I used to think so."

Mr. Salid nodded. "I believe mine does. Though, that's all over now."

I'd never seen him like this before. The pain on his face pulled me closer. I sat beside him and waited for him to continue.

"You know, my son was not much older than you are now," he said, looking off into the ocean.

"Your son?" I asked. "I thought Anas . . ."

"My wife and I had our first child almost twenty-three years ago," he continued. "We named him Jalil after my father. In my country it is a great name. When Jalil got older, he no longer liked the sound of his Islamic name. He wanted so badly to be an American, you see. He wanted an American name, an American upbringing. When we moved here, he insisted that I change his name, but I would not. So, he began to shorten it entirely. When he signed his papers, he kept only the 'J'."

"He signed his name with a 'J'?" I asked, stunned. I thought about how I'd signed my letters in the notebook, always with my first initial. Always with a J.

"Yes." Mr. Salid smiled at the memory, but then his face fell. "He was such a free spirit, my son. When we moved to Los Angeles, he got all these ideas in his head that he wanted to drop out of school and become an actor. I would not allow it. It just wasn't a respectable thing for a man of faith to be. He couldn't understand that. He kept saying that his mother would have been supportive, but as progressive as my wife was, she was a devout Muslim. I was just trying to raise our children how she would have wanted."

I thought about Irsa, about her dreams of becoming a surfer. I could never understand why Mr. Salid was so against it, but now everything was starting to make sense. I realized now that the weariness on Mr. Salid's face was the look of a man who was desperately clinging to a past that would never return to him. I knew all too well what that felt like. Suddenly I understood his struggle.

"I told him that we had to move away, that his brother and sister were being threatened," Mr. Salid continued. "I told him that he had to give up his dreams of becoming an actor and come with us, or else we would have to go without him. We needed to leave the city."

"He didn't come with you, did he?" I asked.

"He would not. I even threatened to disown him from our family, but still he would not come." A cry of anguish escaped his throat. "God forgive me, but I left him there. I left him all alone."

"What happened to him?" I asked, gently. "What happened to Jalil?"

Mr. Salid struggled to collect himself. He wiped his face with the sleeve of his jacket. Then he looked into my eyes as if seeking relief, as if the burden of keeping it inside was too much to bear anymore.

"Jalil hanged himself in his apartment." The words came out a whisper, as if they hurt too much to say out loud. "He killed himself because he had been abandoned. He lost himself, and I left him all alone. I made him choose."

As I looked at him, my own tears escaped onto my cheek. Everything made sense to me now. It was never my own dad writing to me in the mailbox, but Jalil's. Those letters hadn't been an answer from beyond the grave but from a father who had lost his son to unspeakable tragedy. As Mr. Salid stared with vacant eyes out to sea, I realized that the Kindred Spirit hadn't brought our loved ones back to us. It had united a mourning father with a lost son.

"None of you have ever mentioned Jalil," I said.

Mr. Salid nodded. "In Islam, taking your own life is forbidden. We don't discuss such things. It is hard . . ."

"I'm so sorry for your loss," I said, understanding at last.

Mr. Salid shook his head. "My god gave me the opportunity to speak to my son again through this mailbox. He gave me a chance at redemption, and I failed. Do you think that is crazy?"

"I don't think it's crazy at all," I said. "I think the mailbox gives people the closure they've been looking for."

"Closure," he repeated. "I fear I will never have that. I have squandered my chance. My son asked for me. He needed me, and again I was not there. Now I fear he is gone forever."

I thought about the last letter I'd written. I'd been so upset that my dad had not met me at the mailbox. I realized with stinging regret that Mr. Salid had been on his way the morning he found us on the beach. He'd been going to meet with his son. We had gotten in the way. Mr. Salid hadn't just ruined everything for us that morning, I realized. As far as he knew, we'd ruined his only chance at being reunited with Jalil. Now, his anger from that morning made sense. It all made sense.

"I'm so sorry," I whispered.

Mr. Salid patted my hand. "No, it is me who is sorry, Joshua. I was wrong about you. I've been wrong about so many things. I was so afraid that the ways of this country were changing my children that I could not see that I was the one who needed to change. I can never thank you enough for saving my daughter's life. You could have died bringing Irsa back to me. No matter our differences, you are welcome in my home any time."

I took the notebook from under my arm and looked at its crisp, green cover. Then, wiping my eyes, I handed it to him. "We're not as different as you think."

Mr. Salid's eyes widened as he took the notebook from me. "What is this?"

"I think you should read it," I said. "It's my story. It's our story."

His brows furrowed in confusion as he opened it to the first page and began to read. I sat on the bench beside him as a thousand thoughts ran through my mind. The events from this year began to fit together like an intricate puzzle. Every piece fell into place one by one until they all formed a bigger picture. Everything made sense now.

As Mr. Salid flipped through the pages, I replayed the summer in my mind. I saw Irsa and Anas in the water as I watched in awe from the dunes. I saw myself sitting on this very bench when I wrote my first letter. I recalled the first time I'd pulled two surfboards from the sand. I remembered the feeling of utter freedom on the waves beside Irsa and the mystery waiting for us inside a magical mailbox. Everything culminated at this spot. Everything came together at the Kindred Spirit. The In-Between.

When he was finished reading, Mr. Salid looked up at me in shock. He searched my face with questions in his wide eyes.

"It was you?" he asked. "All this time?"

"Yes," I said with a nod. The tears flowed freely now as I watched the realization spread across his face. "We're the kindred spirits. It's us. It was always us."

Mr. Salid let out a cry and gathered me up into his arms. "Oh, my dear boy. I am so sorry for what happened to your father. No child should have to lose a parent."

"And no parent should have to lose a child," I said into his shoulder.

"I'm so sorry," he said again. "I didn't know it was you. I didn't know..."

"I know you didn't," I said, squeezing him to me. "But the mailbox knew."

Mr. Salid held me out at arm's length. "Yes, I believe it did."

"What do we do now?" I asked, unsure of where to go from here.

Composing himself, Mr. Salid looked down at the notebook on his lap. Then he reached into the mailbox and retrieved a pen. He handed them both to me.

"I think it is time to let them go," he said.

I thought about it for a minute. Letting go of my dad was the hardest thing I'd ever have to do, but when I looked into Mr. Salid's tear-stained face and saw our shared grief in his eyes, I knew it was finally time.

"Okay," I said with a sniff as I opened the notebook to a fresh page. Mr. Salid reached back into the mailbox and retrieved a notebook from the new ones inside. We were all starting over, even the Kindred Spirit. Our story was coming to an end.

Looking out to the sunrise, I thought about what I would say. Then I put the pen to the paper one last time.

Dad,

You don't have to worry about me. Everything I was looking for, everything I needed, was right here all along.

I've come to realize that it will never matter how far apart we are. We will always be together in our memories and in our hearts. So, I am letting you go now.

You are not to blame for what happened to me, Dad. I know now that I am in control of my own destiny. You will always be a part of me, just like I will always be a part of you.

We have weathered the storm, and it has set us all free. Though I will never stop missing you, I am finally okay. I'm more than okay, Dad.

I love you more than I could ever say. I always have.

Goodbye.

You are with me always,
J.

Shutting the notebook, I looked to Mr. Salid. He finished his letter and put his arm around me. I looked to the Heavens as the russet sky filled with wispy white clouds.

"I love you, Dad," I said to the horizon. "I will never forget you."

Mr. Salid smiled a sad smile and put his other hand to his chest. "Jalil, you will always be my whole heart. I love you."

When it was time, we took our notebooks to the mailbox. I placed mine at the bottom of the pile like I always had. Mr. Salid put his on the top. Then closing the lid, I grabbed my crutches, and we started our journey home together.

Though my foot weighed me down, my heart felt as light as the grains of sand that danced with the breeze along the surface of the shore. I knew that every step down the beach was another step into a new chapter of my life. I knew that Mr. Salid would be a part of it.

As we were walking away, we both paused when we heard a faint squeak behind us. Turning back to the Kindred Spirit, we stared in amazement. We tell ourselves it was the wind that did it, but deep down we both know better.

For the first time since either of us found the mailbox on that remote stretch of beach, the flag was lowered.

The End

Epilogue

"Hurry up!" I honked my truck's horn beside the Salid trailer. "We're going to be late!"

The summer morning sun beat down as Anas emerged with a cocky smile. He wore a neon-yellow shirt that read, *The Jedinator*. Climbing in next to me, he tossed me my own shirt.

"What is this?" I asked.

He rolled his eyes. "It's our swag. You have to have a stage name."

I read the front out loud. "Switched-on Solo?"

"Awesome, huh?" he beamed.

"I thought we were just going with the Cosmic Cloud? You know, the channel name. We were going to keep it simple."

"Dude, chill." He turned around and pointed with his thumbs. To my relief, the channel logo was on the back.

"I stand corrected."

"Irsa!" Anas yelled, honking the horn. "Hurry up! You're going to miss your big day!"

"Lay off the tuck," I said, pushing him off the horn.

When Irsa stepped outside, my heart skipped a beat. Her new wet suit and matching waterproof hijab looked amazing. She slung her new longboard into the back of the truck.

"Like I would miss this," she said, squeezing in next to her brother.

"You don't look at all nervous," I noted.

"What's there to be nervous about?" she beamed. "I'm going to clutch this!"

The three of us laughed as I put the truck in gear.

"Is your mom going to meet us there?" Anas asked.

"She's finishing up the chicken dip for later," I said. "She's going to ride with your dad."

Irsa shook her head. "He's been slaving over the lasagna all morning. He wouldn't even let me help with the sauce this time. He said it's HIS special sauce now."

"You have to love a man who takes his lasagna seriously," I teased as I pulled onto the main road toward Ocean Isle Beach. "I can't wait to eat it later."

School was barely out for the summer, and the feeling of newfound liberty danced in the air with the sunshine. The beach was once again littered with beach chairs and colorful blankets. It looked as though everyone from school had gathered to watch Irsa compete for the first time.

When we finally found a parking spot, Irsa ran ahead to get registered while Anas and I set up our equipment by the pier. He and I had racked up enough DJ gigs to last the entire summer. When we weren't playing our music for crowds of people, we knew we'd be riding the waves with Irsa at our spot by the Kindred Spirit. This summer we had nothing to hide, no secrets to keep, and nothing holding us back. We had one another, the waves, and freedom.

Once we were set up, Anas and I blasted the music we'd worked on all spring. We used the amps Anas bought with his work money to pump the bass throughout the crowd. People danced and sang along while we all waited for the competitors to take to the water. When they finally did, Irsa dominated the waves as usual.

The crowd seemed every bit as enamored with her as I had been the first time I watched her fly above the water. Anas and I took our seats in the sand beside Mr. Salid and my mom.

"I think she might win," Mr. Salid said as we watched Irsa fly by. "How can she not?"

He was smiling from ear to ear. There was a contentment about him lately that I had never seen before. For the first time since I'd known him, he seemed at peace. We all were.

"Even if she doesn't," I said with a shrug, "I think just being out here is a victory to her."

My mom smiled at Mr. Salid. "It's a victory for all of us."

Anas was deep in thought. "I wonder if she'll share the prize money."

I smacked him in his twiggy arm, then jumped up as Irsa brought her ride home. I jogged to the frothy surf and clapped. Our eyes met for the briefest second, but it was long enough to ignite that familiar spark between us. She smiled at me as I waved.

In that moment I was sure that everything was finally right with the world. I still didn't know if anything would happen between us, and I was okay with that. Watching her glide across the waves was all I needed for now. The two of us were finally free, and that was all that mattered.

I knew that after the competition, win or lose, we would all be there to tell her how proud we were. We would gather at our table and enjoy another meal together. For the first time in years, I had a family again. Everything else would fall into place in time, and we had nothing but time.

For now, I was happy just to live.

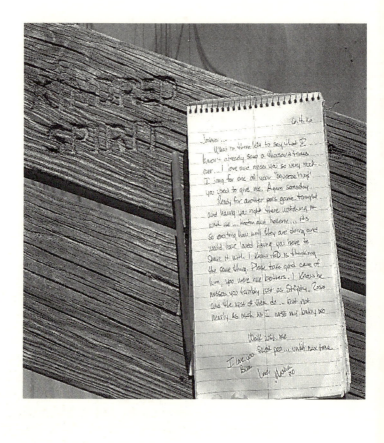

September 29, 2017

Bum - I can't begin to express just how much I miss you being here with me, feeling your hugs, just doing nothing together. At this moment, 2 years ago my world crumbled, stopped, came to a crashing halt. I never could have predicted this happening and that 2 years later I would be writing you this letter. The only thing that keeps me going is the fact that I know that you are in a better place, finally at peace, no more suffering. Thank you for being a huge part of my everyday. I would not have it any other way other than having you here with me. Thank you for so many beautiful years we had together, I cherish them. BTW the butterfly was a nice touch.

I love and miss you so
Sweet pea... my forever sunshine.

missyoujoshua Love Masha xo

Dedicated to the memory of Joshua E. Rizzo.
12/20/1991 – 9/29/2015

Forever in our hearts.

A.L. Crouch

A.L. Crouch, author of the *Guardian* Series, graduated with honors from North Carolina State University with a degree in English. She is now the principal of Ascent Christian Academy in North Myrtle Beach, SC, and an active member of Barefoot Church. She spends her summers formulating tales of suspense and the supernatural, but is always open to whatever God calls her to write. When she's not working to raise up young believers or keeping her readers jumping, she is spending time with her husband and two sons exploring the mountains and coasts.

For more information and other titles by A.L. Crouch visit:
www.alcrouch.com

Check out A.L. Crouch's *Guardian Series*.
Available now on Amazon!

Book One

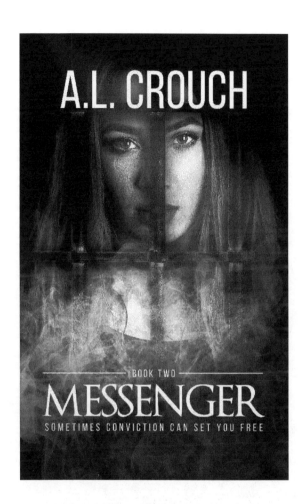

Book Two

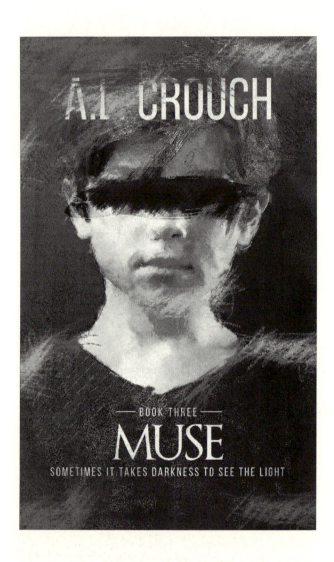

A.I. CROUCH

BOOK THREE

MUSE

SOMETIMES IT TAKES DARKNESS TO SEE THE LIGHT

Book Three

And Coming soon . . .

A.L. CROUCH

BOOK FOUR

DEATH

SOMETIMES THE END IS ONLY THE BEGINNING

Book Four

Made in the USA
Middletown, DE
12 May 2021